LOLA GREGORY

Endgame

First edition

ISBN: 979-8-9910696-0-1

Cover art by Enchanting Romance Designs
Editing by Jenny Rarden from Stormy Edits

This book was professionally typeset on Reedsy.
Find out more at reedsy.com

Contents

Acknowledgments

It feels a little pretentious to include acknowledgments for a book I fully expect will not ever get read. But, here we are. In the event that you are one of the few people I've told about this in real life who are reading *Endgame* to be supportive, or if you have randomly stumbled across it through other means, thank you for reading. It's a surreal feeling to think that the words that I've written are now out in the world.

I wrote the first draft of *Endgame* in 12 days during the height of the pandemic. Lila and King came to me with the subtlety of a lightning bolt, and wouldn't shut up until their story was down on paper. Since then, the story has gone through various tweaks and additions, thanks in part to K and L who are both my friends and my beta readers. Even though spicy scenes make them a little uncomfy, they powered through and gave me the confidence to move forward and publish this book.

Jenny, thank you for your thoughtful edits. Sarah, the cover turned out better than I could have ever dreamed. Thank you for bringing King and Bradley U to life. You both elevated this little book to a whole new level, and I will be forever grateful.

To my guy, thanks for all of the support and the pep talks. And for proofing the book so well it turned into another round of edits. Your knowledge of the beautiful game was essential to making this book feel at least slightly accurate. I love you the most.

Kiddos, thanks for being two of my favorite humans on the planet. In the event that you might one day read this... sorry, not sorry.

Playlist

"Lost in Your Light" - Dua Lipa (feat. Miguel)
"Wild" - John Legend (feat Gary Clark, Jr.)
"bitches broken hearts" - Billie Eilish
"slower" – Tate McRae
"Dead" – Madison Beer
"Symmetry" – Wolfie
"River" – Bishop Briggs
"like that" - Bea Miller
"Say My Name" - Destiny's Child
"Fairplay" – Kiana Ledé
"Bellyache - Marian Hill Remix" - Billie Eilish
"No Diggity" – Blackstreet (feat Dr. Dre, Queen P)
"Save Your Tears" – The Weeknd (feat. Ariana Grande)
"Kiss and Make Up" - Dua Lipa & BLACKPINK

Official Spotify Playlist

Prologue

King Spencer wasn't the most patient person in the world. Perhaps it was because, even as a junior, he was one of Bradley University's star soccer players and was thus used to there being an entire group of hangers-on anxious to ensure that his needs were being met. Or perhaps it was a by-product of his overly privileged upbringing, where there'd been a revolving door of nannies and the occasional housekeeper who all had a vested interest in keeping King's father happy by keeping his only child entertained and thereby out of his hair.

Or maybe it was because he was a grumpy motherfucker whose affect was as fuzzy as a desert full of cacti.

At any rate, it was probably a good thing that dear old dad had cut him off today. King hated the smarmy bastard anyway, and he had the benefit of a full-ride athletic scholarship as well as the money he'd saved while working when he was in middle and high school. Turned out his modest investments had brought about slightly un-modest returns, so King had enough to support himself, at least for the next couple of years. Plus, anything that came from Solomon Spencer always had strings attached.

Just ask King's mother.

King was currently not so patiently waiting for his friend/roommate/team-mate, Jason, to wrap up his shift at one of the local restaurants that were all within close proximity to Bradley U. He was sitting at one of the booths in Jason's section, sipping a comped raspberry lemonade (because he didn't drink any soda or alcohol during the season) as his friend cleaned up his now closed-down section of the restaurant.

He could hear Jason's spirited voice teasing and flirting from the wait station. People typically didn't know what to make of the two when they hung out together. Jason, with the mischievous glint in his blue eyes, gregarious and loud, and King, dark-eyed, quiet unless he demanded to be heard, inscrutable, and impassive unless he was on the soccer field. It was a wonder they hit it off at all. But King was also fiercely loyal, and he guessed his friends put up with all of his other bullshit because they knew he'd always have their backs.

King stretched his long legs so that they were perched on the bench across from him and took another sip of his drink.

That's when he saw her.

She was young, maybe a freshman, possibly a sophomore. Her shiny dark hair was expertly woven into a long braid that fell past the middle of her back. Clad in a black T-shirt with the silver restaurant logo printed on it tucked into a pair of high-waisted jeans, she made her way over to refill the salad bar. The shy smile that she flashed at a customer as she waited for them to finish up struck some sort of a nerve deep within King's chest.

He liked it and he hated it all at the same time.

When she was finished, she disappeared behind an "Employees Only" swinging door, and King breathed out a sigh that lived somewhere in the gray area between relief and disappointment. As he continued to wait, he was definitely not watching for the girl to reappear, nor was he thinking about brushing or braiding her lustrous hair, because that would be weird as fuck. King was more of a hair puller than a hair braider, anyway.

Jason finished up soon after, and as they made their way to King's car, King briefly thought about asking about the girl he'd seen. He assumed that Jason knew who she was; the restaurant wasn't that big. But something stopped him from speaking. Self-preservation, maybe? Or perhaps it was his overarching assholery? He was inclined to believe the latter but had the sinking suspicion it might be the former.

Before he could dwell on it any further, King shut it all down in his mind. He'd come to pick up his friend, and that was the end of it. The girl, her smile, her damn *hair*, weren't anything to be preoccupied with. It was just a strange moment at the end of a strange day.

So, in spite (or because?) of the weird pull he'd felt and the disconcerting appearance of something that bordered on an emotional response that had occurred that day, he didn't step foot in that restaurant again for another year.

When he did? The innocent-looking girl with the shiny braid and the shy smile would become a part of him in ways he couldn't even fathom.

Chapter 1

"Lila, I just sat 15!" The hostess's voice rang through the server station where Lila Alexander was filling up a couple of Diet Cokes and putting one lime wedge along the rim of each glass. "And may I just say, they're probably the hottest group of guys I've helped all night." The hostess fanned herself exaggeratedly and sent an envious look in Lila's direction.

"Sounds riveting, thanks," Lila replied wryly before motioning to the drinks she was holding. "Do me a favor and stick some straws in these and run them to table 11, please?" Lila smiled as she passed the drinks to the eager new hostess, whose name she was pretty sure was Kristi, and then sighed in frustration as soon as said hostess was out of sight.

Friday nights were the busiest nights at The Pub, and she had only been a server a short time. Serving was far more complicated than being a hostess or managing the salad bar, but the bump in pay was worth it. Even when the well-meaning but inexperienced hostess triple-sat Lila's section. Lila pushed a few errant strands of dark-brown hair back into her ponytail then sanitized her hands.

The interior space of the restaurant was arranged in sort of a backward lowercase "r" shape on the east side and a "c" shape on the west in a series of booths that wrapped around a salad bar (because apparently they were still a thing) with a spacious back room of tables that could be rented out for private events, or, in her boss's case, to kiss up to whatever local college sports team wanted to use it.

On a weekend, the front was divided into five sections of five booths each, and the back was divided into four sections. She was working a section in the front and was hyper-aware of her general manager/top boss, who roamed around the restaurant like an overfed cat waiting to pounce on an unsuspecting canary.

She'd worked at the restaurant for about a year, since the beginning of her freshman year of college, to help pay for what her scholarship didn't cover. But the 30-40 hour work-weeks had begun to massively conflict with her 15-hour class load at the illustrious Bradley University. To keep its students competitive, Bradley started its fall semester at the end of August so they could fit in four semesters a year. So instead of enjoying the last couple of weeks of summer like some of her friends from back home, Lila was already back at school and working her breakneck schedule.

This particular night had been especially exhausting, and she was in no mood to deal with another table of cheap college students. But she squared her shoulders and put on her server smile. She tucked away her shyness, hiding it behind a confidence she figured if she faked enough she'd actually feel. Plus, if they were indeed a table of guys, she might be able to flirt her way to a decent tip. Maybe.

"Yo, Alexander, I'll get that table if you want," Jason Carter called before she could approach. "They're all my friends, so if it's no big deal..."

Lila threw a relieved grin his way. "Go ahead and take 'em. It'll give me a 30-second break that I desperately need."

"Hey, thanks." Jason gave his signature wink before veering off to take his friends' orders.

"No prob," Lila called after him, taking the extra moment to breathe.

That crisis averted, Lila went back to grab another table's order, dropped it off, and glanced at table 15 as she walked by. It was a larger, circular booth, designed to fit at least eight people, though there were only five guys at the table. They were all large—athletes most likely—so they filled up the space. They were all handsome in their own way, she supposed, but only one of them drew her attention. His blue baseball cap was pulled low, a muscled leg slightly extended outside of the edge of the booth, but she was focused on her other tables and thus let the information wash over her without really processing it.

Later, when she went to pick up the check at a nearby table, she glanced at him again, her eyes subconsciously finding him and refusing to drift anywhere else. His met hers in the briefest of moments before she quickly averted her gaze, embarrassed to be caught looking. As she turned away, she could almost feel those deep, dark orbs flitting over the length of her body. Dismissively shaking her head and tamping down the color that had risen to her cheeks, she tucked the receipt into her server book as she headed back to the wait station.

The next hour or so was a practice in self-restraint, as Lila forced herself to concentrate on all of her other tables, only allowing the most peripheral of glances toward the guy in the blue hat. Admittedly, though, she felt like a spotlight was on her every time she walked swiftly by. Which was probably due to her own self-consciousness. She wished they'd leave as hard as she wished they'd stay. That *he'd* stay.

The next time she turned the corner, she noticed that the booth was empty. A busser was clearing dishes off the table. She felt a strange twinge in her gut, like she missed the mystery man, which was ludicrous because she didn't even know his name. Hell, she couldn't even gauge what color of hair was hidden underneath his hat. After their departure, the night got even busier, so Lila couldn't really dwell on it.

After closing, Lila sat in the back room rolling silverware with her best friend, Wren Wright. Jason slid in next to them and began to do the same. He slipped Lila ten bucks as a thank-you for letting him wait on his friends. She took it gratefully because it *had* been a rough night for tips.

"So, did ya think any of my buds were hot?" he teased with an impish grin and an elbow to her ribs.

Lila tried to hold back the flushing of her cheeks as she thought about the guy she'd noticed earlier.

Jason, of course, picked up on her embarrassment and pounced on it. "How about it, Alexander? I noticed you scoping them out."

She cleared her throat and tried to combat the redness of her cheeks, which only made it worse, much to her best friend's delight. Wren was constantly pushing her to come out of her shell, and slowly but surely, Lila was emerging. Emphasis on the slow part.

"Seriously, speak now. If you don't, I'll start singing the latest Bieber," Jason threatened with a wink. He knew Lila hated everything Bieber-adjacent.

"You wouldn't dare."

"You know I totally would."

She clicked her tongue. "Jason Carter, you never let up, do you?" She shifted uncomfortably in her seat as Wren watched the exchange with growing amusement.

"Actually, Li, I'm dying to know myself," Wren smirked, her shoulder-length auburn hair bouncing as she raised a carefully manicured brow.

Jason waggled his brows knowingly. "C'mon...out with it!"

"Well, maybe I thought one of them was cute... The one on the end with the hat."

"King?"

"Wait, you have a friend named King? Like, that's his actual name?" Wren interjected. "Is it pretentious, ironic, or both? It's gotta be both, right?"

Jason laughed. "King's actually his middle name, and, given the way he dominates on the soccer field, I'd say it's appropriate. I'm kind of shocked that neither of you have heard of the magnificent King Spencer. He's practically a legend at Bradley. At least among those of us who actually pay attention to sports."

He shifted his attention back to Lila as Wren huffed her disapproval. As a general rule, athletes weren't Wren's favorite. Lila just shrugged, because what the hell did she know about soccer or any of the other kinds of sports ball? Sure, she went to the football and basketball games because they doubled as social events, and she happened to like the occasional soft pretzel, but she didn't know any of the athletes' names. It was bad enough that most of Bradley U's population treated the jocks like they were gods among mere mortals. She didn't want to add more fuel to that particular fire.

Jason didn't let up, though. "Well, Alexander? King's the one you noticed?" he prodded.

Lila lifted a shoulder. "I mean, obviously I don't know his name. But if King was the one wearing the hat, then…"

"I'll keep that in mind."

"You wouldn't dare," Lila laughed, but she couldn't stop the way her heart sped up at his words. Because, as a general rule, guys like King didn't notice socially awkward girls like her. She definitely wasn't going to let Jason know how badly she wished that weren't the case. So instead, she smirked. "Soccer's boring anyway."

Jason clutched his chest in mock horror. "How dare you blaspheme the beautiful game!" He happened to be on the team, too. A defender, she was pretty sure. At Lila's shrug, he rubbed his hands together. "I already have plans. You aren't ready. Trust me."

"I am so going to enjoy this!" Wren replied in response to Lila's look of abject horror. "Come on, Li. You know you need to find the fun, and even though I personally have a 'no athletes' policy in place, there's no reason why you can't dip a toe into the pool."

"Traitor," Lila mumbled as she threw a napkin at her friend amid Wren's and Jason's uproarious laughter.

Chapter 2

L ila trudged up the legendary 150 stairs that most of the students who lived south of Bradley U took to get up to campus, satisfied that they no longer winded her in the same way they had at the beginning of the year. As was the custom with most freshmen, she'd lived on campus her first year in a tiny apartment-style dorm room on the east side of campus with a kitchen and five roommates.

She hadn't known any of her roommates when she moved in but had been pleasantly surprised by how much she enjoyed living with them that year. The summer before their sophomore year started, they all decided to move to the same apartment complex but split up into different groups, with Lila deciding to share a room with a friend of theirs who she'd met during freshman year. Which, in hindsight, hadn't been the best idea. But she liked her other new roommates, and her old roomies were nearby.

She crossed the grid-like campus, expertly designed to ensure that all students could walk the length of it in any direction in 15 minutes or less, passing by a mixture of older buildings from the late 1800s and newer, more modern buildings along the way, each shortened into quirky abbreviations of their actual names. For instance, the student union building's official name was the Jonathan Bradley Student Center, which everybody just referred to as the "Brad."

The administration buildings were situated to the south, the business school building and the athletic facilities to the west, the law school, law school library, and dorms to the east, and the football stadium and basketball arena on the northwest and northeast corners respectively, flanking the buildings housing the science museum and the museum of art. The main library and liberal arts buildings sat in the center of campus, as did the Brad, which was her current destination. After hearing Wren's telltale ringtone, Lila answered her phone.

"Lila, where are you?" Wren's voice came through Lila's phone and echoed through the room, since Lila had already spotted her bestie at their usual table in the large common area of the Brad and was already navigating through the series of tables heading in Wren's direction.

Though best friends and self-proclaimed "soul mates," insofar as they were concerned, Wren and Lila looked nothing alike. Where Lila was shorter than her friend by a handful of inches, angular and olive skinned, with long dark hair and light-brown eyes, Wren was curvy and 5'10", a veritable Jessica Rabbit with a short auburn lob and bright-blue eyes. Though outwardly different, they shared a love for big words, sarcasm, and the pursuit of law school.

"Behind ya." Lila plunked her giant purse that doubled as her backpack down on the huge round table. "What a day... I seriously need a vacation." She twirled her raven hair around her fingers and sighed.

Wren looked at her sympathetically, shaking her head. "So I'm thinking a *Schitt's Creek* marathon and popcorn tonight at my place, yeah?"

Lila nodded vigorously. "At last, we both have the same night off. And forget about homework. I swear I can't do it anymore. It's hard enough trying to do it with all of my roommate drama."

"So Becky is still in the middle of her dramatic love triangle with your next-door neighbors?"

Lila nodded with a groan. "Seriously, I don't know why she thought dating a guy who lives next door was a good idea in the first place, but to then start dating our *other* next-door neighbor at the same time? I can't even with all of the reality TV-esque situations. Plus, she's in a 'I'm only eating wheat toast with no butter' phase, so she's in a perpetually terrible mood. I have no idea why I didn't find a place with private bedrooms. Thankfully Dani and Vicky are normal. Otherwise I would have moved out by now."

Dani and Vicky were both seniors, best friends from way back in the day, and pretty drama free. Dani was in the art program, and Vicky was an aspiring accountant. And both were hilarious and fun and liked to watch movies and hang out. Much to Lila's relief. Because she'd thought that Becky was chill too, until they moved in together.

"Next year, my friend. Next year," Wren promised.

Currently, Wren lived in an apartment about 20 minutes away from campus, whereas Lila lived just south of campus within walking distance. But they'd made a pact to live with each other their junior and senior years...somewhere closer to campus for Wren, with two bedrooms so they'd each have their own.

"Plus," Wren continued, "you know you can sleep over whenever you'd like. Like tonight, for instance. I just made the executive decision."

"I love you, Wrenny."

"Tell me something I don't know." Wren started to gather her hair into a low pony and then abruptly stopped as she noticed a person entering the building.

"Well, look who it is. Mr. King Spencer himself," Wren commented loudly, pointing at King in her typical unsubtle manner.

Inwardly, Lila groaned, for she liked to be as inconspicuous as possible. A hard feat when she was with Wren. She hoped he was out of earshot. Otherwise, she might as well crawl underneath the table and never come out again.

It had been just over a month since she'd seen King and his friends at the restaurant, not that she was counting or anything, and she refused to ask Jason if King had come in again. She wasn't going to give her co-worker the satisfaction of her curiosity.

She nonchalantly turned in time to catch a glimpse of King from a distance, walking with the swagger that was common amongst all of Bradley's athletes. Since she'd found out his name from Jason, she'd done a mild amount of "research" on the soccer player. Apparently, he was the star forward on Bradley's soccer team, a senior who'd redshirted a year, so he actually had another year of eligibility to play if he wanted.

King carried himself as if he hadn't a care in the world, almost daring people to judge him, to see what really made him tick. Lila couldn't fight the little burst of nervous excitement that crept in when she saw him. Dismissively, she turned back, only to feel Wren's perceptive stare upon her.

"You like him." It was a statement, not a question.

"How can I like someone I don't even know? There's just something about him that intrigues me is all; and I highly doubt a guy like that would condescend from his throne of athleticism and date a 19-year-old sophomore." Her sarcasm was apparent.

"Heaven forbid." Wren wrinkled her nose in feigned disgust. "And he'd probably wither away if he heard you utter a word that was over two syllables."

The one thing that Lila and Wren definitely did *not* share was their taste in men.

"Though I suppose he is attractive in the way that *you* seem to find so incredibly appealing," Wren teased. "And I'm woman enough to admit that his ass is a thing of absolute beauty." She whistled. "My heavens, Michelangelo would have spent weeks sculpting and chiseling to try to reproduce that beautiful behind."

Lila simultaneously laughed and blushed because her best friend was all sorts of right about that particular observation. Indeed, King was exactly Lila's preferred physical type. He was at least a couple of inches over 6 feet tall, with a gracefully muscular frame, including the aforementioned ass. His closely cropped dirty blondish hair was just slightly longer on the top, and Lila had a feeling that his piercing dark-brown eyes could eviscerate his opponents with one look. Add in tanned skin, a jawline that would make Zeus weep, and gleaming white teeth, and he was the epitome of the all-around, good-looking athletic type, with just a hint of an edge that Lila found so irresistible. The type that, up to this point, had been almost completely unattainable.

Sure, she'd dated the captain of the baseball team in high school, the year they'd only won one game after winning the state championship the year before, and though she'd tried to be the dutiful, appropriately soothing girlfriend, their fledgling relationship was doomed by the end of the season. Apparently she wasn't "supportive enough" of his needs, whatever that meant. The fact that Lila happened to be debilitatingly shy and thoroughly into academics in high school did not help matters. But she was getting much better at managing her timidity, and Wren never let Lila retreat too far back into herself.

Lila laughed at her friend's semi-serious derision. "Thanks, I am so blissfully happy to receive your blessing. I'll have to promptly find him so that the wedding plans may commence. I better tell Jason. After all, he'll be the best man. Yay!"

"As scintillating as this wedding planning sounds," Wren replied, "we need to get to Nelson's class. Perhaps our illustrious professor will, once and for all, decide who's the greater misogynist: Fitzgerald or Hemingway."

The friends gathered their things and stood up, glancing at each other knowingly. "Hemingway," they said in unison as they burst into giggles.

"Obviously always Hemingway," Lila added.

"The chauvinist of all chauvinists," Wren happily concurred as they headed off to class.

Chapter 3

"Yo, Alexander, can you take two raspberry lemonades to table 18 for me? They need refills ASAP."

Lila swerved to miss another server in the wait station and nodded to Jason, who was already hurrying off to take another table's order. By the time she'd prepped the drinks and headed over to the booth in question, it was too late to realize that King was sitting at the table with another friend, who she was 99% sure was the starting quarterback for Bradley U's football team.

Another thing she observed? The fact that they most definitely did *not* need refills. She slowed in her approach but realized it was too late to turn around. Jason was definitely going down for this once she caught the wily little waiter.

Backed into a proverbial (and literal) corner, she managed to arrange her face into some semblance of a smile, assiduously avoided eye contact, and set the drinks down in front of the two men anyway.

"Jason said you needed these...so here you go."

King briefly glanced up at her nondescriptly, an amused spark flashing through his eyes, and before anything else embarrassing could happen, Lila quickly retreated back to the server station. She found Jason, doubled over in laughter, and gave him a shove.

"Thanks for having me embarrass myself like that. I super enjoyed it," Lila sardonically remarked in reply to the laughter.

"Did they like their refills?" Jason could hardly get the words out. "Sorry, Alexander. I couldn't help myself."

Lila veed her fingers from her eyes to Jason's and back again. "I'm watching you, Carter. And I'll get you back when you least expect it."

Jason just grinned the little mischievous grin that seemed to be a permanent fixture on his face before leaving to go talk to his friends.

Lila wandered into the back room, which had already been closed down for the night, where Wren was wrapping some silverware for the next day's lunch shift. Both of their sections had been closed after the dinner rush, so they just needed to finish up their side work before clocking out.

Wren looked up as Lila let out a soft groan. She read Lila's face like a book. "Let me guess... Jason made you run something to King's table? And your sweet little shy heart almost burst with embarrassment?"

"Yup." Lila grimaced. "Even better? It was drinks they didn't need, so..."

"Jason is such a prankster. We'll have to find a way to get him back." Lila hummed in assent before Wren continued, "Speak of the devil..."

"And he shall appear," Jason finished, poking his head into the room. "Hey Lila, can I borrow you for a second?" He slid into the room and held up his hands. "I promise there are no tricks this time. I just want to introduce you to King and Knight. Wren, you can come too, if you'd like."

"Hard pass. And seriously, what the hell is up with your friends' names, Carter? Like, are they all chess pieces or trust fund douchebags?" Wren questioned wryly.

"Be nice, Wrenny. It's not his friends' fault they have unironically chess-themed monikers. The blame should be upon the heads of the parents," Lila quipped.

"As interesting as this all is, you need to stop stalling and follow me now," Jason said. At Lila's eye roll, he amended his words, saying, "Pretty please, with a cherry on top?"

"Fine." Lila followed him through the French doors and around the bend to where his friends were sitting.

"Server girl," the person who wasn't King said, smilingly. His light-green eyes were a vivid contrast to his black hair. Lila had no doubt he made many a coed swoon just by looking at them. In fact, she felt a little weak in the knees herself, even as she was hyper aware of his silent, stony friend. "So sorry that our boy Jason decided to prank you on our watch. I'm Knight, by the way."

"No worries. I'm used to his antics by now," Lila replied shyly. "Besides, I'm sure he does worse to you all if you're unlucky enough to be his roommates."

She dodged out of the way just as Jason was about to hip check her. "And my name's Lila. It's nice to meet you, Knight."

Knight's grin widened as Jason diverted her attention to King. "Lila, this strong, silent type to our right is King."

"Hi," Lila said.

King gave her a slight head nod in response. A head nod. His expression wasn't exactly unkind, but it definitely wasn't interested either. At least that's how it appeared to Lila. But his eyes were intently examining her, and she couldn't look away.

Picking up on the awkward combination of silence and inexplicably intense eye contact, Knight reclaimed Lila's attention. "So, Li—can I call you Li?" At her nod, he continued, "Are you planning on attending our big party next Friday?"

"The block party where you have to dress up all sporty?"

"That's the one. We affectionately refer to it as Jock Jam, and it's obviously *the* party to attend if you want to dance and have a good time."

Lila's face turned sheepish. "I wasn't really planning on it... I'm not really that much of a dancer. Or a sports apparel wearer."

Knight clicked his tongue in mock disapproval. "Well, I'm afraid that answer's just not gonna cut it, Li. In fact, I'm not only insisting that you come, but that you save me a dance."

His smile and charm were contagious. And honestly, his vibe was so affable, Lila doubted that he had any interest in her other than a potential friendship.

"Well, when you put it that way..."

"Excellent." He took out his phone. "Give me your digits, Lila dear, so that I may text you and remind you of this party you have now promised you will attend. And if you need to borrow any athletic gear. I'm sure that between the three of us, we can hook you up."

While Lila recited her number, she noticed that King's expression had darkened slightly. Almost like he was annoyed. At her? No...that wasn't it. At

Knight, maybe? Whatever it was, Jason also noticed and made a crack about how King should save a dance for Lila too. Once again, King's eyes were on her, silently assessing, his mouth quirked up in the slightest of half smiles.

"I don't think you could handle me, Lila." The timbre of his voice was deep and decadent, and Lila had to concentrate really hard to suppress the shiver that it elicited.

"I guess we'll find out," she quipped with a raised eyebrow, happy that, for once, she had a somewhat witty reply at the ready. She couldn't exactly explain what she felt when she was around King, just that whatever it was, she felt it…everywhere. And it was unlike anything she'd experienced before.

"It's settled, then," Knight interjected, regaining Lila's focus. "You'll come, you'll dance, you'll have a great time."

"I'll come, I'll *attempt* to dance, and I'll have a great time. With a group of my girls so I don't feel outnumbered," Lila amended, much to Knight's apparent delight. He stuck his fist out, which Lila tentatively bumped with hers.

"Deal."

Chapter 4

"I still can't believe that *the* Knight Patrick personally invited you to Jock Jam," Dani sighed dreamily. She and Vicky were clad in oversize matching basketball jerseys that they'd modified to fit like shift dresses along with coordinating Jordans. They were both huge sports fans and had about passed out when Lila had told them that *the* Knight Patrick not only invited her to the party of the year but had also asked for her number. Add in that he'd actually sent her a couple of texts? They seemed in total awe of her.

Wren was sprawled across Lila's bed, hair in two French braids, dressed in her signature boyfriend jeans and tank top with a zip-up hooded sweatshirt to complete the look. "I'm a boxer in training," she'd said in explanation when she arrived.

"You're more than welcome to ride with us," Lila replied, pulling on white knee socks with a couple of navy blue stripes banding the top. Thankfully, it was unseasonably warm for September, with temps in the 50-60s at night, so she could get away with wearing the knee socks with a pair of short navy bike shorts and a long-sleeved white thermal crop top. She threw an unbuttoned Yankees jersey on to complete the look.

"Thanks, but we have to make a pit stop to grab some dinner first," Vicky replied. "But we'll text you when we get there."

Dani and Vicky said their goodbyes and headed out, leaving Lila and Wren in Lila's room. Thankfully, Becky was out on one of her twelve-mile runs, so her weird energy wasn't invading their space.

Lila took one last look in the mirror while donning a white Yankees hat and turned to her best friend. "Well, how do I look?"

"Like every athlete's little fantasy come to life."

"Stop teasing."

"This time, I'm serious." Wren got up and crossed over to where Lila was standing. "You're what we call a late bloomer, my friend. And you're blooming like whoa right about now. Own the hotness."

"Thanks, friend. And thanks for taking one for the...team...to come with me tonight."

"Your pun is noted and thoroughly appreciated, and it is my pleasure to be your wing woman during this night of athletic debauchery."

"I owe you DDPs for life after this." Wren's drink of choice was a Diet Dr. Pepper, always and forever.

"You just might," Wren agreed.

They heard the party before they saw it. Wren had grown up in this college town, so she knew all the sneaky, free places to park. They were about a block away from the nondescript side street that housed the majority of Bradley U's star athletes. Everybody referred to said street as Jock Row, which was basically a narrow half street that ended in a dead end that featured a string of houses that had unofficially become athletic housing because of their proximity to the university's sports facilities and its state-of-the-art gym.

They entered the party from the east. Based on his directions, Knight's house sat at one corner at the end of the road, and Jason and King's house was directly across the street on the other corner. A parking lot stretched between the two houses next to a high cinder block retaining wall that ended the street. That space between had become the center of the party, with large speakers pumping out music. The kegs weren't out in the open, since not everyone attending was over 21, but they were accessible if you knew which houses to enter. Not that Lila had any interest in keg stands.

Wren smiled because if there was one thing she did love to do, it was dance. "Come on, Li, they're playing old school Missy Elliot."

Lila allowed herself to be dragged into the fray and started dancing with her friend. After a while, she felt her phone vibrate from the belt bag she was wearing cross-body style. It was a text from Dani. After sending her their location, Lila shot a text to Knight as well. Might as well let him know they were there.

Since her phone was out, she decided to wrangle Wren into taking a selfie, with the promise that she'd only post it on her Insta stories.

"A selfie isn't a selfie unless it's a Knight Patrick selfie," a jovial voice boomed from behind them before he ducked down into the frame. Lila snapped the photo and then spun around just in time to be lifted up into a hug by the massive football player. "Hey there, Li. Glad you could make it. You better send me that pic." He set her back down and motioned his head toward Wren. "And who is your friend here? I'm assuming your name's not Rocky?"

That actually evoked a small smile from Wren as she introduced herself. Knight put an arm around each of them as Dani and Vicky walked up to them. "Ooh, more friends, Li?"

Lila laughed at his exuberance and at the stunned expressions from her roommates. "Yup. Knight, this is Vicky and Dani. Ladies, this is *the* Knight Patrick."

"Nice to meet you." Knight grinned, and Lila swore their panties melted right off. He dropped his arms and held out a hand to Lila. "Now, if you three will excuse Lila and me for a moment, I do believe she promised me a dance." He motioned his head over to what Lila assumed was his front porch. "You ladies are welcome to head over to the house and grab a drink or whatever. We'll meet you there?"

All Dani and Vicky could do was nod, and Wren smirked her signature smirk and smacked her friend on the ass. "See you two dancing queens in a few."

Knight pulled Lila deeper into the crowd just as a remixed Dua Lipa song began. "All right, Li, let's see your moves."

Lila laughed as they danced together, Knight always maintaining a respect-ful distance. They even worked out a little routine which they performed once they realized a circle of people had formed around them.

"Hot damn, you're fun." Knight smiled as they made their way over to his house after a few songs. "I can see why he's interested in you."

"Wait, huh?" Lila sputtered. "What does that even mean?"

Knight winked and flicked a glance toward a solitary figure leaning against the side of the house. King.

"Hey Li, be a friend and see if you can actually get my boy over there to dance, will ya? He's being so antisocial tonight, and I think you might be able to cheer him up. I'll make sure your girls are good."

"Um...you're not, like, pulling a Jason so I'll embarrass myself, are you?"

"I swear on a stack of footballs," Knight intoned.

"Can you even stack footballs?"

Knight grabbed the bill of her cap and gave it a little shake. "Stop stalling and get your cute self over there."

Lila split from Knight and shot Wren a quick text before heading over to the left side of the house. She tried to calm down her nerves and prayed she wouldn't make a fool out of herself as she approached. His eyes assessed her silently.

"Having a fun time propping up the house?" she asked.

"Something like that."

Lila leaned against the house so they were facing each other. "So why are you out here all by your lonesome? Hiding from all the jersey chasers?"

King's laugh was short but made Lila's stomach somersault nonetheless. "They *are* always lurking around at these things."

"And you don't like all that attention?"

"Not tonight."

"Still gonna see if I can handle your dance moves? I'm pretty sure they're playing 'Get Low' right now. I'd love to see you drop it like it's hot."

King chuckled and looked down at his feet before raising his eyes back to Lila's. "Girl, I *know* you can't. But I have a better idea. Follow me?" He pointed to the backyard of the house.

"You're not planning on murdering me or anything, right?"

"Naw, I only murder on Mondays."

"Nice call on the one-day-a-week murdering. And on the alliteration. It's still a little too murdery for my personal taste, though."

"Fair enough." King pushed off the house and tilted his head. "You coming?"

Lila nodded, her eyes tracing the slope of his broad shoulders as he led her down the path that led to the backyard. There was a full moon out, so the night was surprisingly bright, which was helpful once they reached their destination.

From what Lila could see, there was a cement pad with a few chairs and a grill that was set up against the house, along with a small patch of grass that was surprisingly well maintained for a house full of college boys.

"Be back in a sec," King said, launching up the couple of stairs to a back door. A porch light flicked on, bathing the backyard in soft light. He reemerged with a couple of water bottles in hand and gestured to a couple of lounge chairs that were set closely together.

"Water?"

"Sure, thanks." Lila tried to ignore the strange ways that her nerves fired when her fingers brushed his. She definitely needed to get out more. They both stretched out on the chairs and opened their waters, taking a few pulls in silence.

One of the byproducts of Lila's shyness was that she tended to overcorrect when she felt uncomfortable, meaning she'd become inanely chatty, something she was desperately trying to avoid around King. But as the silence stretched into space and wrapped around them, she felt the familiar itchiness that came right before a bunch of embarrassing word vomit.

Just as she was ready to break with something pathetic like, *So you like to play soccer, huh?* King popped the awkwardness bubble.

"You a Yankees fan, Lila?" His gaze flitted from her hat down the length of her jersey, and Lila felt every heady second of his undivided attention.

"Mostly just an Aaron Judge fan," Lila joked. "My high school ex played baseball and liked the team, and it just so happened that I liked the jersey and the hat and the aforementioned Aaron Judge, so I decided not to throw them out once things were over. Which came in handy for an impromptu-ish party such as this."

"Well, you look good, so I think you made the right decision."

Lila was glad that the light was dim enough that King wouldn't notice the pinkening of her cheeks. "Thanks."

She let herself take a moment to scan over King's plain white T-shirt and navy joggers. "I take it the people who throw the party are absolved from following costume rules? Except I do recall that Knight was wearing a jersey."

"Knight's all about this kind of thing…"

"And, let me guess… You're not?"

"Not always. But hey, we match, so that's gotta count for something."

"I guess you're right. Though, I will admit, I was very much looking forward to your dance moves."

"Like I said, La, you couldn't handle the moves. Not even a little bit."

"La, huh?"

"It suits you."

"Most people shorten my name to Li; this is the first time I've gotten a La. I don't hate it."

"That's good, I guess, because that's what I'm calling you from now on." He leaned in to examine the delicate yellow gold necklace she was wearing. "Is that a crown?" He motioned to the tiny charm that hovered over the center of her sternum.

Lila fingered the small three-pointed crown charm subconsciously. "Yeah. It was a high school graduation gift from my favorite grandma. She said it was to help me feel powerful as I went out on my own for the first time. I rarely take it off."

"I like it," King said with a sexy half smile that made Lila feel all sorts of things. "My name *is* King, after all. Crowns kind of come with the territory." He winked, and she had to suppress a gasp. Because who knew a wink could be anything other than cheesy?

The longer the two continued to talk, the more they had to say. Lila lost track of time and was finally snapped out of her conversation by the vibrations of her phone. It was Wren, saying that she was tapped out on wing womaning for the night. Lila was shocked to see that over an hour had passed since she'd approached King.

"My ride is ready to go, so…" Despite the ease of their conversation, Lila all of a sudden felt awkward again as she stood. King got to his feet too.

"I'll walk you out," he said. He seemed to hesitate, just for a minute, before he spoke again. "So I was wondering if I could get your number? Maybe we could hang again sometime next week, if you're game."

Lila nodded and gave him her number, trying her hardest to play it cool. Unlike with Knight, who she could appreciate was stupidly attractive but who only gave her friendship-type vibes, King created an emotional war of feelings that tore through her body like a gunshot.

They walked side by side up to the front of the house, where Wren was waiting with a grinning Knight.

"Later, La," King said before turning to go into the house.

"Later," Lila managed to eke out to his retreating form.

Wren and Knight shared some sort of a look that they probably assumed Lila wouldn't notice, and then Lila and Wren said their goodbyes to Mr. Charisma himself.

Once they were locked in the safety of the car, Wren turned to her friend. "Okay, Li, spill it right now. Where did you go? And what happened with the inscrutable soccer star?"

Lila shifted in her seat and explained what happened, how Knight had practically pushed her into King's lap. How they ended up talking and laughing together. How he asked for her number.

"So he's, like, taking you on a date?"

Lila hummed. "I don't know. He made it sound like maybe we'd hang out or something. Honestly, it's all still sinking in. The past little while has been absolutely surreal on the social front."

"Like I've been saying, babe, you're blooming. You're hot AF, so of course all of those muscled specimens are going to take notice."

"Thanks for being my wing woman tonight, Wrenny. You know you're the best."

"Eh, it wasn't so bad. I got roped into a game of beer pong, and Knight was decent enough to swap out my beer with DDP because he knew I was driving tonight. And underaged. He's not a bad guy to have in your corner."

"Knight coming through with the DDP. Sounds like it wasn't too bad of a night for you."

"It really wasn't." Wren pulled out onto the road. "So, Denny's Grand Slam and then my place?"

"Obvi," Lila laughed.

Chapter 5

"So I think that's the first time I've actually gotten through a whole movie with a girl without her trying to put the moves on me," King joked. "I must be losing my game."

"Who said you even had any game to begin with?" Lila teased back as she rolled over to face him. His response was to attempt to tickle her ribs until her triumphant smile signaled that she was, in fact, not ticklish at all. She didn't mind the extra contact, though. Not even a little bit.

It had been two weeks since Jock Jam, and King had surprised her by texting her a couple of days after the party to ask if she wanted to come over to his house to hang out. She'd had a blast hanging with King, Jason, and their other two roommates, Will and James. They'd ended up teaching her how to play 5-Card Draw, and she surprised the hell out of all of them by being pretty good at it.

After that, they started FaceTiming every night, talking into the early hours of the morning about all sorts of things. She told him about her family, how she was the oldest of five kids with super overprotective parents who had initially wanted her to go to the local community college and live at home. He confessed that he hated his first name because he was named after his father, who King said was a terrible person.

King made a point to find her on campus around lunchtime so they could hang out. And this particular night, he'd taken her out on their first official date. They'd gone to dinner at a restaurant that was not The Pub and had ultimately decided to head to King's to watch a movie after. Once they'd picked something off Netflix, he had pulled Lila down to lie next to him on the spacious sectional in the main living area of the house. After two hours of spooning and King alternating between lightly tracing the hem of Lila's top and playing with her hair, she thought she was going to spontaneously combust into a confetti of hormones.

His hand found the exposed skin at the small of her back, and he lightly ran his fingers over her body, leaving a trail of goosebumps in their wake. Impossibly, his eyes darkened as he measured her response to him.

"I think I affect you the way you affect me," he murmured, his hand slowly moving underneath her shirt, tracing up her spine.

"How's that?" Lila's response sounded more like a sigh. She couldn't help the way her body arched into his, and she couldn't stop staring at his perfect mouth. Though it'd been a minute since she'd kissed anyone, kissing King was all she was currently thinking about. That, and his hands tracing lines all over her body.

He looked at her for what seemed like forever then leaned in and kissed her softly, his hand moving from her back to span the bare expanse of her stomach, gently pressing her down so her back was flat on the couch. His lips were even softer than she'd imagined, though they commanded hers with a confidence that she completely expected. At first, he softly tasted her, with soft brushes of his full lips and tiny little swipes of his tongue. Lila thought she could live forever in those delicious kisses, until King took them deeper, off the edge to somewhere infinitely more carnal. It was all Lila could do to hold on for the ride.

He moved his mouth down the column of her throat, marking her with gentle kisses and not-so-gentle nips of the skin. When he found a particularly sensitive spot just underneath her ear, she let out a sound that was apparently pleasing to King, because he quickly maneuvered their bodies so that Lila was now fully underneath him and the space between their bodies disappeared.

"Is this okay?" he murmured before moving his hips against hers so that she could feel all of him.

"Yes," she breathed as he began slowly grinding their bodies together as they continued to kiss. His hand had just grazed the outside of one of her small breasts when the front door abruptly opened, with Jason's boisterous declaration of, "Honey, I'm home!" effectively killing the mood. Thankfully, the front door was facing the back of the couch, so Jason hadn't seen them just yet. King quickly pulled down Lila's shirt and repositioned them to their previous movie watching position.

Jason jumped over the back of the couch, landing right next to their feet. Thankfully the lights were off, so Lila's makeout hair wasn't as obvious. "What are you guys watching?"

"Um, we just finished a movie, and I think we're going to call it a night," King replied.

"Party poopers," Jason grunted as they stood up.

"Sorry, J, maybe next time," Lila replied, mostly to divert his attention enough for her to escape without him knowing they'd been fooling around.

"Fine," Jason sighed. Then he turned to look at her and smirked. "By the way, your makeout hair looks pretty epic, Alexander. Sorry to interrupt."

King stayed silent, and Lila rolled her eyes to cover up her embarrassment as they made their way to King's car, Jason's gleeful laughter loud enough that it followed them out the door. Once they were inside, Lila flipped down the mirror to survey the damage as he pulled out onto the road. Her hair was a little mussed but definitely not as wild as Jason had intimated.

"OMG. Jason can be the worst," she groan-laughed as she flipped the mirror back up. "I barely have makeout hair."

"It would have gotten really messy had we had more time alone." King's gaze flitted over to hers, and the desire in his expression caused a rush of heat to settle low in Lila's belly.

She hummed in response as she tried to gather her words. They hadn't really discussed their experience level, because, awkward, but she felt like she needed to let him know that she was out of her depth and trust that he'd respect her boundaries.

The drive to her place passed quickly, and as soon as King put his car in park, Lila gathered up the courage to say what she felt she needed to say.

"So, um, tonight was fun, but I want you to know that that's the farthest I've ever gone physically with anyone before."

King's expression stayed neutral, but he studied her intently, and Lila desperately wished she could crawl inside his brain so she could see what he was thinking about.

"I'm telling you because I just might need to take things slowly. Assuming that's something you're interested in. Because I'm not in the habit of making out with guys that I'm not interested in. I'm not really wired for the whole 'one and done' kind of thing."

"I'd never pressure you into doing anything you don't want to do."

"I appreciate that." She did, but she also focused on what he didn't say. He didn't say anything specific about continuing whatever they'd started. Or that this was more than a one-time, PG-13ish hookup. Lila had the feeling that King rarely said anything he didn't mean and was thus very particular with the words he chose to say. Though she didn't regret her honesty the moment before, she also felt like her lack of sexual experience was probably a deterrent to someone as self-possessed as King.

Her inner monologue was cut off when he leaned in to tuck a loose hair behind her ear and then grazed her lips with his. "C'mon. I'll walk you to your door."

Her apartment complex consisted of four identical 3-story buildings arranged in a square, with exterior staircases leading to the various apartment doors. Lila's was on the second floor, so they scaled the stairs that led to her place.

"This is me." Lila motioned to the door. Then King was in her space, his large hand circling the back of her head as he leaned down to kiss her deeply. Too soon, he withdrew, tracing Lila's bottom lip with his thumb.

"Later, La."

"Later, King."

As soon as she was inside her apartment, she texted Wren, who was waiting on a full report, regardless of how late the hour. Wren was convinced that King was interested in more than just a fling, but Lila wasn't so sure. Though what had happened had felt important somehow, Lila couldn't shake the feeling that their last kiss was more of a goodbye than a hello.

And as the subsequent days began to stretch into weeks with no word from King, Lila realized that she was right.

Chapter 6

Lila left class and headed over to the west side of campus, to the building that housed the Bradley U business school. It was kind of an open secret that the small cafe on the ground floor served the best paninis, and it was definitely a panini kind of day. It had been two weeks since the makeout that had kind of rocked her world, and Lila still hadn't heard a peep from King Spencer.

She was not going to make the first move, nor was she going to bring it up to Jason, who had been badgering her about it at work. No, she was not going to send a text or a DM or anything of the sort, not when her already fragile ego was hanging on by a thread.

In her mind, she chalked his silence up to the fact that she'd probably been a little too open about her lack of experience and was overly assumptive that King would want to continue to hang out after that night. Or maybe she was just a terrible kisser. With embarrassingly small boobs. Her already keen propensity to overanalyze had escalated to a fever pitch, and old insecurities were brought to the fore with a force that was hard to combat.

As always, Wren brought her back down to reality. Wren had reminded her that two weeks in guy time wasn't really that long and that King was the one missing out if he chose to ghost.

While Lila appreciated the sentiment, she knew that her friend was more than a little biased. She was trying to be chill about the whole thing–more adult and realistic. But the truth of the matter was that she'd put herself out there and been open with King, and it seemed like it was coming back to bite her in the ass.

Adopting her "I don't want to chat with anybody" position, she put her headphones in and scrolled through her phone while she was waiting in line. A faint tap on her shoulder caused her to turn around, with an irritated look firmly in place, until she noticed that said shoulder tapper was Knight Patrick. Her annoyed frown turned into a grin that mirrored his as she took out her AirPods.

"Oh, Knight! Hey. Fancy meeting you here."

Knight laughed lightly. "It's nice to see that smile, Li. For a second, I thought you were going to rip my head off."

Lila winced playfully. "Sorry about that. Wasn't really in the mood to chat with randoms today. Or get hit on by someone who asks if I can spare some Chapstick."

Knight wrinkled his nose. "That's happened before?"

Lila nodded.

"Some dudes need lessons in the fine art of talking to someone without being completely creepy."

"Agreed. Thus the AirPods."

"Understandable. I guess it's a good thing we're like best buds now that we've bonded over our superior dance moves and overall awesomeness. I would also like to note that you are an excellent texter. It's becoming a lost art, really, and your wittiness-to-emoji ratio is second-to-none."

"Agreed about the best buds thing. And thank you," Lila replied with a smile as they moved up the line. Knight Patrick was rapidly becoming one of her favorite people. It was a shame that Wren wasn't typically into athletes, because Lila had a feeling that underneath the muscular exterior, Knight was just Wren's type. They made small talk as they waited in line, Knight filling her in on the business classes he was taking, how the football team was faring, and then Lila shared something funny that had happened in her last class, until it was time to order. Knight insisted on paying for her lunch.

"Seriously, Li, put your money away," Knight said, cutting off her protestations and giving the cashier his card.

"Well, thank you," Lila murmured, suddenly keenly aware that lots of eyes were focused on her and the star quarterback. It was kind of difficult not to notice the stunningly attractive Knight and his imposing frame. The contrast between his dark hair and grass-green eyes alone was positively drool-worthy.

"Honestly, it's just my selfish attempt to round up some company for lunch," Knight joked, oblivious to all of the attention as he motioned to a small table nearby with his head. "Shall we?"

"We shall."

They ate in companionable silence for a minute or two before Knight took a large swig of his bottled water and then asked the question that Lila was hoping he wouldn't ask. "So, how are things with you and King? Word on the street is that Jason interrupted a sexy moment." He brandished his strong brows like a weapon and his green eyes glittered with something in the neighborhood of mischief and delight.

Lila gulped down the bite of sandwich she had been chewing on and waited another beat or two before she answered. "Um, so yeah, that is a thing that kind of happened. Though I'm sure Jason has grossly over exaggerated the particulars."

"So things are going well?"

Lila had assumed that Knight and King were pretty close, so she was surprised that he seemed to be in the dark about the fact that King had gone radio silent.

"Um, he hasn't, like, texted me or whatever since that night. So I'm assuming...no?" She quickly corrected herself so her previous statement didn't sound so much like a question. "I mean, it's not a question. It's obviously a no. I think we're done hanging out." She cringed a bit as she shrugged. "Or whatever we were doing."

Knight made a sound in his throat that sounded a lot like irritation. "So you're telling me that he maybe more than kissed you and then ditched you?"

"Um. Given that fact that I haven't heard from him, I guess?" Lila felt uncomfortable, old insecurities creeping back in. "Look, I mean, I'm probably not the typical kind of girl he goes for, so I get it. I'm not wired to just hook up, I guess."

She shifted in her seat, crossing then uncrossing her legs. "Anyway, can we talk about something else? More football maybe? Whether or not you have a special lady in your life since we last spoke?"

Knight looked her over somberly for about half a second, and then his affable grin was firmly back in place. "Your wish is my command. How much do you know about fourth-down conversions?"

Later, after their lunch was finished and they exited the building together, Knight caught Lila by the elbow. "I consider you a friend now, Li. Almost like the sister I never had. And I've got your six, okay? King or no King."

"Thanks, Knight. Same." She leaned in and hugged him around his middle and said goodbye, heading to her next class with a smile on her face.

* * *

When Lila returned to her apartment later that afternoon, she inadvertently interrupted Becky's newly established meditation time, which apparently took up the entirety of the apartment's communal space, so she waded through the smell of burning incense to get to their bedroom. Vicky and Dani had wisely cleared out, and Lila luckily had a dinner shift. She made quick work of changing into her work clothes and pulled her hair back into a ponytail before slinking back out the front door with a quiet "Good-bye," while Becky was chanting with her eyes closed.

Wren was off that night and Jason was working in the section next to hers, so she had to continue to deflect any questions he posed about King. When there was a lull in the rush and they were both wrapping silverware in the wait station, Jason poked her with his elbow.

"C'mon Alexander, you've gotta give me some details about what's up with King. I mean, I was there to see all of that sexy energy happening in real time," he chuckled and gave a fairly decent shoulder shimmy. "He never says anything about anything, so it's up to you to give me all the dirty details."

Lila worried at her bottom lip for a minute so that she wouldn't break down and interrogate her coworker. She played it as cool as she could. "I haven't heard from him since that night you came home and we were watching the movie on your couch," she replied evenly with a slightly raised shoulder.

Jason's face lit up with confusion, which then settled into a knowing understanding, and it was almost disconcerting to see his expression when it wasn't filled with mischief or humor. "Ah" was all he said, his voice unsurprised but with a slight edge to it. Frustration, maybe? Based on Knight's and Jason's similar reactions to her response, Lila wondered if perhaps King was as inscrutable to his friends as he'd been to her.

Lila really, *really* wanted to ask him to elaborate, but she refrained. What King did or didn't do wasn't any of her business. Luckily, she didn't have to discuss it further because she got another table. Unfortunately, they were close personal friends of the restaurant manager, Bryan Blaine, and so she spent the next 45 minutes catering to every little whim they had.

But seriously, who orders a pizza with melted cheese *on the side?* Monsters, that's who.

She managed to control her eye rolls, even as Bryan made an appearance to try to flex in front of his friends. He put an unwanted hand on her shoulder and steered her toward the table. "I trust that Lila is taking care of you all tonight?" he simpered with an inordinate amount of simper.

One of the guests wrinkled her nose and said, "She did make me wait exactly 67 seconds for a Diet Coke refill, but I guess that other than that, she's been fine."

Lila loved it when they talked about her like she wasn't standing right there. Creepy Bryan still hadn't removed his damn hand from her shoulder, either.

She had to suppress yet another eye roll at the asinine response. Because she'd been hustling for that table all night. She also knew they'd use this arbitrary (and, she'd argue, totally reasonable) wait time as an excuse to tip like shit. Lila managed her best server smile and apologized once again and explained to them *once again* that she'd already added an additional discount on top of their friend discount.

That seemed to appease Bryan, though she knew she'd get a lecture at some random day in the future. The last time that had happened, he got upset with her about her poor service to a table that wasn't even in her section that night. So she hadn't even been their server. But the boss is always right and all that, at least where Bryan was concerned. Luckily, the kitchen managers and most of her co-workers were awesome, so that's why Lila stayed. Plus, the kitchen managers were cool if they took food home at the end of a shift. Usually just something from the salad bar or a mini pizza or something, but it helped Lila keep her food costs down and made up for the shifts where she made lower tips.

At last, the table from hell left, leaving her a ten percent tip on a discounted ticket, and Lila suppressed a groan of frustration. She went to the server station and snuck a look at her phone, trying to tamp down the waning hope that King had suddenly decided to text her. Yeah, she was aware of how pathetic it was. Kissing King Spencer had kind of messed with her head. And also maybe her lady parts.

No texts from King, but a text from Wren in response to Lila's earlier text about Becky and her "mediation station."

WREN: *I can't believe she was using the whole room to burn incense and do headstands.*

Lila looked over her shoulder to ensure nobody was watching and fired a text back.

LILA: *Hey, at least she was fully clothed this time. Not that I'm opposed to nudity. I just prefer to not be bombarded with my roommate's naked backside doing downward dog in our bedroom. I will never be able to unsee that. Ever.*

Wren's response was immediate.

WREN: *Sounds like a sleepover is in order, especially since there's no class tomorrow.*

LILA: *Yes, please. I'm off in about 30.*

WREN: *See you soon. Bring DDP. Please and thank you.*

LILA: *I mean, it's the least I can do.*

WREN: *You are an angel among us mere mortals.*

LILA: *Tell that to Becky's ass.*

WREN: *Too far.*

LILA: **insert maniacal laughter here**

Lila slid her phone back into her purse and stashed it back in the cupboard where employees' stuff lived during their shifts. Her last table had blessedly left her an amazing tip, so the night ended on a high note.

After a quick run to the local gas station that had the best fountain Diet Dr. Pepper, Lila was off to Wren's with the hope that when she returned to her apartment the next day, it would smell a hell of a lot less like burnt patchouli.

Chapter 7

"You're an asshole, you know that, right?" Knight said as he entered King's room and flopped down on his bed.

King swiveled his desk chair around to face his friend, though he couldn't mask the annoyance on his face.

"I'm not even going to pretend I know what the hell you're talking about."

Knight threw a pillow at his face. "I'm talking about Lila, man. Did you really ghost her?"

King frowned. He didn't appreciate being called out, and he really disliked it when Knight talked about Lila with such familiarity. So instead of processing all of that, he evaded. "What, are you two besties now or something? How is this any of your business?"

"As a matter of fact, we *are* friends, and because she's my friend, I've got her back. You totally hit that and quit that, bro. Which is a pretty shitty thing to do to anybody, but especially to somebody like her. She's kind. Genuine. She's not fucking around."

"I did not hit that and quit that," King countered. "We barely tapped second base."

Knight rolled his eyes. "Semantics. Also, don't act like such a dick. I thought you actually *liked* her. If I had known you were going to treat her like a one-and-done situation, I never would have encouraged her to hang with you in the first place."

"If you like her so much, why don't you date her?" King baited his friend, though the very thought of Knight and Lila together romantically made him seethe.

"Real mature response, bro. You know that's not our vibe, though sometimes I wish it was because she's pretty damn great."

King growled, though he did realize his friend had the moral high ground here. He had pretty much ghosted Lila after their date. He didn't like getting attached, and that night had been heading in a direction that he didn't want to go. Especially when Lila had talked about her lack of experience. Before she'd said that, he was just in the moment...wanting to show her just how fun their time together could be.

Her honesty in the car had thrown him, made him feel uncomfortable for some reason. Like her expectations were too high, that he'd let her down. So he'd distanced himself to let things cool a minute. Which hadn't gone exactly to plan since she was still in his damn head. And he'd be lying if he said he wasn't secretly glad that Knight wasn't interested, because he was— Nope, King wasn't going to go down that road.

"Why is she telling you our business in the first place?" King redirected.

Knight rolled his eyes. "The only thing she said to me is that she hasn't heard from you since you went out. I connected the rest of the dots myself."

The moment was tense enough as it was, but Jason's sudden entrance into King's room just added another layer to his irritation.

"What are we talking about, dudes?" Jason leaned against the doorframe, his tricky grin a near permanent fixture on his face. Jason took a moment to assess the two and then perked up. "Ooh, this is all about Alexander, isn't it?" He turned his attention to King. "Is Knight getting ready to kick your ass because you ditched his new best friend?"

"No comment, asshole," King responded. He could feel the tension in his face from subconsciously clenching his jaw and immediately tried to relax.

"I mean, I work with the woman in question, and I hear things." Jason shrugged. "If you were going to pull your whole commitment-phobe thing again, why couldn't you have picked somebody who knows the score? There are plenty of options in that category."

"Agreed," Knight chimed in.

King grunted sullenly. "Maybe I just got busy for a minute and have every intention of seeing her again."

Now he was just arguing to argue because Jason was getting on his last damn nerve. It had nothing to do with the fact that he'd been thinking about Lila's plush lips and how good they'd look wrapped around his cock since the minute he'd dropped her off.

"And if by a minute you mean three weeks…" Jason trailed off when he caught King's glare. "Look, text her, don't text her, what the hell ever man, just figure your shit out, okay? I'm going to find Will. He's way more fun than either of you guys right now."

As soon as Jason left the room, Knight let out a big sigh and stood up. "Look, King, we all have our stuff that we have to deal with. You have your reasons for doing the things you do, and I'm here to support you, unless you're fucking someone over on purpose. Because that shit isn't cool no matter what." Knight paused, debating something. "You two just seemed to have something together. Like magnets or something. Hell, you seemed different. Lighter. So I guess I'm wondering why you'd run away from someone who makes you feel that way."

King shrugged, unsure of how to respond. Because the answer to that question was highly complicated and not something he wanted to think about, ever. Even as he fought it, King was starting to feel the pull to her again. Maybe enough time had passed that they could have fun again, and it wouldn't get too heavy or serious.

He couldn't picture a time when hooking up with Lila would get old, though. That might be a problem.

"All I can say is, if you're going to fall into your typical noncommittal pattern of running, just keep going. Leave Lila out of it. Because she deserves better than that."

"She does," King agreed, and whatever control he'd had over the situation finally snapped. Without giving it more thought, he grabbed his phone and pulled up Lila's number, his finger hovering over the green button on his screen.

"What are you doing?"

"Calling her."

"Like, you're actually calling, not texting?"

"Yup."

"Well. Maybe you do actually like this girl. Who talks on the phone anymore?"

"I like her voice," King slipped, and Knight's smile grew smug.

"Mmhmm. I'll leave you to it, then." Knight gave him a light punch to the shoulder. "Go get 'em, tiger. I'm pretty sure you have some groveling to do."

King took a breath and hit the screen. It rang once...twice... five times. He wasn't about to leave a message, so he was ready to hang up when the phone picked up.

"You better be calling to apologize to Lila. Otherwise I'm hanging up right now," a voice that was decidedly not Lila's whisper-barked at him. He assumed it was her best friend, Wren, but he wasn't positive.

"I'm guessing this is Wren?"

"You presume correctly. Lila's currently grabbing us drinks in the kitchen, so you have like five seconds to convince me to pass along the phone. Because, trust me, she wouldn't have answered."

"So why did *you*?"

"Great question, one I refuse to answer. You now have approximately two seconds."

"I just want to talk to her, Wren. It's up to her whether or not she wants to talk to me."

"If she doesn't?"

"Then she doesn't." King didn't like that idea, though. He hadn't realized how much he wanted to hear her voice.

"Hold on." He could hear the phone shuffling and low voices, and then...

"Hey, King."

"Hey, La. How've you been?"

"Fine, thanks. You?"

"Fine." He let the silence stand, waiting to see what she'd say next. Whether or not she wanted to continue the conversation.

"Well, now that we've established that we're both fine, I should probably... Ow! Dammit, Wren!" she hissed. "You have bony elbows."

King stifled a laugh as he pictured the tall redhead coming for her girl.

"Come on a drive with me?" he blurted out, somewhat surprised at himself.

"What, like, now?"

"If you're free, yeah."

"I really don't…" There was a loud crashing noise followed by a few scuffling sounds.

"She'll be ready in fifteen," Wren breathed into the phone before hanging up.

Okay, then.

* * *

King drove them to his favorite spot overlooking the whole valley and the lake just beyond it. He liked to come up here when shit with his family got to be too much or when he just wanted a minute to breathe. It was unintentional, him bringing her here, but when he pulled out of her apartment complex, he'd driven to this spot as if on autopilot.

He stretched in his seat, taking in the fact that Lila's body language was completely closed off. They hadn't said anything beyond "hi," and he wasn't certain how to fill in the empty space. She was hunched forward, elbows resting on her knees, intently gazing out the windshield. King made it a point to be measured with his words, but there was something about Lila that had dropped his guard. But all of the progress had been undone since they last saw each other.

"So you're probably wondering why I haven't called you until now," King abruptly murmured.

"Nope," Lila lied. At least, he hoped she was lying. She glared out the window. "I'm mostly just embarrassed that I allowed myself to be honest and vulnerable with you. I thought…" She shook her head, a tiny sound of frustration escaping her lips. "Never mind. It doesn't matter."

"It matters," King replied.

She raised a skeptical eyebrow, which King noticed she did a lot. It kind of drove him crazy, in the best and worst of ways. He waited, hoping she'd continue to talk to him.

Finally, she spoke, her full attention directed at him. "I just thought you might be different from all of the other guys around here. Obviously I was mistaken." She repeated the brow raising and returned her focus to the view.

King drew in a breath. "Well, you definitely know how to put a guy in his place." He leaned into her space, just slightly, so she'd turn back to face him. "Did you think that it might be possible that I was trying to figure all of this out and I needed a little time is all?"

"A little time for what exactly?"

"Just thinking about stuff."

"Glad you're not being super vague or anything."

King tried to suppress a frustrated groan. In the moment, he couldn't decide if he was stupid or smart for trying with this girl. "Look, I'm trying to be honest here."

"Okay, so be honest, then." She crossed her arms over her chest and scanned him expectantly.

"I'm sorry for the radio silence. I just don't really do this whole 'dating' thing. Ever. So this is new territory for me. I just... I didn't expect you."

Her face was adorably confused. "What does that even mean?"

"That I didn't expect to like you like this. To want to talk to you every night. To find you on campus and chill between classes." He frowned. "That's not typically been my experience with members of the opposite sex around here."

"If you feel that way, why ghost me? I thought we were, at the very least, friends. I liked you." She studied his face for a minute. "I still like you, in spite of myself."

King's stomach tightened, and he couldn't tell if it was in dread or relief. All he knew was he was treading on the thinnest of ice and he didn't want her to disappear from his life. So he decided to go for what he wanted, consequences be damned.

"Look, La, I like you too, but I don't want the labels. You know, boyfriend/girlfriend. Can we just be what we are and have fun and not stress?" King looked into Lila's eyes. "I mean, we have fun together right?"

"We do," she conceded. "I don't need a label, but I do need you to be straight with me. I don't want you to make a fool out of me. Honesty no matter what.

As long as you can do that, we're good."

"That's fair," he replied. He took a moment to scan over her face, down her body, taking her all in. "Now that we've agreed, does that mean I can kiss you?" Because, shit, he needed to kiss her.

King could see Lila's pulse thrumming and her eyes dilating as she nodded, and damn if it wasn't the sexiest thing he'd ever seen as he leaned over into her space and took her mouth. He hadn't realized how much he'd missed the feeling of her softness yielding to his hardness. Even though they'd only kissed once. Their chemistry was heady, something he'd never experienced before.

The center console of the car became an issue, so King adjusted his seat so it was set all the way back and lifted a surprised Lila onto his lap so she was straddling him.

"Okay?" He cupped her face in his hands while he waited for a response.

"Better than okay." Lila smiled as she leaned in to kiss him softly. He gripped her hips with his hands tightly, encouraging her to move over him. He couldn't remember the last time he'd bothered with fooling around. Had it ever felt this good?

King's first year with the females at Bradley U had been a comedy of errors. Luckily, he learned fairly quickly to discern between those who enjoyed hooking up and getting off with no strings and those who would be surreptitiously poking holes in your condoms if they thought you had a shot at going pro. He avoided that second category at all costs.

That Lila didn't fit into either group was not something King was too concerned about at the moment, not when her tight little body was eagerly grinding against his. He could feel the brush of her erect nipples against his chest, and he wanted them in his mouth. But he knew he needed to take it slow with Lila; to let her show him what she wanted.

Almost as if she could read his thoughts, she broke their kiss and rocked back, taking his hands in hers, and guided them up her body to her chest.

Her expression was apologetic. "I'm sorry they're so small."

"Don't insult the girls," he chided. "They're perfect." Then he teased her with his fingers, flicking his thumbs against the hard buds, eliciting the most incredible sounds from his not-girlfriend.

His hands roamed and explored the lines of her body over her clothes then underneath her shirt, and he couldn't help but imagine what it would be like if there were no barriers between them. King threaded his fingers through her tantalizing hair then found the spot on her neck that he remembered drove her crazy and sucked... Hard.

Her body stiffened even as she moved against him more frantically, and he read her body like a book. "You close, baby? Do you need me to help you come?"

"I don't... I haven't..."

King raised her chin up, shocked. "You haven't had an orgasm before? Not even by yourself?"

She shook her head as a faint blush rose to her cheeks. "Let's just say that being painfully shy and having conservative parents ensured that I haven't... explored too much." Lila blew out a breath, and her shoulders sagged. "Sorry, I'm making this awkward."

The last thing King wanted her to feel was embarrassment, so he focused instead on making her feel good.

He lifted her chin up and grazed her bottom lip with his thumb. "You have nothing to be embarrassed about. Not with me, okay?"

She nodded.

"So you haven't come before. Let's see what we can do to change that, La."

One of his hands found her hip again, and he helped her move over his erection, making sure she hit the spot she needed. He lost track of the time as she moved over him, his focus solely on her as he struggled to keep his composure.

His free hand wandered over the contours of her body. The slope of her back, the curve of her waist, the soft strands of her hair that never failed to drive him crazy. Every part of her tempted him in ways he'd never quite experienced before.

Eventually, King's hand drifted back up to her breasts, his fingertips once again exploring her as she sighed. Lila looked down at him through her lashes, and that look was almost enough to make him lose his shit right then and there.

"Take what you need from me, La," he grunted. "I want to see what you look like when you lose control."

Lila's movements quickened, her soft sounds drawing his attention back to her mouth, which King wanted to devour. He kissed her hungrily, doing with his tongue what he hoped he'd get to do with his dick one of these days. Listening to the sharp intake of her breath, he sensed she was close to the edge. And when he gently pinched her nipple, she cried out as her orgasm hit her.

King was damn near close to exploding too, but he let her ride it out as he tried to keep his shit together. Because that was the hottest thing he'd ever fucking seen.

Her face was beautifully flushed when she came back down from her high. "That was..." She shivered. "I mean, I didn't know it could feel that way."

"You liked that?"

She nodded shyly, which King found sexy as hell.

"That's nothing compared to what it'll feel like when I'm inside you."

"When?" Lila teased.

"I think it's inevitable, don't you?" He again ran his fingers through the soft strands of her hair. "But not until you're ready, of course."

"Maybe. Probably," Lila conceded. "But we'll cross that bridge when we come to it." She pointedly gazed down at King's sizable erection. "Can I help you take care of that?" Her cheeks reddened. "Or...I could watch you take care of it yourself?" How she could ask such salacious questions so innocently was a mystery, but King was there for it.

"I don't want you to feel pressured to take care of me. What just happened between us was all about you, but I enjoyed every minute of it."

She teased the button fly of his pants with her index finger, her nails scraping over each button with a small metallic snick. "What if I want to make you feel good? What if it's something that I'll enjoy too?"

Damn, this woman. "If you want it, you can have it, baby," King gritted out.

Lila gently unbuttoned his pants, her eyes zeroing in on the outline of his dick underneath his boxer briefs.

King pulled down the waistband of his underwear, freeing his erection.

"Whoa, King, you're so…" Lila gulped. "Like, is that the normal size for a dick, or is yours an exceptional specimen?" She seemed to think about it for a minute. "I'm thinking it's 100% the latter."

"Lila, you always say the nicest things," King replied with a chuckle. "You want to touch me?"

She nodded eagerly.

He removed his T-shirt, leaving his chest and torso bare. Then he guided her hand to him, showed her how he liked to be touched, and let his hand fall free. She used both of her small hands, using firm strokes that brought him to the edge much faster than anyone else ever had, himself included. *Because it's her.* King pushed that thought away as Lila sped up the rhythm of her hands, and King felt his balls tighten.

"I'm so close, La. Don't stop." A moment later, he was coming all over his abdomen.

Lila looked fascinated by the mess they'd just created. Her eyes were wide, her breaths short, as she gazed down almost reverently, softly tracing a finger down the center line of his abs. When she put her finger in her mouth and sucked, her bright eyes locked with his, King growled, because where had this bold, sexual version of Lila come from?

"I like the way you taste, King."

Dammit, she was killing him.

"Woman, if you don't stop being sexy as all hell, I'm going to have to throw you in the back seat and fuck your brains out."

Lila blushed, and it was fucking glorious. "I'm thinking that'll probably be happening sooner rather than later."

"But not tonight," King said.

"Not tonight," she agreed.

He used his shirt to clean himself up then threw on a hoodie that he'd stashed in his back seat. Then he drove her back to her place, dry humped her against her door for a good fifteen minutes, and then made plans to meet up with her for lunch the next day on campus.

And he couldn't wipe the smile off of his face even if he tried.

Chapter 8

"Yeah, right there," Lila moaned softly. "Ohhh, that feels so good, King. So. Good." Her head rolled back to rest on the arm of the couch as she continued to make soft, satisfied noises.

King laughed as he continued to rub the arch of her foot. They were at his place, her feet in his lap. She'd just gotten done with a double shift and hadn't sat down once in that entire 12 hours, so he offered to rub her feet.

"For real, King, if the whole soccer thing doesn't work out for you, I think you just might be able to make a career out of massage therapy, with an emphasis on feet."

"I'll keep that in mind," he deadpanned. They'd been hanging out a lot the past few weeks, carving out time for each other around their busy schedules. In addition to school, Lila worked at least 30 hours a week, and King was in the middle of fall soccer season. His very sexy make-out buddy had come to most of the home games, usually with Wren in tow. He liked having her there, a lot, and appreciated that she didn't try to get all over him in public like a lot of the other girls he'd hooked up with. The ones who came wearing his jersey, acting like he was going to wife them up or something. Though, he wouldn't exactly mind if Lila showed up to a game wearing his jersey.

"I'm sorry I couldn't come to your game today." Lila's voice broke him out of his head. "But I saw your stats. A hat trick, huh?"

"Second hat trick in a row, if we're being technical about it."

"So modest."

"That's me, Mr. Humility." He started rubbing her calves, eliciting even more groans.

"Humble and so good with your hands," Lila breathed.

"And my fingers." King looked at her knowingly as she blushed. He loved making her blush. Which wasn't happening quite as often, as she was becoming bolder and bolder with her sexuality. They hadn't had sex yet, but he'd become very familiar with her perfect tits and had made her come with his fingers many times. He was desperate to try with his tongue. They were taking things slow-ish.

Normally, if a girl wasn't into the whole sex thing, there'd be no hard feelings or pressure, but King would've moved on to someone else who was into a casual one-time thing. He'd never invested this kind of time, nor had he gotten to know a girl the way he'd gotten to know Lila. Because they didn't just fool around. They talked. For hours. They talked and laughed, and he found himself telling her things he hadn't thought he'd tell anyone. He wanted her to know him, and in turn, he wanted to know her, too.

"How are things with the un-ironically named Becky?" King asked. They usually spent time at his place because Lila's roommate was kind of a nightmare. Plus, King had his own room, so they could have privacy when they wanted it.

"Ugh." Lila covered her face with her hands. "She threw out my cashew milk and Vicky's cow's milk yesterday because she said that she couldn't have her soy milk near any other kind of milk."

"Seriously?"

"Yup," Lila groaned. "Then she forgot that she'd scheduled dates with both Andy and Joe at the same time, so there was fist fighting involved. Actually, it was more like spirited slapping, but you get the idea."

King chuffed out a laugh at that image. "You really need to move."

"Tell me about it. If I could get out of my contract early, I would. Stupid off-campus housing rules."

"Which thankfully don't apply to athletes," King ribbed.

She threw a cushion at his face. "Thanks for rubbing it in. I super appreciate it."

"Anytime."

The front door opened, and Knight and one of his roommates, a giant defensive lineman aptly named Bear, came through the door. Knight zeroed in on Lila and grinned widely.

"Little sister!"

She turned her head to him and smiled. "Hey big bro. How's the bye-week treating you?"

"Well, look at you becoming a super sports fan. So proud of you, Li. I feel like our imaginary shared parents would definitely approve."

"Just soccer and football for me, thanks. Baseball and I still have to go through some counseling together. And basketball would be much better if they still wore those mid-thigh-length shorts from the 80s." She waggled her eyebrows as Knight and Bear laughed.

Now that it was firmly established that Lila and Knight's relationship was entirely platonic, King wasn't as bothered by their friendly dynamic. He didn't feel as threatened as he had in the beginning, which was a relief because Knight was one of his closest friends.

Lila sat up and removed her feet from King's lap, crawling over to sit next to him. He slid an arm around her waist and rearranged her right on his lap. He twirled a lock of her hair around his finger absentmindedly.

"You guys wanna come sit?" King asked, even as his friends were taking the empty space that Lila had just abandoned.

Before long, Lila had everybody laughing their asses off as she shared some server horror stories from her shifts that day. When she got up to go to the bathroom, Bear nudged King in the ribs.

"Seriously, dude, your girlfriend is super fun. You've gotta hold on to that one; she's like a unicorn. Beautiful, funny, smart. You lucky bastard."

For some reason, the word girlfriend rubbed him the wrong way. It was a box, and he didn't want to feel trapped inside. "She's not my girlfriend. We're just hanging out."

He avoided the glare he knew was coming from Knight's direction, because, well, he already knew what his friend thought about his whole anti-girlfriend stance. Especially since Lila was involved.

"Suuuuuuure," Bear scoffed. "You were just rubbing her damn feet. Playing with her hair. You're booed up and loving it."

"For real, man. I don't do girlfriends. They expect too much. This is just for fun, nothing serious."

Knight cleared his throat, drawing King's attention to Lila, who'd come back out from the bathroom. Based on the fact that her smile seemed forced and didn't reach her eyes, he could tell she'd heard some, if not all, of what he'd just said. But that's what they'd agreed to, right? She'd said she was okay without labels. So why would she be upset?

Her expression did strange things to his insides. Like he didn't want to be responsible for causing it, but he also suddenly felt trapped.

"You coming to the Halloween extravaganza this weekend, sis?" Knight asked as she moved to sit back down next to King.

"Unfortunately, my boss wouldn't let me take the night off." She rolled her eyes. "So, unless by some miracle I get cut early, I probably won't make it."

"You should have told him you were personally invited by the star athletes of both the football and soccer teams."

"Believe me, I tried," she groaned. "I even had a costume ready to go." She shrugged. "Oh well. I can always save it for next year."

"Holding you to that." Knight pointed at her. He was a junior this year, so he'd be around for next year's party. And although King was technically a senior, he was planning on still being around too, taking an extra year so he could play his last season of soccer. And hell, another year of school meant that his double major of economics and computer science would make him a more marketable candidate for an MBA, provided he didn't get drafted to an MLS team.

Later, when King was walking Lila to her car, he noticed she still seemed off. Before she could open her door, he boxed her in against the side of it. "Everything okay, La?"

She avoided his eyes as she said that things were fine.

"I need your eyes, girl."

She reluctantly looked up at him, their height disparity on full display because she was wearing flat shoes rather than the heels she wore when she wasn't working.

"What's wrong?"

She sighed. "I think I'm wanting things I know I can't have, is all. Don't worry about it. It's not your problem; it's mine."

"Wanting things like what?" King was pretty sure he knew, but he wanted to hear her say it.

She took in a breath then looked up at him boldly. "Things like being your girlfriend."

King stiffened. "But we agreed…"

"I know what we agreed on. But we also agreed to be honest, and that's honestly how I'm feeling."

She looked down at her feet. "I'm sorry, King, I can't control it. But I don't have expectations. Just because I'm feeling a certain way doesn't mean things have to change."

"It doesn't," King lied. Her confession *had* changed everything. She could say that nothing would change, but deep down he knew that they would anyway. He could feel the tightening of his chest. Having a girlfriend meant being trapped. Even if that weren't the case, King still wouldn't know what the hell to do with a girlfriend if he had one. It's not like his parents were a model of healthy relationship behaviors. And admittedly, if you looked up the definition of "girlfriend material" in the dictionary, there was probably a damn picture of Lila Jane fucking Alexander.

She deserved more than what he could give her. He'd always known that, but now? He knew what he had to do. His stomach dropped as the idea took shape in his mind. But he knew it was necessary.

Temporarily pushing the feeling away, he kissed her, hungrily, memorizing the shape of her body with his hands, the softness of her skin, all while knowing it would be the last time he'd be with her this way. What he had planned wasn't going to be pretty or pleasant, but it would be what was for the best—for him, but especially for Lila.

Chapter 9

ila sneakily checked her phone. It was Halloween night, and the dinner rush had hit early. Consequently, the restaurant was pretty quiet, with only a small smattering of older patrons and a few groups of teens. She saw a text notification from Vicky, who she knew was at the Halloween party Knight had mentioned last week. Her heart sank as she took the message and the photo in.

VICKY: *Sorry, girl. Just thought you should see this.*

The attached photo showed a shirtless King grinding on a tall blonde clad in lingerie and what looked to be some type of angel/fairy wings. Lila felt sick to her stomach. Even though she knew she had no real claim to him, she didn't think that he was capable of being so carelessly cruel. Because they hadn't just been physical with each other. They'd been friends, too.

When she'd left his place a week ago, she'd thought that things were fine. But when she didn't hear from him at all, and when he left her congratulatory text about his away game win on "read" without replying, she had the sinking feeling that things were, in fact, the complete opposite of fine.

She couldn't have imagined that he'd already have moved on to someone else, though. Not that they were together or anything…except they kind of had been, labels or not. They'd spent so much time together, it seemed implausible that he would have been seeing anyone other than her. The image felt like a knife to the ribs, and she desperately tried to tamp down her sudden tears.

"That scumbag," Wren hissed over her shoulder as she took in the photo.

Lila's breaths became more labored as she felt a few tears spill over.

"Seriously, Li, I want to cut off his balls and make him wear them as earrings. Nobody does this to my bestest and gets away with it."

Lila laughed through her tears. "That was graphically violent and shockingly specific, my friend. But thank you for always having my back."

"Always," Wren affirmed. "In fact, we're getting out of here, and you're going to make this jerkface sorry he ever messed with you."

"I don't know about that..." Lila's voice trailed off as Wren abruptly left the server station and headed back to their kitchen manager. Her grin was beatific when she returned. "Because it's so slow, I just convinced Nick to let the both of us go home, and we don't even have to do side work."

"Just like that, huh?"

"He owed me a favor, and I just cashed in." Wren grabbed Lila's hand. "Come on. We've got a Halloween party to crash."

After a stop at Lila's for a quick costume change, she and Wren found themselves crossing the threshold of Knight's house. Lila had donned a skintight black catsuit, spike-heeled boots, and a whip, à la Michelle Pfeiffer's Catwoman, which she was keenly aware was a part of a certain fantasy of King's that she'd hoped they would have the opportunity to explore.

She left the cowl draped at the back of her neck, though, so she could look the bastard in the eye and not hide behind a mask. Wren had even dressed up, borrowing a fitted red dress from Dani's closet, which, coupled with her fierce expression and her black leather jacket, made her a veritable Cheryl Blossom from *Riverdale*.

"Okay, let's find the bastard," Wren practically growled, her eyes zeroing in on the throng of bodies that filled all of the open areas of the great room.

Knight found them first, his eyes pained, his face conflicted, even as he tried to smile. "Hey ladies! This is a pleasant surprise. I thought you both were working?"

"We got off early," Lila said.

"Well, let's go to the kitchen to get you something to drink. Or maybe the basement to play some pool?"

Lila sighed. "You don't have to run interference, Knight. Just tell me where he is, okay?"

Knight pinched the bridge of his nose in frustration. "He's drunk, Li. He never drinks during the season. I tried to... But he wouldn't..." He trailed off.

Lila touched his forearm gently. "Just tell me where he is, Knight. I'm a big girl. I can handle it." *Fake it 'til you make it, right?* But when her eyes finally landed on King, she couldn't help the feeling of devastation that ripped through her gut. Knight's eyes were full of empathy and compassion.

"He's an idiot, sis. A fucking idiot."

She raised up to her toes to kiss his cheek and turned to her best friend. "Shall we?"

Wren led the way, people automatically parting the way for her tall, commanding presence.

When they were close, but not too close, to where King was still dancing with the blonde, Wren turned to Lila. "How do you want to play this, Li?"

Lila squared her shoulders, the sudden adrenaline pumping through her body giving her the extra push she needed to do what she needed to do. "Wait here."

King noticed her at the moment she tapped the scantily clad blonde on the shoulder. "I'm so sorry to bother you, but do you happen to be friends with Chelsey?" She'd taken a stab at the name and was pleased when the blonde nodded. Lila motioned over her shoulder in the general direction of the bathroom, "I think she's had one too many and needs an assist."

The blonde turned to King and rubbed her hand over his bare abs dangerously close to the waistband of his pants. "Gotta go take care of my friend real quick, handsome. We'll continue this later."

"Yeah we will," King replied, smacking her ass as she left. But his eyes? They were on Lila, taking in her costume with an unbridled ferocity. And while Lila was pretty impressed by the blonde's dedication to girl code, she still felt jealous as hell. Even though King had been looking at her while the blonde sauntered away.

"Having fun?" Lila stepped into King's space.

Whatever heat had been in his eyes dulled to stone. "I was, until you interrupted."

"My apologies," Lila said with the hint of a sneer, trying to keep her feelings in check.

"What are you doing here, Lila?" It was back to Lila, then. No more La. That hit her right in her feelbads, and Lila did her best to keep her expression even. She wished then she'd actually put on the rest of her costume. That she was wearing a mask. Anything to shield her from the pain this conversation was wreaking.

"I just had to see it for myself." She sucked in a breath. "You could have at least had the decency to tell me that you were done."

"Was my silence not enough of a sign, Lila?" King replied tonelessly. "Besides, there was nothing to end. We were never together anyway."

The force of his words pushed Lila back a step. "Nothing to end, huh? So that's how you're choosing to play it." She laughed humorlessly, shaking her head in disbelief. Because who was this person in front of her? Maybe she really didn't know him at all.

He didn't even have the balls to look her in the eye. "Yup."

Her anger coursed through her body like a firestorm. "Screw you, King."

At that, his dead eyes honed back in on hers, his face twisted into a horrific caricature of a smile. "Not happening, sweetheart, not even if you beg me for it."

She cringed feeling the moisture accumulating in her eyes, but she stubbornly held her tears at bay. "Who are you right now, King? What have you done with my friend?"

"Don't pretend that we shared some sort of connection, Lila. And we're not friends. We never were."

"That information would have been useful to know before I let you put your hands all over my body. *Inside* my body." Not to mention the number he'd done on her heart. Dammit, her stupid heart. She'd known better than this and had fallen anyway.

King just shrugged. Then, as quickly as she'd disappeared, the blonde was back, deftly sliding around Lila and repositioning herself on one of King's toned thighs.

"We done here?" He smirked at Lila as he put his hands on the blonde's ass and squeezed. Blondie giggled with delight, and Lila swallowed the bile that had accumulated in her throat.

Instead of answering, Lila turned on her heel and walked away, not even stopping when she passed Wren. Her friend's long strides caught up with hers in no time, and soon, they'd exited the house, the cool autumn air a shock of a different kind.

She waited until they were in the car, Wren's arms wrapped firmly around her, before she fell apart.

Chapter 10

L ila exited the RBG building and made her way to the Brad. She'd just finished her last final of the semester and breathed a sigh of relief. Luckily, it had been an essay test, which was her personal favorite. She was a political science major with an English minor, and so she'd just gotten to write a paper about the intersection of American exceptionalism and toxic masculinity in 20th century literature. It was a blast.

In the time since her now legendary face-off with he who shall not be named, there was an unspoken agreement that she was granted joint custody of Knight and Jason, along with the rest of their friend group. She initially thought that they were going to all drop her too, but Knight made sure that didn't happen. Jason, for all of his mischievous ways, also surprised her when he apologized for introducing her to King in the first place.

When she was still hanging out with King, she'd gotten into the habit of meeting up with them all for lunch. That continued, though she only made an appearance on the days that she knew King had class or would otherwise be away from that area of campus. Wren would also accompany her on the days their schedules aligned, which helped bolster Lila's confidence.

She approached the table of the impossibly good-looking athletes, knowing that jealous eyes were upon her. The fact that the football team was playing in a major bowl game and the soccer team had the best record in their conference heading into the second half of the season were just two more reasons all of the players were getting even more attention from the student population.

Jason spotted her first. "Yo, Alexander! How was the final?"

She slid down in an empty seat between Will and Bear. "It went well, I think.

I got to be all nerdy and analytical, which is basically my favorite thing in the entire universe."

Jason chuckled and asked if she'd be willing to swap shifts at work. While they were working out logistics, a large disposable coffee cup, complete with lid and two skinny straws, was placed down in front of her. She smiled and glanced over her shoulder. "Hey, big bro."

Knight smiled down at her. "A hazelnut hot chocolate with extra whip for my favorite little sis." Then he rounded the table and took a seat.

She took a sip and moaned in delight. "You are officially my favorite person, Knight Donovan Patrick."

He shot her a wink from across the table and then started talking bowl game strategy with Benny, one of the wide receivers. She sipped contentedly, catching snippets of conversations and contributing when engaged. She shot off a text to Wren, who was working a lunch shift, because they had plans to hit a movie after she got off work. The hairs on the back of her neck raised, and she sensed a shift in the energy around her. She looked over at Knight, his tense expression telling her everything she needed to know.

King Spencer was officially in the building. And there were no empty chairs to be found.

It had been over a month since that hellacious Halloween night, and the once-searing pain that had radiated in the center of Lila's chest had tamped down to a dull ache. They'd managed to avoid each other up until now, and she knew that it was time to establish their new normal, to show him that she wasn't going anywhere.

Everybody was watching the two of them to see what was going to happen, and before King could say anything, Lila picked up her drink and stood up. Then raised her eyebrow at Knight, hoping he'd pick up on what she was planning to do and be okay with it.

"This seat's open," she said over her shoulder as she made her way over to Knight. He patted his knee, and when she sat, he wrapped an arm around her waist. She didn't spare King another glance as Knight and Benny roped her into a discussion about the best movies from the nineties.

She tapped her chin thoughtfully. "I'd say that *Silence of the Lambs*, 10

Things I Hate About You, Clueless, and *Pulp Fiction* are all in my top ten. Ooh, and *My Cousin Vinny.*"

"Those cover a lot of bases, Li," Knight laughed. "I never thought I'd hear *Silence of the Lambs* and *10 Things I Hate About You* brought up in the same sentence."

"Well, now you have." Lila took another pull of her hot chocolate. "Hot damn, Knight, this is so effing good."

"Only the best for you, Li. Besides, we're celebrating. One more semester down, am I right? Also, thank you for taking the time to proof that paper for me. You are quite literally the best. I know I'm not the only one at the table who thinks so."

Will, overhearing their conversation, chimed in. "Seriously, Lila, you saved my ass. I ended up getting a B+ on my humanities paper. Thanks so much for taking a look at it."

"You're very welcome, Will I Am." Lila smiled. "It was the least I could do after all of the stats help. That is a class that I will not miss." There were a couple of sympathetic rumbles from around the table because they'd been there, done that, plus that particular stats professor had a superiority complex and made the required general class absolutely miserable.

"But you're still getting an A, right?" Knight bounced her a bit on his knee. Lila pursed her lips. "Probably."

"Atta girl. Look at you, going for that 4.0."

"I mean, it might be an A minus. We'll just have to see what the damn curve is," Lila grunted. Because she really wanted that A. The last A minus she'd gotten was in the seventh grade, so she wanted to keep her streak alive.

Benny whistled. "Damn, Lila. You're telling me you're not only smokin' hot, but a genius too?"

"Oh stop it," Lila said, while jokingly motioning for him to continue. While she didn't ever look at King directly, she kept feeling like he was looking at her. When the guys started enthusiastically talking about their fantasy sports leagues, Knight leaned in to whisper in Lila's ear.

"Your boy's been staring at you this whole time."

She tilted her head so she could whisper back. "He's not my boy."

Knight's chuckle rumbled through his chest. "You should probably tell him that, because he looks like he's about ready to murder me."

"I'm sure it's because he's mad we're still friends. You know what happened on Halloween. Whatever was between us is done."

"And I support you 100%, Li. You deserve the world."

She ruffled his hair lovingly and then checked her phone. Wren had just gotten off work, so it was movie time.

"Wren's ready. Gonna go," she said. Knight kissed her on the temple before she stood up and said her goodbyes to the group. She threw away her empty drink and headed out the south entrance of the building.

Lila stepped to the side of the path so she could pop her earbuds in and almost dropped them as she startled at the sound of a deep, dark voice.

"So you're with Knight now, huh? Can't say that I'm surprised."

Her head snapped to the left where King was standing, a hardened glare on his face. After a month and a half of radio silence, he'd chosen this moment to follow her? To goad her?

She rolled her eyes. "If we were, it'd be none of your business, King."

He scoffed. "That's not a denial. Were you with him when you were with me?"

Lila had had it. She whirled on him, eyes ablaze. "I'm not even going to dignify this bullshit line of questioning with a response, because not only is it wholly offensive, condescending, and ridiculous, it's also none. Of. Your. Damn. Business."

She paused and drew in a breath. "And we weren't together anyway, right? So what the hell does it even matter?"

King crowded her so her back was against the red brick wall, caging her in with his arms. He leaned down so that they were nearly eye to eye. "It. Matters." King's expression was an intense combination of irritation and intimidation.

Lila rolled her eyes to stave off the intensity of his glare. King didn't let up.

"Are you with Knight? Yes or no?"

Lila refused to be intimidated. "Why don't you go ask him? Since you seem to be so concerned about his well being and all."

She couldn't lie, his frustrated growl was music to her ears. But there was pain there, too. Just briefly. It flashed across his face like a streak of lightning and was gone just as quickly.

Lila knew she didn't owe King a damn thing, but she wasn't heartless, either. So after she ducked under his arm and started down the path, she stopped and turned back, just for a second, and said, "No."

And tried not to notice the way King's shoulders seemed to slump in relief.

Instead, she popped her AirPods in, cranked up her angry music playlist, and walked home.

Chapter 11

Holiday break flew by quickly, and Lila enjoyed spending time with her parents and four younger siblings. She'd returned to the same house she'd spent the bulk of her childhood in—the one that was always filled with freshly baked cookies, the laughter of siblings and friends, and her parents' adorable, perhaps slightly nauseating, PDA.

Bradley U was about 50 miles away from the suburb where she grew up, providing just the right amount of distance between her and family. Because even though they were pretty damn great, Lila relished the opportunity to be on her own, completely autonomous. Her parents were well-meaning but overprotective, and her siblings delightful but in a different phase of life. Though she tried to make the drive home at least once a month for extended family Sunday dinner, she didn't really visit on the weekends because of her job. The break from school and the family time had been just what she needed to recharge before second semester started.

She'd especially enjoyed spending time with her 16-year-old sister, Layla. Layla and their mom were the only ones who knew the basics about King, mainly because they'd surprised her one day at work and he happened to be there at the same time they were. When they saw him interact with her, they knew something was up. That all happened before the Halloween disaster, however.

Layla was the only one who knew exactly what had happened, and Lila hoped to keep it that way.

It was the first day of class for winter semester. She was currently sitting in her democracy and social justice class, which she'd wrangled Wren and

Julia, one of her roommates from freshman year, to take with her. When they'd scanned the small auditorium style room for seats, Lila spotted King's roommate, James, and Nate, who was the soccer team's goalie, trying to get her attention.

"Come sit by us, ladies," Nate crooned, his eyes taking in her friends with unabashed interest. So she found herself flanked on one side by her friends, and on the other by two soccer players. Their professor jumped right into the deep end of the pool, so Lila concentrated on furiously typing out notes.

As they were all packing up their stuff, James leaned in, just a little bit. "We miss having you around, Lila. King's been such an asshole lately. You seemed to mellow him out."

"You mean he's being an even bigger asshole than his normal level of assholeishness?" she remarked sardonically as they all filed out of the row and headed out of class.

James laughed and slowed his stride so they were walking side by side. Wren, Julia, and Nate were following close behind. "Exactly. Plus, we all miss hanging out with you. Even if that means you're kicking our asses in poker."

Lila returned his laughter and waggled her brows. "I am pretty good, aren't I?" She lifted a shoulder. "There's no rule that we all can't still hang. You're always welcome to come into the restaurant. Jason isn't the only one who can hook you guys up. Plus, I work more than he does because of all the sports ball he plays."

"True, true." He turned back to Nate then nodded in the direction of the athletic facilities. "This is us. Later, Lila."

"Bye, guys," Lila and her friends said as the two men made their way west.

"So Nate is pretty hot and tall enough," Julia sighed. Julia was even taller than Wren, standing at 6'2", and was a dead ringer for Naomi Campbell circa 1992. Nate was at least 6'5". Needless to say, even when she wore heels, Lila was always the short one amongst her group of statuesque girlfriends by a large margin.

"He was totally scoping you out during class," Wren said with a smirk. "Lila, you need to make this happen."

"On it," Lila replied as she quickly pulled up his Insta and typed out a DM.

Nate's response came so quickly, it was almost comical. She looked (way) up at Julia. "Can I give him your number?"

"Absolutely." Julia nodded in the serious, almost solemn way she adopted when she was analyzing information. Then the corners of her mouth turned up and her excitement became more visible.

"Done." Lila turned to Wren. "Need a date coordinator? Because apparently I'm really good at it."

Wren rolled her eyes lovingly. "If you happen to find someone who wants to have intellectual conversations about legal theory and wears the hell out of a pair of glasses, sign me right on up."

"I think we both know you've already found somebody like that," Lila said knowingly. Wren had long been holding a torch for her childhood best friend turned first love, Aaron. He'd taken off right after their high school graduation, for...reasons. But theirs was a complicated history, one that Wren kept a tight lid on, and Lila was one of the few who knew the whole story about why he left.

The short version? He'd made plans to come to Bradley with Wren but then had taken off without a word to her, leaving a brief note for his family. That he'd been battling a secret addiction to pain medication was something that only Wren had known and why, she suspected, he'd disappeared in the first place.

Wren sighed but didn't contradict her. Julia had another class, so she waved her goodbyes and headed across campus.

Lila slid an arm around her friend's waist. "DDPs at the Brad?"

Wren put her arm around Lila's shoulders. "Only if you're buying."

"Obvi."

They stayed that way as they walked east toward the Brad. Wren's arm tightened around Lila as she whispered, "He's back, Li."

That stopped Lila short. She dropped her arm and reached up to grab her friend's shoulders. "Aaron's back?"

Wren nodded. "I don't know what to do."

"We need to continue this conversation over drinks and perhaps a cinnamon roll or five," Lila murmured.

"Agreed."

So they made their way to the Brad, grabbed reinforcements, and sat down at their usual table. Wren desperately tried to keep it together as she filled Lila in on what had transpired in the past few weeks. How Aaron had showed up at her parents' house late one night and wouldn't leave until she showed up. Wren's family lived across town, and so she'd made the short drive in record time.

"He wants to... I mean... He thinks we should..." Wren breathed.

"You mean that he finally realizes that leaving you for two years was the worst idea ever and that he misses the hell out of you and wants you back?"

Wren's exhale was wobbly as she took a long pull from her drink. "Yeah, pretty much."

"And how do you feel about that?"

"I don't know how I feel about it."

Lila slid the giant cinnamon roll she'd just bought in front of her friend. Wren took a huge bite, then another, and took her time swallowing. "He promised me he's clean now. That he needed to get well on his own, and now he's doing better." Then she looked at Lila with a pained, guilt-ridden expression. And Lila had a feeling she knew why.

Lila placed her hand on Wren's. "It's okay if you want to move home, Wren. It's okay if you want to be closer to him. I want you to be happy. And we wouldn't be farther away from each other than we already are. It's just in the other direction."

At that, Wren started crying, which was a rare sight. "I'm sorry, Li. I really wanted us to have the whole roommate experience together. But I can't *not* do this."

Lila wrapped her arms around her friend. "I know, and that's what I want for you, too. Aaron's been a part of your life for a long time, and you deserve to do what you need to do. I'd be mad at you if you didn't. Besides, it's not like we can't still have sleepovers and stuff. We'll still see each other all the time. I'll find somewhere great to live that doesn't involve sharing a room with someone who thinks that waking up at 3:00 a.m. to run is a good idea. Everything's going to work out the way it's supposed to." Lila gave her friend her best intimidating stare. "But if he hurts you? His ass is grass."

"I love you to the moon, you know."

"I know."

"Thanks for being in my corner, Li." Wren held up her cinnamon roll, which Lila bumped with hers.

"Forevs and evs."

Chapter 12

As stoppage time wound down, King dribbled the ball around the defender and shifted the ball from his right foot to his left. He sent a lateral pass to Will, who then quickly tapped it back to King, who kicked the ball hard. It bent perfectly, hitting the top left corner of the goal. The keeper had gone the other direction and hit the goalpost in frustration. They'd finally broken the 0–0 stalemate with their biggest rival, and King's teammates crowded him excitedly. The ref's whistle signaling the end of the game came a few seconds later, and the crowd cheered loudly.

"Hell of a game, Spencer." Coach Klopp nodded sharply as King headed to the locker room. Even though it was still damn cold in February, it was the first game of the second half of the season, and Bradley U was currently at the top of their conference standings with no losses and only one tie.

"And no penalties, praise the Lord," Jason chimed in, smacking him on the ass.

King grunted. The last few fall games had ended with a couple of yellow cards and some other stupid fouls. *All the games after Halloween*, his brain mocked him.

He didn't think about that night if he could help it. And he definitely didn't fantasize about the way Lila had looked in her costume. Shit, he'd had a more-than-half-naked woman grinding on his leg, and it had done absolutely nothing for him. As soon as he saw Lila, though? He got so hard it made him angry.

The whole month following that stupid night, King had made a point to avoid the Brad at times when he thought he'd run into Lila. He focused on soccer, where he could work out his pent-up aggression on the field, and school, where he studied for his finals with an energy he'd never had before. Though he'd always been a pretty good student, he had the feeling that perfect grades just might be in his grasp this time around.

He'd honestly thought he was doing okay until the day Lila had gone out of her way to sprawl all over Knight's lap. Despite himself, his stomach had turned to acid and his vision blinked red. So he'd followed her out the door without even thinking about it first, and she'd knocked him on his ass once again. With her proximity, her coldness, her indifference. The weight that was lifted off of his chest when she'd said there was nothing between her and Knight also made him angry. He couldn't afford to want anyone, to need anyone. He shouldn't give a shit if Lila and Knight were together. But he did.

Dammit, he did.

After he knew that Lila and Knight weren't fucking around, he couldn't help but drive by her place a few times. Or maybe more than just a few. It was like his car just drove there automatically, kind of like the day he'd taken Lila up to the overlook. He chose not to analyze why it happened or why his chest seemed extra tight any time he caught sight of a brunette with long hair who resembled her.

Then he'd had to endure the holiday break with his dysfunctional family. His dad acted like the cheating, entitled asshole that he was, and his mom desperately tried to keep up appearances and pretend that everything was okay as they hosted their annual lavish holiday farce. Being an only child didn't help things. There were no siblings to commiserate with, nowhere to escape. The fact that his father called him "Junior," like he hadn't cut off and ignored his only child, and his mother insisted on referring to him as "Solomon" like it was a designation of distinction, only deepened his sense of entrapment. Solomon Spencer Sr. was a liar, a philanderer, and a shitty parent, and King wanted to excise the burden of carrying around that name every damn day.

And now, even though he hadn't seen either of his parents for the better part of two months, he still dreaded the text he'd receive from his sperm donor. Either praise for scoring or beratement for assisting. In Solomon

Spencer's world, selfishness reigned supreme. There was nothing else.

King showered and dressed quickly, not in the mood to socialize. Of course, Jason, Will, James, and Nate had other ideas. They intercepted him in the parking lot.

"Get in, loser." Jason snickered at his own movie quote. "You're coming with us to The Pub."

King gritted his teeth. "The fuck I am."

Nate rolled his eyes and opened the back door. "Seriously, dude, get your ass in the car. My lady's waiting on us." Yup, Nate was dating Julia, one of Lila's former roommates and one of her closest friends. King loved the evil eye she shot him every time she came over. It was a super-fun time for him. But he got into the car, trying to convince himself that he wasn't secretly hoping that Lila was working.

He'd catch glimpses of her on campus, and he hated the way she still twisted him into knots. Hated how he still pictured the way she looked when she'd been with him. How he knew there was a secret side to her that he knew no one else had seen.

King remembered the night they'd gone the furthest with each other, their clothes discarded on the floor, with just the thin barrier of their underwear between them. That was the night Lila had taken him into her mouth and given him the best blow job of his life. She'd done some research, she'd said. Because of course she had. He could still picture her on her knees, looking up at him with trust and a helluva lot of lust, as he placed his hand on the back of her head. Her attention was powerful and heady and terrifying.

The thought of someone who wasn't him experiencing her in her most intimate moments made his frozen heart drop to his feet.

Because their group was too big to fit into a single booth, they were seated in the back room of the restaurant. Julia and a couple of friends King hadn't met were already seated, and her smile lit up her whole face as she got up to jump into her boyfriend's arms.

"Great saves tonight, babe! You looked so good out there."

Nate chuckled and leaned in to whisper something in her ear that made her eyes widen before she ducked her head into his neck. Once everyone was seated, Wren approached the table.

"Hey everybody. I hear congratulations are in order?" she said with a smile, much to the delight of his teammates, then made quick work of getting everyone's drink order. "I'll be back with those and a couple of appetizers, compliments of Bryan the Bradley fan."

Bryan Blaine was the owner/general manager of the restaurant and obsessed with Bradley U sports, so they could always count on some sort of discount or perk when they came in to eat. Which was probably why they all ate there so often.

Soon, Wren was back, with Lila in tow. She notably dropped drinks and an appetizer off at the other end of the table, her eyes refusing to drift over to King's side, and as Wren placed his drink down, she whispered, "Don't even think about messing with my girl today, or I'll spit in your food and not feel even remotely bad about it," and then moved on as if she hadn't just threatened him with her saliva.

Lila's smile was genuine as she said hi to Julia and her friends, as well as his teammates on that side of the table, her gaze sweeping over him briefly, a small, perfunctory smile on her face, before she made a quick exit as Wren circled around to grab food orders.

"I feel so bad she's working on her birthday," King overheard Julia whisper to Nate.

"Wren?"

Julia shook her head. "Lila. Wren told me she actually asked for the shift. Probably to have an excuse to not come to the game tonight. You know she likes to go and support most everybody, but it's hard too, for obvious reasons."

Nate made a sympathetic noise, but then his eyes drifted to King, so King abruptly nudged Jason and drew him into a conversation about next week's opponent. Halfway through the meal, he got up to use the restroom. He walked through the front part of the restaurant and out a side door that led to a hallway that housed the facilities.

After stepping out of the men's room, King leaned against the opposite wall, needing a quiet moment to himself. Seeing Lila again threw him for a loop. Instead of his interest waning, it constantly seemed to grow each time she darted in and out of his life. Damn if it wasn't the most confusing feeling in the world.

If King was being honest with himself, there was a part of him that wanted to track her down, to apologize, to try to start something real with her. The problem was, he wasn't sure he was capable of it. He couldn't subject her to all of his damage and then have it all crash and burn anyway.

It was easier to hurt her now and have her hate him than to attempt the impossible and have her think she could fix what was irreparably broken. The last thing he wanted was for her to pity him, and if she knew everything about him, she would. She'd pity the fact that he'd never seen a functional relationship in his life. She'd pity the fact that he couldn't even utter his first given name without feeling like throwing up.

The door to the women's bathroom opened, and a startled Lila put a hand to her chest. "King! Hi. Um, fancy running into you here. Of all the hallways, am I right?" She forced out a sound King assumed was meant to be a laugh. Her eyes drifted down to the floor then tentatively back up. The awkward silence between them hung in the air.

"So...not to be rude or anything, but is there a specific reason you're creeping right outside of the women's bathroom?"

"That was unintentional." King smiled, just a little bit, because he'd missed flustered Lila. Flustered Lila said and did awkward things, and it was one of the things he loved—liked—about her. Past tense. Definitely not now, still. The tension that he'd been carrying through his jaw? That hadn't lessened because she just half-smiled at him. Not a chance in hell.

"Well, sorry to interrupt your deep bathroom-hallway thoughts, I'm just going to go..." She trailed off, a thumb pointing over her shoulder at the door leading back to the restaurant. King stayed silent as she turned and began to walk towards her destination.

Before King could process what he was doing, he jogged to catch up, gently catching her by the wrist.

Lila stiffened as she turned back to face him, and King immediately dropped his hand. "Sorry, uh, I just wanted to say happy birthday."

Her brow furrowed in confusion as she mulled over his words and then uttered a soft, "Thank you," before turning again.

"Wait." King's voice sounded frenzied, desperate, to his own ears.

Lila turned to him once again, her face unreadable in the dim hall light. "What is it, King?"

Instead of replying, he slowly backed her into the wall. When their bodies were flush, he cupped the back of her neck, his thumb running a path along her jawline. His other hand found the slight curve of her hip, and his fingers squeezed involuntarily. King felt her body tremble, saw her throat bob, her pupils already blown. The electric charge between them was still just as palpable, just as overwhelming as it had always been. He could see the hunger within her, knew that he probably reflected back the same damn thing. And suddenly, all of the reasons he'd been telling himself to stay away from her vacated his mind, replaced by an aching, desperate need that utterly overtook him.

"What are you doing?" Lila whispered. "Because this back and forth, I can't..." She trailed off as King leaned in closer, lowering his head so their mouths were almost touching.

"I've tried my hardest, but I don't want to stay away from you anymore, La," he murmured against her lips. "I'm sorry about Halloween. I was a dick to you. And I know I don't deserve it, but I want another chance to kiss you and fuck you and just *be* with you. So damn much it's hard to breathe." He moved his thumb down from her jaw to touch the delicate crown charm dangling from her neck.

Lila stared at him for a minute then tentatively traced her hands up his chest, and he closed his eyes at the sheer pleasure of it. He knew she could feel his hardness against her stomach.

"You've driven by my place, haven't you?" she whispered, eyes searching his, brows furrowed together in such a way that made King want to smooth them out as he nodded in reply.

"Why?"

"Couldn't stay away," he confessed softly, his thumb moving to ease those lines of tension. "I can't fight this thing between us anymore. Can you?"

She groaned in frustration, the battle clear on her face. Finally, she spoke. "I can't fight it anymore either. I should, but I can't. Because this"—she moved her hips against him slowly—"feels so good." She sighed and tilted her head back until it softly tapped the wall. Then she leveled her doe eyes on him. "Why do you always feel so good?"

At the sensual tone of her words, his control snapped. His lips were on hers before his brain could tell him to stop, consuming every inch they had access to.

He moved his mouth to her neck, kissing her the way he knew she loved.

"Shit, King, the way this feels..." she murmured.

It feels like coming home. The thought rose, unbidden, and he pushed it away. Because there was no way in hell he was ever going there. He broke away, his voice rumbling in the back of his throat. "No labels."

She arched a brow then nodded. "Nobody else as long as this lasts."

"Agreed." He leaned back in to kiss her again, knowing that they needed to get back to reality but needing more of Lila's luscious mouth. "You coming over tonight?"

Her eyes darkened, her face running a gamut of emotions, all warring for dominance. "Yes."

* * *

King was already opening his front door before Lila was done knocking. After she'd gotten off her shift, she'd gone home to quickly shower and change and was looking delectable, dressed down in a pair of light-pink sweats. She seemed to hesitate, unsure of how exactly to greet him. So he pulled her against him and left her breathless with a kiss that started off sweet and got dirty real quick.

"Hi." He smiled.

"Hi yourself," she stammered, trying to catch her breath. "That was quite the greeting."

"Nothing but the best for the birthday girl."

"Actually, I think we're past midnight, so technically it's not my birthday anymore."

"It's over when I say it's over," King growled playfully. "Plus, you haven't gotten your gift from me yet." At her suspicious look, he clarified. "It's more of a 'show,' rather than 'tell' kind of a present."

Her face lit with understanding...and arousal. "My favorite kind of gift."

Hand in hand, they quietly padded up the stairs to King's room. Once he'd clicked the lock into place, he stalked over to her cautiously and took her in his arms, hugging her tightly. He inhaled her unique scent and let his hands roam over her body as she made soft sounds of contentment. "I've missed this," he murmured into the juncture between her shoulder and her neck.

"Same." Her hands found his, and she guided them to the hem of her top. He lifted it over her head and about passed out when he saw the delicately sheer black lace bra she was wearing underneath. He'd been with her before, but he'd never really *seen* her, not like this. His eyes devoured her, his fingers tracing along the lines of her lingerie as his mouth slanted over hers. King loved the way she opened for him, how she matched the strokes of his tongue with hers. He thrust his knee between her legs so she could grind on him while he teased her with his fingers.

When his hands rounded her back to brush against the clasp of her bra, he paused, waiting for her permission to proceed. At her nod, he removed it from her body, first tracing the roundness of her breasts with his hands then replacing them with his mouth. Her tits were the perfect mouthful, and King loved the way Lila's body writhed as he lavished her beautiful body with his lips, tongue, and teeth.

He laid her down on the bed and then sat back on his heels to remove his shirt. He lowered himself on top of her, supporting most of his weight with his forearms, and hissed when he felt the brush of her nipples against his bare chest.

"Are you ready for your present, La?"

"This isn't it?" she teased then moaned as King ground their sexes together.

"I want to taste you." He reached down to cup her between her legs. "Here." She tensed, just the slightest bit, and King removed his hand. "We don't have to if you don't want to, La."

"I want to, believe me." She shifted, her eyes avoiding contact. "I'm just a little nervous that you won't like what you see or whatever."

He lightly gripped her chin, lifting her face to meet his. "Trust me, I'm going to love what I see. I'm going to love what I taste. I'm going to love it because it's you, Lila Alexander."

"You say the nicest things," Lila said with a knowing smirk, bringing King back to that hot night in his car. But there was also a tenderness in her eyes that made King feel utterly exposed. Instead of dwelling on it, he slid down her body, removing her sweatpants first so he could take in the miniscule black lace thong she was wearing. He ran his tongue over the lacy material, eliciting a surprised-sounding moan from her. He pushed the fabric aside and swirled his tongue around her clit then dragged it lower.

"Fuck, La, you're perfect." His restraint abandoned him the moment he tasted her. He ripped off her underwear and dove back in, his tongue alternating from teasing her clit to penetrating her center. And when she came? He didn't want to come up for air. He wanted to live between her legs.

Reluctantly, he moved back up her body and kissed her hungrily.

"I liked that present," Lila whispered, her cheeks beautifully flushed, her body languid and relaxed.

King laughed as he ran his fingers through her hair. "I'm glad. Nothing but the best for you, La."

"King..." She hesitated, and he stiffened with worry.

"What is it? Are you okay? Did I hurt you?"

"No, nothing like that. You were amazing. I just..." Lila's amber eyes held his. "I don't want you to stop."

King stilled. "Are you sure? Because once we do this, there's no going back."

"I know. I'm ready, King. I want to have sex with you. If you want to, that is."

He grinded his erection over her core in response. "I want to, La. Fuck." He leaned down to kiss her deeply. "I'll be right back." King went into his ensuite bathroom to grab a clean towel and retrieve a strip of condoms from the vanity drawer.

When he returned, he paused a minute, taking in the beautiful naked form stretched out before him. The crown charm of Lila's necklace caught the dim lighting from the lamp in the room, and her raven hair was spread out in beautiful waves. All of a sudden, he was nervous. He wanted her first time to be perfect. He'd been careless with her before, and she was giving him another chance. He wanted to show her he was sorry, that he understood that this meant something. What, he wasn't sure. But this wasn't a meaningless fuck, not to him.

King dropped the condoms on the bed then leaned over to lift up her hips. He put the towel underneath her. "For when you bleed," he said, stopping to kiss the inside of one of her thighs.

Then he stood up and shucked off his pants and briefs in one swift motion. King ripped a condom off of the strip and opened the package with his teeth. He could feel his erection swelling to the point of pain as Lila hungrily took in the image of him rolling the condom on.

"Keep looking at me like that, and this will all be over before it's even begun," King said, only half joking, as he climbed back over her body. He started sliding his length over her, getting her ready for him.

"Can't have that, can we?" She smirked, moving her hips to meet his. Her tongue swiped at his lower lip, so he took her mouth again as he picked up speed. Then finally, *finally,* he positioned himself at her entrance, making slow, purposeful movements as he sank into her inch by inch, stretching her as he went.

Her moans were a mixture of pleasure and pain as he continued to sink inside. Once he was fully seated, he held still. "Okay, La?"

She breathed shakily. "Better than okay. But I think I need you to move now, King. Make me feel good."

And so he moved, his fingers linking with Lila's as he started with shorter strokes that continued until her pleas of "harder" and "faster" took him to another place, one where he was claiming her all for himself. They fit together, somehow, and as King got closer and closer to his release, he changed the angle so that he could grind against her just where he knew she needed it. Because he wanted her to come again. He *needed* her to come again.

As soon as he felt her spasm around him, her unintelligible, pleasured sounds signaling that she'd shattered again, King felt himself come undone as he finally let go.

Chapter 13

Lila's cheeks heated as she gingerly padded down the stairs with King. All three of his roommates were in the kitchen eating some form of breakfast. Judging from the streak of mischief in Jason's baby blues and the knowing looks on Will's and James's faces, she immediately intuited that she and King hadn't been quiet last night.

If someone had told her 24 hours ago that she'd be at King's house, minus her virginity, she would have laughed in their face. But here she was, freshly fucked and deliciously sore, hand in hand with her "no labels" sex...buddy? Companion? Demon? In front of all of his roommates.

"Coffee, Alexander?" Jason asked with half a smirk.

Lila wasn't sure if King wanted her gone but given the fact that they'd had sex not once, but three times the night before, she was in desperate need of some caffeinated sustenance.

"Yes, please."

"You look like you didn't get a lot of sleep last night," Jason snickered as he handed her a cup.

Lila sipped her piping hot beverage instead of replying. Normally, she'd dilute it down with milk and sugar, but mornings like this one called for the strong stuff. Again, she wasn't sure how to navigate the whole "morning after" routine. She was trying to take her lead from King. He shifted so he was standing behind her, his body flush with hers, one of his arms braced against the kitchen island in an almost...possessive(?!) way. *Okay then...*

"Shut up, Jay," King growled, his free arm gently encircling Lila's waist from behind in such a way that her body instantly responded. He leaned down and kissed her neck. "Can I have a sip of that, La?" he whispered in her ear. Holy shit, this guy was going to melt her insides if she wasn't careful.

Suppressing a shiver, Lila turned in his arms so that she was leaning against the counter and facing him. As soon as she saw his expression, whatever nervousness had been floating around was abandoned and replaced by an arousal so intense, it flooded her veins. She passed the mug to him, and he took a sip, his eyes never leaving hers. They continued the back and forth for an indeterminate amount of time. It could have been a minute; it could have been ten. But they continued to look at each other long after King placed the empty coffee cup on the counter.

Everything about this man was intense. But there was a gentleness deep underneath the surface that Lila had seen for the first time the night before, when he'd handled her with such care. When he worshiped her body and prioritized her pleasure over his own. When he'd gotten a warm washcloth and cleaned her up after their first time. She needed to be cautious, because if she allowed her thoughts to fully go there, she would fall for him, *hard.*

"Is it just me, or is it getting warm in here?" Will joked, successfully breaking them from their sexy staring contest.

King made a sound somewhere between a grunt and a groan at the same time Lila laughed. Which, to her great delight, elicited a small smile from King. She circled back around to face the others and made an effort to chat with them about soccer prognostics for the rest of the season and questioned them about their classes. She also agreed to pick up a couple of Jason's shifts because the scheduler at The Pub had forgotten that soccer had started up again. All the while, King caged her against the counter, his thumb lightly stroking her hip bone, and she could feel every inch of his very impressive and very hard dick pressed against her ass. Soon, the other three abandoned the kitchen, leaving Lila and King alone. He spun her around to face him, cupped the side of her face, and leaned down slowly.

"I have coffee breath," she whispered.

"So do I," he said right before he lightly nipped her lips with his teeth then soothed them with the tip of his tongue. "Open for me, La."

She didn't refuse him. She didn't think that she'd ever be able to again. Not when he kissed her like the world was burning down and she was his only source of water. Soon, he lifted her onto the countertop and nestled himself between her legs, creating just the right amount of friction between their bodies to drive her insane.

"I want you," Lila breathed, briefly breaking their kiss.

"Are you up for it? I worked you hard last night." King looked down at her with a concerned expression that was tinged with lust.

Lila tried not to let King's awareness of her comfort light her up like a Christmas tree but miserably failed. "I'm ready for you to work me hard again, King. Fuck me, pretty please," she cheekily replied with her best attempt at puppy dog eyes.

He laughed softly against her mouth, hoisted her up, and wrapped her legs around his waist. Without breaking a sweat, he led them up the stairs back to his room, where he made quick work of stripping her out of her clothes. She returned the favor, and soon they were on his bed, ferocious, passionate, and yes, loud, as he flipped her onto all fours and took her from behind.

Too soon, she was coming, hard, and she felt the weight of his collapsing body as he followed. Lila didn't hate it. King kissed her between her shoulder blades before he carefully pulled out, going into his bathroom to throw away the condom. She was admiring his amazing ass when her phone buzzed.

Lila reluctantly rolled over to where her phone was lying on King's nightstand. It was then she noticed she had about ten texts from Wren and a couple of missed calls.

"Shit," she whispered.

"What?" King asked as he got back into bed and sidled up next to her. She rolled to her side so they were almost nose to nose. "Is there an emergency or something?"

Lila hummed. "Nothing like that. Wren's just been calling and texting since last night. I hope she's not worried."

"She know you were coming over here?"

"Maybe," she hedged, insecurity creeping in unbidden.

"Maybe?" King gently prodded. His brow was furrowed, just a little bit, almost like he was hurt.

She reached out to smooth the lines down on his face. "Okay, yes, I told her, just for safety purposes. But if you don't want me to tell her we had sex, I won't." Lila's gaze sank to the sheets. "If you want to keep things quiet, I mean."

"You're not a dirty secret, La." He looked mildly offended at the idea, which surprised the hell out of her. "Neither am I."

She sighed in relief. "Okay. I just wasn't sure if this was a one-time thing or a secret thing or whatever. I mean, it's fine if it is, I—"

King cut her off with a kiss that left her breathless.

"First off, this isn't a 'one-time thing.' I'm pretty sure it's already been a four-time thing. And I have no intention of stopping, not when it's already this good. Do you?"

"No."

"Good," he grunted.

"Glad that's settled, then," Lila deadpanned before shooting off a text to Wren, assuring her that she was alive and well and properly fucked.

"Wanna go get breakfast?" King asked as he absentmindedly ran his fingers from her shoulder down her arm and over the curve of her waist and hip.

Lila's stomach growled in response, and they both laughed.

"I'll take that as a yes." He grinned.

"That's a hell yes, apparently," she responded.

They spent the rest of the day together, and it wasn't until much later, when the sun had already set and King had walked Lila out to her car and was kissing the shit out of her while grinding on her against said car, that she fully realized the magnitude of the fact that this whole thing had an expiration date. She pushed the thought from her mind and decided that regardless of whatever the future held, what they had now was worth it, no matter the cost.

Chapter 14

King propped himself up on his pillows as he watched Lila braid her hair. It wasn't the worst way to wake up, with a beautiful woman standing in front of him in the lacy matching underwear sets she'd started sporting more and more of since they'd started sleeping together. The blow job she'd given him a few minutes ago hadn't hurt either. She'd kept her golden eyes on him the whole time, the intensity of it practically knocking the wind out of him.

He felt settled for the first time in his life. Though it had only been a couple of weeks since they'd taken things back up, they'd spent almost every night together. Much to King's delight, Lila had become somewhat of a sex fiend, and he was more than happy to indulge her whenever the mood struck. Hell, he was actually relieved to discover that her drive seemed to match his. Because he wanted her all the damn time.

"Working on Saturdays is so boring," King whined as Lila started to get dressed.

She smiled at him through the mirror that hung on his closet door. "But working during the day means I get to come to your game tonight, so…"

"I guess that's an okay trade." King stretched and then reluctantly got out of bed. He was naked and already half hard again, and he sauntered up to stand behind Lila. She took in his nakedness as he approached and made a frustrated sound.

"Tease," she groaned, turning to face him. He kissed her and pressed his body against hers. "Ugh, I really don't have time," she sighed, reaching out to stroke his length as she kissed him back. Then, much to his dismay, she let him go and stepped out of his arms, moving around the room to gather her discarded clothes from the night before and grab her bag.

"If I had my way, we'd be fucking all day," King growled, only slightly grumpy that they couldn't have a quickie.

"As lovely as that sounds, I've gotta pay for books. And rent. And you need your energy for your game tonight." Lila stood on her tiptoes to peck King on the lips. "I'll see you then, okay? Give 'em hell out on the field." She paused at his door. "I'm still waiting for my invitation to get banged inside the locker room, so…" She blew him a little kiss and exited the room quickly before he could chase her down and throw her back on the bed. Or mercilessly tease her for using the word "bang."

King threw on some boxer briefs and a pair of sweatpants and headed downstairs to grab breakfast. Will and James were already in the process of making their game day smoothies, and Jason shot a look at King from where he was perched on the sectional.

"Should we have Lila start paying rent, King?" Jason teased as Will and James laughed.

"I mean, the earplugs she brought over were nice, though," Will conceded. He'd made a comment about how loud they were one night when they were all watching a movie, and Lila had shown up the next day with cookies and a bunch of packs of disposable earplugs. King was pretty sure his roommates liked her more than they liked him, which meant they were excellent judges of character.

"Yeah, your girlfriend is kind of the best," James agreed.

King grunted, "She's not my girlfriend." For some reason, every time he heard the word, his heart sped up and his stomach bottomed out. Still.

"Tomato, tomahto," James retorted as he held out a glass to King. "Shake?"

"Thanks, man."

They spent the rest of the day prepping for the game, watching some film of the other team, and doing a little lifting.

Right as the game was about to begin, King felt a sense of intense relief when he spotted Lila in the crowd. He'd just had a run-in with his father, who'd surprisingly shown up at the game with a woman who was not only *not* his mother, but was probably around King's age.

"King, this is my secretary, Daphne," his father had said with a cruel sparkle to his eye. "She's a big soccer fan, so I told her she could be my plus one for the game."

"Whatever explanation helps you feel better, Sol," King had grunted. He'd been calling his father by his first name more and more, partially because he knew it drove Solomon batshit crazy.

"Watch it, boy," his father had sneered before heading off to his seat. It was too bad for Sol that his son now had him by a few inches and about 30 pounds of muscle. Otherwise he probably would have popped King right there in front of everyone.

King pushed the dark thoughts out of his head as his team won the coin toss and set up for kickoff. They were playing a team who had a really dirty defender. Stone Maddox was known to go for the knee and/or the Achilles, and so King needed to be on his guard.

It appeared that Solomon's presence was turning out to be a bad omen.

The entire first half, Maddox kept trying to trip King up, coming dangerously close with an illegal slide tackle that the referees chose inexplicably not to card him for. After Bradley U went up 1-0 at the beginning of the second half, Maddox got even more aggressive. Normally, King would exchange some good-natured banter with his opponents, but not today.

After another near miss, where Maddox went for King's knee, this time earning him a yellow card, King exploded. He shoved Maddox and punched him in the face. Maddox threw King to the ground, but one of the refs got between them before Maddox could retaliate further. But the damage was done: King's outburst earned him a red card, which meant he was out of the game, his team had to play a man down, and he was automatically benched for the next game. Luckily for him, Maddox earned another yellow card, and because he'd already gotten one, that meant he was also ejected from the game with the same consequences.

King didn't make eye contact with his coach or his teammates as he left the field and headed for the locker room. He angrily tore off his jersey and threw it against the lockers, raking his fingers through his hair as he paced back and forth.

He let out a frustrated yell as he tore his boots off and threw them too. They ricocheted off the wall and landed with an angry thud.

"King?" The soft, tentative voice made him stop in his tracks, and he turned toward it.

"Lila?" For a minute, he thought he was hallucinating. It wasn't exactly easy to get into the locker room. But she was definitely standing there, looking gorgeous, her eyes filled with emotion. King shook his head in disbelief. "What are you doing here? How did you even get back here? You're not supposed to be back here." His voice sounded overly harsh, and he saw Lila flinch just a little bit.

She inched toward him, her movements cautious, like he was an injured animal or something. "I have my ways" was all she said as she approached. When she was standing right in front of him, her soft exclamation of his name just about did King in.

The adrenaline and testosterone from the game was still coursing through his veins as he advanced on her, attacking her with his mouth, his hand wrapping her braid around his fist. "I need you," he growled as he ran a hand up her thick tights and then underneath her skirt. Thank fuck she was wearing a skirt. "Right now." Then he ripped her tights right down the center seam.

"I'm yours," she said as she pushed him down so he was sitting on the bench that ran the length of the row of lockers. He quickly slid his shorts down so his dick swung free, and before he could say anything else, Lila had sheathed his cock and impaled herself on it. He thrusted upward in brutal strokes that bottomed out every time, and she took everything he gave her and gave it right back. Too soon, he was covering her mouth to muffle her cries as she came, and he followed right after her.

She pressed her forehead against his and then went to move off of him. "Stay," he grunted, wrapping his arms around her tightly.

"As long as you want me to," she whispered, her breaths still labored from what they'd just done. The silence stretched as their breaths slowed and their bodies stayed connected.

"My father's here tonight," King finally murmured against her neck. "With someone who isn't my mom."

Lila cupped his face with her hands and gently stroked his cheekbones. "What an asshole," she said disgustedly.

"Yeah, that's Solomon for you. A lying, cheating, abusive asshole."

Lila ran her hands through his hair, her nails scratching the buzzed sides just how he liked. "So it wasn't just the bastard on the field. It was your dad being here too."

"Yeah."

Lila leaned in to kiss him gently then reached back and undid the clasp of her necklace. She fastened it around King's neck. "To remind you that you are *not* your father. You're a king."

His eyes felt suspiciously glassy. "La, I—" But then the sounds of the game ending pulled them out of the moment, and Lila jumped off of him quickly as he pulled off the condom and tucked himself back into his shorts.

"There's a side door over there," King whispered, kissing her quickly. "It'll put you on the east side of the field."

"I guess we can check locker room sex off the list," she said softly with a mischievous smile. "And you owe me a new pair of tights, Spencer. See you at your place." Lila happily skipped out the door, taking his obliterated heart with her as she went.

Chapter 15

February 28

LILA: *Nice of you to not only replace my tights but to throw in those lacy extras as well. Wanna see me wearing them later? Maybe 8ish?*

KING: *Hell yes.*

* * *

March 1

KING: *Tonight. Pink lace.*

LILA: *What's the magic word?*

KING: *Ten*

LILA: *???*

KING: *The minimum number of times I'm planning on making you come. If you wear the pink lace.*

LILA: *FINE. *smirk**

* * *

March 2

LILA: *Note to self: pink lace is always a good idea.*

KING: *Told you, La.*

* * *

March 3

    LILA: *Late night at work, gonna crash at home.*

    KING: **thumbs down**

    LILA: *I'll make it up to you, I promise.*

    KING: *It's cool.*

* * *

March 4

    KING: *You definitely made it up to me. Gonna be thinking about that tongue of yours all day.*

    LILA: **tongue* *eggplant* (That's sex emoji for you're welcome.)*

* * *

March 5

    LILA: *Sorry you didn't get to play tonight, but happy the team was able to pull out a win even without your expertise on the field. When do you all get back? Got something new to wear that you might be interested in. *eyeballs**

* * *

March 10

    King: *Come over?*

    LILA: *Well hello King, it's nice to see you got home from your away game safely. Was slightly worried until I saw Jason at work.*

    KING: *Been busy. You gonna come through?*

    LILA: *Any reason why I haven't heard from you?*

    KING: *Just been busy, La. And really interested in seeing what you wanted to show me the other night.*

    LILA: *Noted. You've been busy. And you like me in lingerie. Any chance you'd wanna grab dinner first? I feel like I haven't seen or talked to you in a minute.*

    KING: *Already ate. But saved room for dessert.*

LILA: *Well, when you put it that way... gonna grab a bite and then I'll be over.*

* * *

March 11

LILA: *Thought we were supposed to meet for lunch today?*
LILA: *Everything okay?*

* * *

March 13

KING: *Things are fine. Busy.*
KING: *I'll lyk about lunch.*

* * *

March 16

KING: *Movie? Sleepover?*
LILA: *Just got home from work and am super tired.*
KING: *How about if foot rubs and orgasms are involved?*
LILA: *Be over in about 30.*

* * *

March 17

LILA: *We all waited for you for like an hour at the bowling alley and you never showed. I hope everything's okay. Going home now.*

* * *

March 19

LILA: *Really starting to wonder if you're okay.*
KING: *Fine. Just busy.*

LILA: *What happened the other night? We were all worried about you.*
KING: *Just had stuff to do. Lost track of time.*

***

March 25
KING: *Coming in tonight to eat. Maybe I can have you for dessert later?*
LILA: **thumbs up* Sleepover?*
KING: *Can't. Got an early morning practice. But we could still have fun for a minute.*
LILA: *Hopefully longer than a minute. *smirk**

***

March 31
LILA: *Did you come to the restaurant today?*
KING: *Yeah. Had to pick up Jason.*
LILA: *Any reason why you didn't come and say hi?*
KING: *We were in a hurry.*

***

April 1
KING: *Hi.*
LILA: *...*
KING: *I'm outside your place. Drive? Ice cream?*
LILA: *Only if brownies and caramel are involved.*
KING: *And sex.*
LILA: *Presumptuous of you. But also accurate.*
KING: *I'm outside your door. Open for me?*

***

April 2

    LILA: *We celebrating that win tonight?*
    KING: *Raincheck*
    LILA: *K*

* * *

April 3

    KING: *Sleepover?*
    LILA: *So we're celebrating?*
    KING: *Or something.*
    LILA: *I'm intrigued. Also coming over.*

* * *

April 9

    LILA: *It's not every day I get awoken for some sexy time at 2 am, but I'll take it.*
    KING: *I'm just glad I missed all the incense. And the naked yoga. Though I'm not opposed if you want to try that out sometime.*
    LILA: *Becky doesn't often sleep over somewhere, but when she does...*
    LILA: *Thanks for all the orgasms, btw. Super nice of you.*
    KING: **thumbs up* *smiling devil**

* * *

April 13

    LILA: *Must keep missing you during lunchtime. Wanna meet up for lunch sometime this week?*

* * *

April 15

LILA: *I'm thinking today is a panini day. Gonna meet up with Knight. Want to join us?*

* * *

April 17

LILA: *That was quite the game tonight. Waited for you after, but the guys said you'd already taken off. Celebration later?*

Chapter 16

Dread settled low in Lila's belly as she looked over the last few texts she'd sent King that had all gone unanswered. In the two months since they'd christened the locker room, he had slowly been withdrawing. It had been incremental at first, but as the weeks had gone on, he had been less and less responsive. They spent less time together.

At first she excused it by convincing herself that it was because they were both so busy; Bradley U's soccer team was slated to play in the national championship in two weeks, and King had been throwing himself into the sport with a fervor she'd never seen before.

The sex was still amazing, though now, whenever it felt like it was more intimate than mere fucking, King would disengage for a few days, sometimes a week. At first, Lila thought she'd be able to handle the ebbs and flows of their arrangement, but it was starting to really wear on her.

Every time she convinced herself he was done, that she was okay with accepting that he was done, he'd call or show up at her place or the restaurant, and they'd spend the night together, making up for lost time, reaching for each other in the early hours of the morning and as the sun rose. They also filled up the empty spaces between by talking to and holding each other in ways that felt decidedly more relationship-y than Lila would have thought King was comfortable with. But she didn't push him. She didn't tell him she'd fallen for him again. Harder this time than the time before.

When she had his full attention? She glowed. When he turned away? She withered. Lila knew that she deserved better, but he was like a drug to her. The worst part? She loved him. She was completely gone for this man.

Unfortunately. Which was why she kept going back and why she kept letting him in, even when he let her down.

"Hey," Wren said as she slid into the seat next to Lila's. Their Pop Culture in America class was about to start, and Lila couldn't help but notice the dark circles her best friend was sporting.

"You doing okay, babe? You look tired."

Wren sighed. "It's Aaron." Her breath stuttered. "He's using again. Heroin this time, which scares the hell out of me. He refuses to acknowledge it's a problem and won't go to rehab."

"Dammit," Lila groaned. "I'm so sorry, Wrenny."

"It's tearing me apart, Li. I loved him, you know? The old him. I don't even recognize the person he is now. I've tried so hard to help him, but I can't do anything if he doesn't help himself." Wren paused, her gaze dropping to the ground. "I told him we were done. For good this time."

Lila leaned over to wrap her arms around her friend. "Come on. Let's get out of here."

"What about class?" Wren sniffed.

"Please, we're both going to ace this class, and we need to go get you a DDP ASAP. Plus a huge-ass ice cream sundae."

They quickly snuck out of the back of the room as their professor was entering from the front. They giggled as they headed down the hall, and for the first time in a long time, Lila felt lighter.

Since Lila had walked to school, they made their way to the student lot where Wren's car was parked, which also happened to be right next to the athletic facilities. As they approached, Lila felt the gut punch of seeing King, standing casually and talking with two coeds. One of them was standing quite close to him, her hand resting on his arm in a gesture that looked like it was the furthest thing from platonic. They were still a ways away, but she'd know King anywhere. He still kept his hair pretty short on the sides but was growing out the top so that it waved and curled in the most enticing of ways. Lila loved running her fingers through those golden strands, naturally highlighted because he spent so much time outside.

"Isn't that..." Wren trailed off when she saw Lila's face. "Dammit. I'm sure it's nothing. They're all probably just friends and he's going to call you tonight and you'll have hot marathon sex."

"Yup, I'm sure that's it. Yay for all the sexing that will happen in the near future."

Lila couldn't take her eyes off him as they got closer. Part of her wanted him to see her, to see how he'd react. The other part of her hoped that Wren would veer them off to the right or the left before he noticed them.

When she heard the enthusiastic, "Li! Wrenny!" from a deep voice behind them, she braced herself just in time for her to be lifted up by her other bestie, Knight. He'd put one arm underneath her and the other underneath Wren and lifted them up in an awkward, but delightful, backward hug. It was that moment when King's eyes snapped up to meet hers. And they were unreadable, cold. He scanned her briefly and then turned away without further acknowledgment, walking into the building and leaving the two girls he'd been talking to behind.

Lila tried not to let her devastation show as she turned around with what she hoped was a genuine-looking smile. "Hey, bro."

"Sister." His green eyes shifted over to Wren. "Sister's best friend."

Lila couldn't help but notice the longing in Knight's eyes as he took in her best friend. She'd suspected for a while that he had a thing for Wren, but he'd never confided in Lila about it. But he never dated, and she suspected her beautiful redheaded friend was the reason why.

"Just wanted to ensure that you're in for the spring edition of Jock Jam." Knight's eyebrows danced. "We just got clearance to hold it next Friday. So you both better be there or be square."

Wren surprised her when she said, "We're in." Knight's smile grew, and he said his goodbyes as he headed to the gym.

Once they'd driven to their favorite local ice cream shop, a Diet Dr. Pepper and a hot fudge sundae in front of Wren and a peanut butter and chocolate ice cream shake in front of Lila, Wren dropped the bomb.

"I'm going to do a semester abroad. In Europe," she blurted out. "Actually, it's technically three because of our school's ridiculously short spring and summer semesters. Also, shouldn't they just call them terms at some point?

Like, how does that even work? You know? So many other schools handle this differently. It's like an intricate scholastic mind puzzle."

"You're rambling." Lila smiled at her best friend fondly.

"I'm rambling," Wren confirmed. "All of said rambling is to avoid saying that I get back right before holiday break. So I'll be gone for seven months total."

Lila processed the information like a wave, letting it wash over her before she reacted. She sensed that her friend was already hanging on by a thread and knew she needed to be supportive even as her heart broke just the slightest bit.

"Look, Wrenny, I'm not going to lie and say that I won't miss you or that I didn't wish that I could go with you, but I understand why you need to do this," Lila said. "I think putting some distance between you and Aaron will be a good thing. The best thing."

"Agreed."

"But I'm going to miss the hell out of you. You better FaceTime me and send me lots and lots of postcards. Also a souvenir or five would be greatly appreciated."

"Check, check, and check plus," Wren said while writing invisible check marks in the air.

"And maybe send Knight a few postcards too," Lila added nonchalantly before taking a bite of her shake. She was delighted to see her friend's alabaster skin redden. "He's a good guy, Wren. My other best friend, and I love the hell out of him just like I love the hell out of you. Maybe someday, when you're ready, you'll let him shoot his shot. Or throw his pass, as it were."

"Yeah...maybe. Someday," Wren said before digging into her sundae, the subject officially closed.

Chapter 17

I t was the night before Jock Jam, spring edition, and Lila still hadn't heard from King. Not even after their strange exchange in the parking lot. She could read the writing on the wall, but she wanted to hear it from him. Wanted him to have to say the words to her face, instead of just shrinking away like a thief in the night. He'd ghosted her once, and she wasn't going to let him do it again. Not this time.

She inhaled and exhaled a couple of times before knocking on his door. Since he had been dodging her texts, she knew she needed to just show up in order to catch up with him. Will had assured her that King was home, so she gathered her courage as she waited for the door to open.

King opened the door shirtless, his hair wet, his trim waist wrapped in a low-hanging towel, because of course, she'd be forced to look at his post-shower hair and perfect torso while the final nail in the coffin was driven in. He looked surprised and a little wary, but she cut him off before he could say anything. "Can we talk? I promise this won't take long."

He examined her for a minute before he nodded and stepped aside so she could enter.

"Do you want to, I don't know, put on clothes or something? Or sit down, at least?" Lila asked nervously. Because his body affected her, and there was nothing she could do about it. Especially after a two-plus week drought of feeling that perfect body against hers. Damn him and his perfect abs and mouthwatering Adonis belt.

"Naw, I'm good. Besides, you said this wouldn't take long." King just stood there, making no move to sit down, so Lila stood there a minute, letting his indifference steel her resolve.

She inhaled. "So, I basically just wanted to come here and hear you say it. Your silence has been pretty definitive, but I wanted to be totally sure."

"And what, exactly, would you like me to say, Lila?" The cold way he said her given name made her want to cry.

"That you're done with me, with this. I don't expect you to give me a reason, because a reason would imply that this meant more to you than it apparently does, but I thought that, after everything, you'd at least tell me to my face."

"You're right. I guess I do owe you that, all things considered." He shrugged.

"So, to make things perfectly clear, we're done here?"

King crossed his arms across his chest. "We're done," he affirmed.

Lila sucked in a painful breath. She'd expected it, but it still hurt like hell. "Great. Good talk. Can I, um... Could I please have my necklace back?" She couldn't bear the thought of him keeping it, not after this.

King's nostrils flared, just a little bit, and Lila wondered why that request would make him angry. After all, he was the one calling this. He was the one who'd been ignoring her, who had been too chickenshit to end things before now.

He looked at her for a beat then replied, "I lost it."

"You...lost it?" She couldn't help but hunch over slightly and place her hands on her stomach, just for a second. Because his confession felt like an actual blow to her body. She'd given him her most prized possession, and he hadn't even cared enough to keep it safe. It had been disregarded and discarded, just like her.

"Yeah. Sorry. I can give you some money for it or whatever if you want."

Lila felt her eyes water and desperately begged her tears to hold themselves at bay. He would not have the pleasure of seeing her break. She straightened her spine, pasted on a tight, fake smile, and looked him dead in the eye. "Don't bother," she said in a tone she hoped was nonchalant. "It's not important."

He didn't respond, just studied her, his expression inscrutable.

"I guess I'll see you around, then. Or not," Lila said, and then she turned and left without waiting for a response. She walked across the street to Knight's and pulled out her phone.

LILA: *You home?*

KNIGHT: *Yup*

LILA: *Would you please open your door, then?*

He opened the door, and she didn't even get inside before she started sobbing. "Sorry," she said between hiccups. "This is so embarrassing."

Knight wrapped his arms around her and gently led her inside. His house and King's had almost identical layouts, so the foyer similarly opened to a big great room and kitchen area with a large TV and a sectional. But his other roomies were all watching something, so he shielded her from them as best he could and led her up to his room.

Once she was sitting on the edge of his bed and Knight had rolled his desk chair over so he was sitting across from her, he spoke. "Can you tell me what happened, Li?"

"King," she shuttered. She lowered her face into her hands and tried to calm down. She recapped how King had been pulling away and how she'd called him on it, how he'd ended things. And then she mentioned her necklace, and Knight gritted his teeth.

"The necklace from your grandma? The one you love?" He made an angry sound when she nodded.

He got up. "Okay, Li. I've gotta go take care of something, and I will be right back. Please just hang out, and then we can go grab a bite, okay?"

"Okay," she sniffed. Once Knight had left the room, she called Wren and gave her the update. Her response was similar to Knight's, only with more swear words. By the time they hung up, Knight was back, the knuckles on his right hand bruised.

Lila stiffened. "Knight, what did you do?"

"What needed to be done. Bastard had it coming."

"But that's your throwing hand!"

"Season's over. And, as you recall, we won our bowl game, thank you very much. Besides, I pulled it a bit. His eye's gonna be black but not too swollen. He's still got an NCAA championship to win."

"Are you guys going to be okay? The last thing I want to do is cause problems between the two of you. I know you go way back."

"This was all a part of us working it out. Trust me." Knight's smile was 90% brotherly concern and 10% sympathy.

"You're a good man, Knight Patrick. One of the best I know." She quirked a brow in his direction, "Now, when are you going to tell Wren how you feel about her?"

"You picked up on that, did ya?"

"Obviously. Though admittedly, it took a minute. Maybe more like half a second." She winked.

Knight sighed. "I'll tell her when she's ready."

"Well, let me say, on the record, that I'm shipping this whole scenario hardcore. It would be absolutely blissful if my two favorite people ended up together."

"Noted." Knight extended a hand and pulled Lila up to standing. "Now, before we go eat, let's get you something for tomorrow's party." He held up a hand before she could protest. "You're coming. And you're going to have a great time."

"Plus, you want to see Wren."

"That is very perceptive of you."

He held out a large Bradley U football team T-shirt that had his name and number on the back of it. "Wear this with a pair of those over-the-knee boot thingies, assuming you have some." At Lila's nod, he continued, "Guys will be drooling all over you."

Lila's mouth formed a small smile as she absorbed his enthusiasm.

"Are you going to want this shirt back, or can I modify it for fashion purposes?"

"Do your worst. I've got like 70 million of these."

"Challenge accepted. Got another one I can give to Wren?"

His eyes sparked at the thought of that. "Hell yes."

Chapter 18

"**W**ell, if this doesn't feel vaguely reminiscent of something we've done before..." Wren commented dryly as they walked into the party from the same direction they'd come from in the fall. They were both wearing the shirts that Knight had given Lila the day before, and over-the-knee boots.

Lila might have mentioned that said boots were kind of Knight's idea, which is ultimately what got Wren into the footwear in question, though she'd never admit it out loud. His shirt was long enough on Lila that she was wearing it as a dress. Wren's legs were too long to wear the shirt alone, so she'd paired her navy tee with a pair of similarly hued booty shorts. Knight was going to lose his damn mind when he saw her.

Julia was somewhere in the crowd with Nate, but Lila worried about seeking them out directly, given the fact she wanted to avoid King at all costs. She caught glimpses of Vicky and Dani in the crowd and waved as they weaved through throngs of people to get to where the makeshift dance floor was.

"Tonight, we dance our asses off," Wren intoned. "I leave in precisely three weeks, and we are going to live it up until then."

"You don't have to tell me twice," Lila replied with fake solemnity.

Whoever was on music duty was killing it with early aughts classics, and the friends, indeed, danced their asses off. Knight found them, his eyes almost bugging out of his head when he took in Wren in her boots, wearing his number on her back.

"Knight, Wren, get together for a pic," Lila demanded as she snapped a few photos with her phone. Then she had Knight hold the phone to get a selfie of the three of them. Then Wren took a photo of Lila and Knight, and then he snapped one of just her and Wren. Once she got her phone back, she surreptitiously sent Knight the images of him and Wren, and he mouthed a thank you as soon as they pinged on his phone.

"So picture happy tonight, my friend," Wren teased knowingly.

"Just trying to document all the fun times, and leave the bad ones behind." Lila lifted a shoulder.

"Well let's get to it, then."

Soon, Julia and some of her former roommates made their way over, as did Dani and Vicky, and they all made a circle that they took turns dancing inside. Soon, though, Julia drifted over to Nate, and Knight had managed to wrangle a dance with Wren. A dance that became *several* dances and then a trip to "grab water" that they still hadn't returned from. Lila had done an inner happy dance when she saw Knight place a hand on the small of Wren's back as they made their way inside his house.

Tired from dancing, she drifted to the edge of the designated dance floor, in search of bottled water.

"Alexander!" Jason's boisterous voice rose above the volume of the music. He was standing on his porch with James.

Lila waved and made her way over to them. "Water?" She mimicked taking a drink. James hooked a thumb over his shoulder, pointing inside the house. She shook off the feeling of awkwardness that was radiating in the air, wishing she'd instead gone in the direction of Knight's house. *Too late now.* Weird that she'd been there just yesterday, but she pushed that thought away as quickly as it came.

Lila scanned the packed room and finally laid her eyes on the water bottles. "Victory," she mumbled to herself as she walked over to grab one. It wasn't until after she'd taken a long drink that she felt eyes on her, boring holes in her back.

Don't look, Lila. Don't. Look.

She looked.

King was sitting on the couch, his arms draped over the tops of the cushions. An unidentified pastel-haired girl was straddling his lap, and...

Was she nuzzling him? With her nose? It'd be a weird sight under normal circumstances, but Lila wasn't thinking rationally. No, she was super jealous. So jealous it was infuriating. His eyes read onyx in the dim lighting, his left blackened by Knight's fist, which gave Lila a modicum of satisfaction, even though it was petty. And because the fates hated Lila, apparently, King's intense, glittering eyes were focused entirely on her.

Fuck. That. Shit. She was so done with allowing this guy to mess with her head.

Lila's brow arched as she allowed herself to absorb the entire scene. Hate slithered slowly into her veins, decaying all the love she had felt for him, and somehow it made the whole situation easier. After all, weren't love and hate just two sides of the same toxic coin?

Pastel girl was now making a big show of dry humping one of King's legs, and Lila tipped her bottle to him in silent cheers. His eyes narrowed slightly, his face a mask except for the almost imperceptible tensing of his jaw.

Gratefully, her phone chimed, and she turned away from the ridiculousness she'd just witnessed to check it. She placed her capped water bottle between her legs (because there was no way in hell she'd ever put her drink down at a college party, even one thrown by her friends) as she pulled her phone out.

WREN: *I'm officially calling in my one AOC of the year. Are you okay, or is there a McConnell situation?*

Lila's eyes widened as she took in the text. "AOC" was the code they reserved for an instance where they could ditch the other for the night, no questions asked, unless the ditchee declared it a McConnell situation, which meant they were in an unsafe situation in which to be left. The handful of times this had been invoked, there had been no problems, and Lila was determined there wouldn't be any on this night, either.

LILA: *I'm so proud of you. Hell, I have no doubt AOC would be proud of you. No McConnells in sight, so you are a go.*

WREN: *Text me when you get home. *heart**

LILA: *Obvi. *heart**

LILA: *Remember: safe sex is the best sex. There are Magnums in your glove compartment. *eggplant* You're welcome.*

WREN: *eyeballs* *flushed face*

She smiled down at her phone before tucking it back into her bag and retrieving her water. As Lila bent down, the slits she'd cut a few inches up the sides of her shirt/dress displayed the long line of her right leg, and she noticed a random guy checking her out. Lila caught his eyes and shook her head emphatically, motioning for him to stay put.

Unfortunately, he didn't get the hint and approached her anyway. Before he could even open his mouth, she said, "Please turn around. I'm not interested. Nor am I in the mood to be ogled. Thanks."

"Bitch," he muttered. Before she could respond, she heard a crash, a high-pitched "Hey!" and then the interloper was wrested away from her and thrown against the side of the couch. In Lila's periphery, she could see pastel girl gingerly rising from a spot on the floor, one of her hands rubbing her ass. Then it hit her. *King fucking Spencer.*

"Get the fuck out of here," King growled at the ogler. His black shark eyes and grim expression apparently terrified the guy, and he couldn't run out of the house fast enough. Which was probably the smartest thing he'd done in his whole life.

Lila huffed out a sound of frustration. Part of her wanted to believe that his over-the-top actions were because he was jealous, but she knew better and hated that her mind even wanted to go there. She snapped her eyes up to King, prepared for battle. "I had it handled. But thanks for that fine display of toxic masculinity. It'd been at least fifteen minutes since I'd last seen one."

She tried to maneuver around him, but he reached a hand out, and his fingers kissed her abdomen as he tried to stop her. She jumped back as if burned. Physical contact was the last thing she needed right now. "Don't touch me, King."

He tucked his hands into his pockets. "Sorry." He didn't sound sorry. And he sure as shit didn't look sorry. "Maybe next time you should consider wearing something other than a shirt that barely covers your ass and you won't have any problems."

He knew very well that the shirt hit mid-thigh, her ass completely covered, because she'd worn similar shirts of his in the exact same size. Plus, he had eyes and could see it for himself. Regardless, she could and would wear whatever the hell she wanted. Getting harassed was on the harasser, not the harassed.

"Ooh, let's add slut shaming and victim blaming to tick off all of those toxic masculinity boxes, shall we? It's a toxic trifecta. Well done, *Solomon.*"

As soon as the words left her mouth, she regretted them.

Dammit, Lila.

King reared back, the pain evident on his face. Lila sighed, suddenly so, so tired, and held up her hands in surrender.

"Shit, I'm so sorry, King. So sorry." She sighed and rubbed the skin of her forehead between her brows before looking him in the eye. "I shouldn't have used that name. Ever. I know the pain it causes you, and it doesn't matter what you've said to me or how you've treated me. There's no excuse for what I just said. It won't happen again, I promise."

His face twisted into a remorseful expression, and it was just too much. "La..."

"Just don't, okay? Please just leave me alone. Before either of us says anything else we regret."

His jaw popped as he clenched it tight, and he nodded before turning to leave. Lila didn't watch him walk away.

She shot Vicky and Dani a text so she could hitch a ride home with them. After they got back to the apartment, she bid them goodnight and shot Wren an "I'm home" text before stripping off her boots and shucking off her bralette. She was too drained to manage anything else. Lila sighed tiredly as she crawled into bed, unwillingly subjected to Becky's weird white noise machine playing what was allegedly supposed to be "womb sounds." Unlike other nights, however, she eschewed her earplugs and let the sheer exhaustion of the night's events pull her under.

Later, Lila awoke to the sound of shoes hitting the floor and the sensation of someone sliding next to her in her college-issue twin bed. Womb sounds officially off, she figured it was at least 6:00 in the morning, which was the time Becky always woke up to do her second Saturday morning run. She turned to face her best friend, who was still dressed in her outfit from the night before.

Wren's face was streaked with mascara, the tip of her nose pink, her expression weary.

"Want to talk about it?" Lila whispered.

"Not right now," Wren murmured.

"Okay." Lila put a comforting arm around her friend, and then they both fell asleep.

Chapter 19

It had become obvious throughout the week that Knight was not doing okay. Whatever had happened the night of Jock Jam had left the normally amiable Knight moody and reclusive. And since Knight was always there for King, even when King was acting like a jerk, King was there for Knight, no questions asked. He waded through the empty beer cans, pizza boxes, and takeout containers that littered Knight's room as he yanked the covers down off of his friend.

"Rise and shine, gorgeous. We're going to be late for our final if you don't get your ass in gear." King sniffed. "And take a damn shower. You stink."

Knight groaned and tried to pull the covers back over his head. "Fuck off, Spencer. My head is killing me."

King ripped off the covers in response, thankful that his friend didn't sleep in the nude. "Seriously, man, do you not care about athletic eligibility? You miss this final, and your ass is grass next year. The final is half the damn grade."

"Fuck! Fine." Knight finally sat up, slowly, and rubbed his eyes. King thrust some Advil and a glass of water into his hands.

"Take these and jump in the shower. I'll make you some coffee. It's a damn good thing you have a photographic memory, or you'd be screwed."

Knight grumbled and headed toward the bathroom. As soon as King was satisfied that Knight had actually started the shower, he headed downstairs to make some coffee. Based on what he'd heard from the other guys, the night of the party, Knight and Wren had gone upstairs together, and no one was sure what had happened after that.

A few minutes later, Knight staggered down the stairs, dressed and smelling a hell of a lot better. King slid a cup of black coffee in Knight's direction then took a sip of his own. He cleared his throat, unsure of how to play it. Knight had always been like a brother to him, including kicking his ass when his ass needed kicking, and King wanted to reciprocate.

"Look, if you don't want to talk about what happened, I get it. But I'm here if you need to talk to somebody."

Knight grunted, and King could see the naked emotion on his face. "Thanks, man. I...uh, shit." And then he started crying.

King was around the island in a flash and banded his arms around his friend. He held him while he cried, his large body shaking the both of them. "I've got you, okay? Whatever's happened, I've got you."

Knight calmed and stepped back, swiping a hand over his eyes. "Thanks, King. I appreciate that. I just... A lot happened that night. I thought that maybe things were finally falling into place, but then..."

"Then, what?"

Knight rubbed his temples and sighed. "She called me Aaron."

"Aaron, as in her ex, Aaron?"

Knight nodded.

"During sex?"

Knight nodded again with a wince.

"Well, damn."

"Yeah." Knight sniffed. "And then the fucker actually had the balls to call her right after, super high and confused. Which is awful, obviously, because he needs help."

He sucked in another breath before continuing. "I helped her find him and get him back to his parents' house. But afterwards, she just shut down. Didn't acknowledge what she'd said or what happened between us. It was like it was nothing. Like *we* were nothing."

His friend drew in a shaky breath. "I think I love her, man. But it's obvious she's not ready for that. She's dealing with her own shit. I think things might be too complicated and fucked up for it to ever work out. She's leaving next week, and I just... I feel like shit about all of it. And it's been hard for me to deal with. I didn't think that love could make you feel so damn miserable."

King could empathize. He wouldn't wish that kind of pain on anyone. "I'm sorry, Knight, really. I feel your pain. But maybe her leaving will give her the time to get over her shit while you get over yours." He shrugged. "I have to believe that a guy as good as you has good things coming his way."

Knight's smile was small, but it was there. "King Spencer, I think that behind that asshole exterior of yours is a pretty decent human being."

"Yeah, well, don't tell anybody, okay? I've got fear to instill and people to push away."

"People like Lila."

King grunted in frustration. "You know that's different. I'm not the kind of person who deserves a happy ending. Especially not now."

This wasn't the first time they'd talked about it. King had tried to explain everything to Knight the evening his friend had given him a well-deserved black eye, but it had been difficult to verbalize. Knight was aware of how dysfunctional King's family was, but that night, King shared just how much that dysfunction had messed with him, too.

"She deserves so much more than a guy with a fucked-up family who wouldn't know a functional relationship if it punched him in the face. Pun intended," King had remarked wryly as Knight grabbed an ice pack from the freezer and tossed it in his direction.

Knight had pinched the bridge of his nose and looked skyward for a moment. "King, you were already in a relationship with her, whether or not you choose to admit it, and it seemed like things were pretty damn great when you weren't making a point of acting like an asshole."

"I need her to hate me. It makes it easier for me to stay away."

Knight blew out a frustrated gust of air. "Look, I care about both of you, King. But you hurt her, so much. And you're hurting yourself, too. It doesn't make any sense. You two are so good together." He shook his head. "Look, I can't get in the middle of this anymore. This is between the two of you. But I'll keep punching you if you keep acting like a dick. And if you keep making her cry."

"Fair," King had conceded, even as his stomach bottomed out. He hated himself for making Lila cry.

As he went to leave, Knight had turned around and said one final thing: "I hope one of these days you stop getting in your own way, King. Because you are capable of so much more than you give yourself credit for."

As if Knight knew where King's brain went, he repeated his words from that night, verbatim, thanks to his perfect memory.

King smirked. "So you've said before."

Knight's expression turned determined. "We're going to be okay, King. Both of us. We're going to figure our shit out."

King glanced at the clock. "And make it to our final on time."

"Yeah, also that."

"If you do better on this than me without actually studying, I'll kick your ass," King joked.

"You can certainly try," Knight replied with a smile, some of the former brightness returning to his face.

It was then that King had the sense that, at least for Knight, things would eventually be okay.

Chapter 20

The locker room was charged with a combination of testosterone and anticipation as King and his teammates readied themselves to take the field to play for the NCAA Championship. Bradley U's team had played nearly flawlessly during the season, but they were up against the reigning champs, the same team they'd fallen to in the semis last year.

Unlike regular season games, where they could end in a tie, this final match would go on until there was a clear winner. Meaning extra time and then a shootout if the score was still tied after the additional minutes were played. King was planning on doing everything in his power to ensure that his team took care of things in 90 minutes.

He touched the crown charm of Lila's necklace under his jersey. Yeah, he hadn't lost it. He just couldn't bear to return it. Not after she'd so lovingly given it to him.

To remind you that you are not your father. You're a king. Those words and the gentle way she'd fastened the necklace around his neck had been playing a constant loop in his brain.

That moment had been the best and the worst of his whole damn life. Because that was the moment when he knew that he loved Lila Alexander. That he'd always love her. It was also the moment he realized he had to let her go. He'd become too dependent on her. He craved her. Her mind, her body—hell, even her scent. The longer it went on, the worse it would be when she finally realized how broken he was and left his ass. So he might as well end it while he still had part of his heart left.

Which turned out to be bullshit because he was already all the way gone for that girl. And he'd thoroughly fucked things up. Destroyed the best thing in his life.

"Ready for this, Spencer?" Jason's words and accompanying shoulder punch snapped King out of his thoughts.

"Ready to kick some ass," he replied, game day face firmly in place. This was the last time he was going to play with Jason, Nate, and James. They were all seniors, and this was their last shot at the title. And even though King was eligible to play next year, it wouldn't be the same playing without his teammates.

Coach Klopp gave them his standard stern pregame speech, and then they were heading out to the field. Thankfully, this year, the semis and finals were played at the professional soccer stadium in the next state over, and the drive was only three hours. Because of this, Bradley U navy and white filled most of the seats, with little smatterings of maroons and yellows, which were the opposing team's colors.

King tried not to wonder about whether or not Lila was in the crowd. He knew through the grapevine that a few of her friends had made the drive, but he'd made a point not to ask if she was joining them. It wouldn't make a difference, anyway. They were done...for good this time. And he wasn't going to dwell on the fact that his asshole sperm donor was here, but this time Sol at least had the decency to bring his wife to the game, instead of one of his mistresses.

The next 90 minutes were a battle. It rained on and off throughout the game, making the field conditions less than ideal. In spite of that, Nate protected the hell out of the goal, Jason defended like a boss, and Will and James represented in the midfield. King had a couple of shots on target, but the score was still tied 0-0 going into the 90th minute.

As the rain started up again, King knew that if they didn't get it done right, then during stoppage time, they'd most likely be headed for a shootout in unpredictable conditions. He subconsciously rubbed the necklace underneath his jersey as he sped to get open for a pass. *Five minutes and counting.*

Will had managed to retrieve the ball from the opposition and was moving it upfield. Then one of their rivals executed a clean slide tackle and took over possession. *Two minutes and counting.*

The other team advanced the ball to Bradley's goal box—within scoring range. Their forward maneuvered around the Bradley defenders and got a shot off. Fortunately for Nate, the forward slipped in the wet conditions and Nate made an easy save. He stood up quickly and ran to the edge of his goal box, scanning the field for someone open to throw to. King caught his eye, and Nate nodded almost imperceptibly. He made a move like he was going to roll the ball to James but then launched it over everyone's heads. King stayed in line with their rivals' last defender so he remained on-side as he trapped and cradled the ball with his foot.

You are not your father. You're a king. Lila's words came to him as he flipped the ball up and over a defender and reclaimed possession of the ball as soon as it hit the grass. He dribbled once, and then positioned his body over the ball. Time seemed to slow down as King took a deep breath and looked up at the goal. He picked a spot in the upper left corner and struck the ball hard with his laces. The momentum of his shot and follow-through brought him to the ground. As he fell, he saw the keeper jump and stretch toward the corner, but the shot was perfectly placed and out of his reach. The crowd and players were holding their breath and King heard the sweet sound of the ball hitting the back of the netting.

Before King could get up, his teammates were piling on him, their cheers triumphant, even though they still had about a minute left to play. They got to their feet and set up for kickoff. The referee blew his whistle to restart the match, but as soon as the player in maroon kicked the ball to his teammate, the ref's whistle blew again, and the Bradley U soccer team officially became the national champs.

They all cheered and sang the Bradley U fight song. The crowd had rushed the field, so it was a sea of school colors and celebration.

King stiffened when he felt a hand on his shoulder. Solomon. Solomon with a guy he didn't recognize. His mother was standing a few feet away, ever deferential to her husband.

"Way to finish, Junior. This is Guy Nelson, a scout for the Seattle Sounders."

Automatically, King shook the man's extended hand.

"We think you have a lot of promise, King, and think you should consider entering the SuperDraft this year."

King clenched his jaw and forced himself to breathe before he responded. "Thanks for coming, sir. I'm sorry. I'm still not sure what I want to do. I have another year of eligibility to play, and right now, I'd like to focus on our win and go celebrate with my team." He didn't even look at his father, whose creepy light-blue eyes were probably glowing red right about now.

Guy didn't miss a beat, "Of course, son. But give what I said some thought."

"Will do. Thank you, sir," King managed to say before heading back toward his teammates.

Then he saw her.

She was standing next to Julia and Nate, who were having an epic, slightly indecent, celebratory makeout. A few of their other friends were there too, taking selfies and dancing around. But not Lila. She was standing still, her legs looking like they were a million miles long in the skirt she was wearing, with an umbrella in her hand. An amused half smile lit her face as she watched her friends. She hadn't noticed King yet.

King tried to will his body forward, but he was stuck right where he was. He wanted her eyes on him. Hell, he wanted all of her on him. Seconds later, her expression changed, and her face turned towards his.

He wasn't sure if they stared at each other for minutes or mere seconds, but she was the one who finally broke eye contact, a lifted left eyebrow and a slight dip of her umbrella offered as her final parting gifts.

The crown hanging from his neck felt heavy.

You are not your father. You're a king.

Maybe it was time he started believing that.

Chapter 21

"Can you tell me why you're here, Solomon?"

King internally cringed as he sat across from the counselor that he'd been assigned to as a part of Bradley U's Counseling Services. The room was painted in what he assumed was supposed to be a calming light-blue shade. But all it reminded him of was the blue-haired woman he'd allowed to be all over him at Jock Jam. The one whose name he didn't know and whose face he couldn't even remember. He remembered what Lila's face looked like when she saw him, though. The disappointment and the hurt. He was pretty sure that image would be burned into his brain forever.

He nervously rubbed his hands on his knees. "Could you call me King, please? It's my middle name and what I like to go by. When people call me by that other name, it's...uncomfortable for me."

She wrote something down in the notebook she was holding before looking back up at him, her smile apologetic. "My apologies, King. I assure you, it won't happen again. The whole point of this center is to ensure that you're able to find a safe space, and I appreciate you taking the initiative to set that boundary up front."

Dr. Hatch seemed almost grandmotherly...if said grandmother rocked a white pixie haircut and reading glasses attached to a rainbow-striped beaded chain.

"Uh, thanks," King muttered. Dammit, why was this so hard for him?

"You seem to attach a lot of meaning to your name. Could you tell me a little bit about that?"

King cleared his throat, feeling the fight-or-flight response rising in his body. But he tried to wade through the feelings instead of pushing them away. *Might as well just rip the Band-Aid off...*

"Okay, so, I'm named after my father. He named me after himself and calls me Junior. And I *hate* it. I hate *him*." King swallowed the lump in his throat as he processed what he'd just said.

Dr. Hatch nodded encouragingly, giving him the confidence to continue.

"The first time I caught him having sex with someone who wasn't my mom was when I was seven." He gulped down another lump in his throat. "Of course, I didn't understand what was happening then, but the older I got, the more and more I understood just the kind of man my father is. He's never been faithful to my mother the entire 25 years they've been married. And the worst part? My mom knows. My mom knows, and it kills her, yet she still stays with him. She's always on his side, even when he treats her like shit."

He could feel a few errant tears tracking down his face, and he swiped them away angrily. "This one time, I packed a bag for me and for my mom. So we could leave and start over. And when I told her what I'd done, she slapped me across the face and told me to go to my room."

"How old were you when that happened?"

"Ten."

"So it would be fair to say that you grew up in a home that was emotionally, verbally, and physically abusive?"

"I'd never thought about the emotional part of it before, but yeah, I think that's fair to say," King responded.

Dr. Hatch wrote something down and then steepled her fingertips under her chin. "I'm so very sorry that the two people in your life who should have protected you, who should have loved you above anything else, didn't care for you the way they should have," she said kindly but thankfully without pity.

"Thank you," King replied. Then he shook his head. "Honestly, I'm afraid that I'll turn out just like him, that I'll end up hurting the people I love. That's why I..."

"That's why you what?"

"I loved someone—hell, I still love her—and I ended things. And now everything feels hollow. We just won the national championship in soccer, and the only person I wanted to celebrate with was her."

"Have you told her how you feel?"

King shook his head. "I'm pretty sure she hates me now. I mean, I pretty much did everything in my power to guarantee that she despises me. I let her think I didn't care, that I didn't want to be with just her. That I was interested in other people. None of which is true."

"Why do you think your default is to self-destruct rather than to trust?"

King mulled that over for a minute. "I honestly don't know. Maybe it's because I was feeling too dependent on her or because I realized I was in love with her. I just could picture myself letting her down or overwhelming her with all of my shit, and those thoughts gutted me. She's way too good for me, anyway."

"No relationship can ever be perfect, King. In spite of your best efforts, there will be times when you unintentionally let your partner down. The important thing is whether or not you're willing to put work into it. Allow it to grow. To communicate with honesty and integrity, even when it seems difficult. To acknowledge harm and be humble enough to apologize."

King thought about Lila's face when she'd angrily called him Solomon. How immediately she looked stricken and remorseful. Like the last thing she wanted to do was hurt him. And then she'd sincerely and instantly apologized to him, even though he was the one who had goaded her and prodded at her until she broke.

"That actually makes a lot of sense."

Dr. Hatch smiled. "I'm glad you think so. All that said, I do think you have some healing to do, and some narrative reframing definitely needs to happen if you sincerely want to overcome these inclinations. But if the desire is there, I think that you'll get to a place where such a bond will be met with feelings of love and safety instead of uncertainty and fear, whether it's with this particular person or someone else down the road.

"Regardless, you need to become comfortable with who you are individually and be secure with your own personhood, whether you desire to seek a partnership or not. The most important relationship you can have is with yourself."

She adjusted her glasses and looked right at him. "Are you willing to put in the effort to grow, King? If so, I'd love to keep seeing you to help you as you work all of this out."

"I'd like that," King replied, agreeing to meet with Dr. Hatch twice a week for the next couple of months. As he left the counseling services building, he could feel the weight on his shoulders lightening, just a little bit.

Chapter 22

Lila hugged Wren a final time before watching her walk through the automatic doors leading to the airport terminal. They'd made the most of their time together, managing to have fun while still studying for and taking their finals. And they'd been able to make the trip to see the Bradley soccer players win the national championship, though she didn't exactly want to dwell on the fact that she'd had some pretty intense eye contact with King, which only served to remind her that she was nowhere near over him. The bastard looked particularly edible when muddy and soaking wet, much to her dismay.

When Wren had finally told Lila about what happened with Knight, Lila hugged her and reassured her that things would unfold the way they were supposed to. Knowing that Knight was hurting too, she snuck into his house and cleaned up his room while he was out taking a final. It was an absolute sty, and she felt awful that both of her best friends were feeling so wretched. She was optimistic, though, because there were some intense feelings happening. But she also knew that they both had stuff they needed to sort through and hoped that the time apart would be healing for them both.

Before pulling away from the curb, a text from Knight came in.

KNIGHT: *Everything go okay with the big sendoff?*

LILA: *About to start driving. Calling you now.*

She put her AirPods in and started the call before she pulled out into traffic. Knight answered on the first ring.

"Someone's excited to talk to me," Lila teased. "He who never actually talks on the phone."

Knight's laugh sounded almost back to normal. "Always, Li. How did everything go? She get off okay?"

"I mean, there was no getting off, but I did throw a vibrator into her suitcase."

"Who are you, and what did you do with Lila Alexander? All of a sudden you're making sex jokes and talking vibrators."

"What can I say? It's been an interesting and transformative year," Lila giggled. Then she sobered up. "She's okay, and I think this experience is going to be good for her. And, don't worry, I'll keep tabs on her address so you can send her snail mail."

"People still do that?"

"If they don't, they totally should," Lila asserted. "There's something wonderful about a handwritten missive. Letter writing is a lost art."

"Okay, now you're sounding more like the Lila I know and love."

"Glad I could come through for you, bro."

"Question."

"Answer."

He chuckled. "Have you found a place to live yet? Isn't your lease up in like a week?"

Lila's heart sank. For some weird reason, she had yet to find an apartment to rent for the spring/summer. A lot of her friends were graduating, and the few that weren't already had places secured. Which meant she might have to move home with her parents for three and a half months and commute to work and school, all while trying to find a place for the fall. Which was, needless to say, less than ideal.

"I'm going to take that contemplative silence as a no."

"Perceptive of you, Knight. Very perceptive. At this rate, I'll have to move home with my parents and be subjected to their well-meaning but wholly puritanical views on sex and dating. I'm also about 99 percent sure they'd give me a curfew, too."

"Sounds horrific."

"You have no idea."

"What if I told you I had a solution for you? A place to live with fun roommates and your own private room and semi-private bathroom."

"I'm listening."

"You should move in here," he said triumphantly. "Jaxon and Mark graduated, so their rooms are open. The rooms are already furnished, as you know, and the mattresses have already been swapped out and the place thoroughly decontaminated. Plus, you already know Bear, so you're two for three in the roommate department already."

She mulled it over. It wasn't the worst idea ever. Living with Knight would be fun. And Bear was super chill. Though she did have questions about the bathroom arrangement.

"Good points, all. But what about this whole shared bathroom situation? Like, I wouldn't be sharing with either you or Bear because you already share one, yes? So I'd have to share with some random guy?"

She cringed at the thought. She had three little brothers, after all. Falling into the toilet in the middle of the night because they forgot to put the seat back down? Not awesome.

"Yes, you are correct that you would have to share a bathroom with a dude, but he will be thoroughly vetted by me, so he won't be a creep. I'll also threaten to kick his ass if he leaves the toilet seat up. And, just so you know, there are both inside and outside locks on the bathroom doors. So you can lock it when you're inside the bathroom for privacy, and you can also lock your door from the inside of your room so no one can enter it from the bathroom."

That made her feel marginally better. If she could handle a house full of females during shark week and a naked roommate in lotus pose, she could handle sharing a bathroom with a guy. And the truth was, she didn't really have any other options at this point.

"You really think this is a good idea?" she asked, uncertain.

"I think it's one of the best ideas I've ever had. Plus, you can't beat the commute. You can move in today if you want. The other room will probably be vacant until fall semester starts anyway, because a lot of people go home for the summer."

Lila could only think of one reason why she'd refuse, and he lived across the street from Knight. But she was bound to see him at some point anyway, wasn't she? There was no avoiding it when they shared a best friend. She also wasn't positive he was still planning on living there anyway or that he would even be returning back to school. So Lila decided to throw caution to the wind and go for it.

"Okay, Knight. I'm in."

"This is going to be the best summer and senior year ever," Knight cheered.

"Junior year for me. But I guess senior year for me too, since I'm hellbent on graduating in three years."

"Genius pants."

"Says the guy with the eidetic memory."

"It has its positives and its negatives."

"Touché, my friend. Touché. All right, I'll pack my shit and be there later tonight."

"Need any help?"

"Nah, I don't have that much stuff. It shouldn't take me too long."

"Then I'll pick up the Ben and Jerry's and have it ready for you."

"See, this is why we're best friends. You get me."

"I really, really do."

They said their goodbyes, and Lila made her way back to her apartment. Vicky and Dani had already moved out, and so it was just her and Becky until the end of the week. She wrinkled her nose at the sight of Becky's white noise machine.

Definitely not going to miss those womb sounds, she thought with a smile as she packed up her stuff. The benefit of attending a university that required off campus housing to be furnished with, at the bare minimum, a bed, a dresser, and a desk, was that she had no heavy furniture to move. Just her clothes and toiletries and a few decorative items she'd added to her room and the apartment. It only took a few trips to her car, and then she was ready to go.

Not wanting to be a total jerk, she wrote Becky a little note as a way of saying goodbye, stuck it on the sound machine, and then drove over to her new place.

Chapter 23

"Lila!" The chorus of deep male voices greeted her as soon as she walked in the door. Bear, Knight, and Will were all sitting on the U-shaped sectional in the front room and eyed the bags in her hands expectantly. She'd been living with Knight and Bear for a couple of months now, and it had become a bit of a tradition for her to bring them home food if she was working a closing shift. When Bryan, the owner of The Pub, found out that she was living with Bradley U athletes, he basically gave her carte blanche to take home what she wanted. Which definitely helped her score some major points with her roomies.

Surprisingly, she'd only seen King a handful of times, mostly in passing. She suspected that he and Knight had purposely coordinated hanging out with each other when she was at work, on campus taking a few classes to ensure she could graduate early, or otherwise not at the house. Which was a relief, because her heart was still doing that stupid thing where it did a series of cartwheels in her chest and then promptly bottomed out whenever he was in her proximity. Or whenever she heard his name. She didn't quite know what to do about that, but she'd gotten a lot better at suppressing it. Hopefully one day, the feeling would fade altogether.

"You all expecting something?" she teased, even as she moved over to the kitchen island and started taking to-go boxes out of the bags. "Knight, there's ribs tonight. And Bear, some of those spicy hot wings you're obsessed with. Will, I know you're a sucker for those oatmeal chocolate chip cookies, so there are some of those as well."

Bear dug into the wings. "Seriously Lila, if I were into chicks, I'd marry you tonight."

"High praise, Bear. High praise, indeed." Lila went over to the fridge and grabbed a rose lemonade. Her guys, as she'd come to call them, knew she liked them, and they weren't always available at the grocery store, so whenever they saw them while out shopping, they'd grab a pack for her. It turned out that living with a house full of males wasn't so bad, especially since the parties were on such a smaller scale since it was summertime. She missed Wren and her girls, but that's why FaceTime, What's App, and Marco Polo existed. There were multiple threads happening so they all still felt connected.

"So Lila darling, we were talking about going super throwback and having an epic *Die Hard* franchise movie marathon tomorrow night. Most of the guys have never seen it. Because obviously they don't have excellent vintage film tastes like you and me," Knight said between bites. "You in?"

Lila winced. "As much as I would love to revel in the excellence that is John McClane, I can't. I have plans."

The guys started grumbling, and Lila elaborated. "Seriously guys, I have actual plans. I'm going out with Eli again."

That's right, she was dating again.

Sort of.

She'd met Eli a few weeks before when she waited on him and his friends. He'd been charming and kind and had asked for her number at the end of the night. Eli's trim build, side-parted dark-brown hair, and clear-framed glasses were attractive in a sort of tweed jacket with elbow patches kind of way, and he didn't cringe when Lila used multisyllabic words. So that definitely worked in his favor.

Eli was a few years older than Lila and was attending Bradley for graduate school. Pursuing a master's in public administration, she was pretty sure. Perhaps it was because he was older, or because he hadn't attended Bradley for his undergrad, but Eli allegedly had no interest in any of the sports teams, which suited Lila just fine. They'd gone out on a few dates, kind of fooled around a little bit, and it was...fine. His kisses felt nice-ish, albeit a little slobbery, but they definitely didn't make her burn like she did when she kissed certain other people who she refused to name. But maybe that was okay. Maybe that's what she needed at the moment.

"Invite him to join," Knight said.

"I don't know about that... You guys are awesome, but you're kind of extra sometimes. Like, I don't know if Eli can handle all of this energy." Lila waved her hand around in a circle and laughed.

Bear held up a finger. "Hold on a minute. How about a compromise? Why don't you go out to dinner or whatever you were going to do and then come back and join us for a bit?"

Lila didn't hate that idea. She mulled it over. "Yeah, I think that actually sounds fun. Besides, it's probably time he met you guys anyway." *If they even made it past their next date.* She got out her phone and started texting.

LILA: *The boys want us to join them for part of a Die Hard movie marathon after we go out to dinner tomorrow. You amenable to that idea?*

ELI: *I don't think I've ever seen an entire Die Hard movie, but I suppose there's a first time for everything. Plus, it would be nice to get to know your roommates. I'm in. Pick you up at 7?*

LILA: *thumbs up*

She looked up from her phone. "All right, we're in. We're going to go to dinner and then will head back here."

The guys did sort of an awkward three-way high-five and then shared some sort of a look when they thought her head was turned. Too bad her peripheral vision was second-to-none.

"Seriously though guys, go easy on him, okay?"

"Easy as Sunday morning, Li," Knight said with a smirk. "Besides, if he can't handle us, he's not the guy for you anyway. You're like a 20 out of 10, so the bar is pretty damn high."

"And now I have a battalion of older brother types ready and willing to defend my honor like it's the 1950s," Lila teased.

"Naw, we just care about you." Knight slung an arm around her shoulders.

"Your care is noted and appreciated." She stifled a yawn. "K, I'm beat, all. My bed is calling me. Try to keep the gaming to a decent decibel level," she said sarcastically, because there's no way that was happening. Normally she'd be up watching them play.

"Night Li," they all yelled as she laughed all the way up the stairs. She hoped tomorrow worked out okay, that they'd go easy on Eli. That it wouldn't be a complete disaster.

* * *

Well, this was a huge mistake.

Lila and Eli hadn't even crossed the threshold of the doorway before she sensed a difference in the energy of the room and those stupid stomach gymnastics she was trying to get rid of decided to make themselves known.

King.

A lone wolf standing in the kitchen, under the dimmed pendant lighting over the island (yeah, this house was fancy like that), eating a folded slice of pizza. Lila reckoned that it was probably his signature thin crust Italian sausage and jalapeño combination that he'd previously introduced her to and that she now craved all the damn time. Especially after mediocre meals like the one she'd just eaten. Distracted, Lila stopped short, so Eli ran into her.

"Oops, sorry, babe," Eli said, apparently thinking that calling her "babe" was an appropriate identifier in this scenario. She'd let him know later that it definitely was not. And when he slid an arm around her shoulders? Lila didn't love that either. Was there just some sort of weird vibe that was floating around in the air tonight? Or had it been way too long since she'd hung out with her ladies? Probably a bit of both. Thankfully, she didn't think that anybody had heard them because the volume of the TV was so loud.

She flipped the overhead light on to get everybody's attention. Someone paused the movie, and suddenly the full force of their scrutiny was solely aimed at the two of them. And Eli's arm was still around her shoulders.

"Lila!" they all declared, and she couldn't help but smile. Damn, if she didn't love this big pack of guys.

She subtly stepped out from under Eli's arm, and he mercifully didn't try to touch her again. "Hey there boys." She pointed to her date. "Everybody, this is Eli. Eli, meet the boys." She pointed at everybody and named them. "That's

Knight, Bear, Demarcus, Will, Benny, and over in the kitchen is King."

"Nice to meet everybody," Eli said.

Knight patted a place next to him. "Saved you guys a seat. Eli, you're next to me. I need to make sure that your intentions toward my little sister are noble."

"He's your brother?" Eli whispered, confused.

"Not literally, but pretty much, yeah." Lila shrugged. She didn't want to get into it, and she was getting wary of all the eyes on her. Well, of just one set in particular.

They made their way over to Knight, and as promised, Knight wrangled Eli into sitting next to him. The space next to Lila was open, but she didn't think much of it because the guys all liked to manspread.

Demarcus hit the lights and Bear pushed play on the movie, and Lila leaned her head back to enjoy the dulcet sounds of Bruce Willis crawling through air ducts saying, "Yippee ki-yay, motherfucker." Which never got old, ever.

Whether it was the intimidating physicality of Knight's presence or the fact they weren't alone, Eli mercifully kept his hands and arms to himself. Dinner had been okay...but Lila felt like their dating experience had run its course. Eli was nice, but just not for her.

Everything was fine until somebody vaulted over the back of the couch and landed right next to her. She didn't have to look to know that it was King. She hadn't been this close to him since the last time they'd... *Ahem.* The juniper and citrus scent of his fancy body wash hit her nostrils, and she angled her body more towards Eli. He did not smell as good, but she was feeling a little off-kilter.

Damn her heart and its cartwheelingness.

It also didn't help that the air conditioning was apparently working overtime tonight and the house was currently the temperature of an icebox. So she was cold on top of everything else.

She suppressed a shiver then flinched when she felt the weight of fabric being draped over her shoulders. King had taken off the zip-up hoodie he'd been wearing and wrapped it around her without a word. Her initial instinct was to shrug it off, but she *was* cold, and she didn't want to make a scene.

Plus, enough time had gone by that they could totally be in the same room together and just be friendly. It was *fine.*

Lila glanced over her shoulder, her eyes quickly landing on his chin. "Thank you," she murmured.

He nodded.

She threaded her arms through the sleeves and then zipped it up. Hell, Lila even put the hood up for a minute. She was instantly warmer, and also in her own personal purgatory, because now she was surrounded by King's scent in the dark. With the man himself close enough to touch. She couldn't help the heat that was pooling low in her belly, so she tried to just ignore it.

When his powerful thigh brushed up against hers? She tried not to picture the beauty that were his quads. Muscular and powerful and lickable and...

Stop it, Lila.

She moved her leg so they weren't touching anymore and had to repeat the action a couple more times before the movie ended.

She leaned over to Eli. "I'm ready to call it a night. Can I walk you out?"

He nodded, stood, and then held out a hand to help her up. She reluctantly took it and was dismayed when he didn't drop it once she was standing.

Yeah, this guy needed to go.

Once they were outside, Lila disengaged their hands. Awkwardness hung heavy, and she tried to think of what to say. "Thanks for dinner and for being willing to share our date with a bunch of *Die Hard* fans."

"They were nice. Make sure you thank them all for me."

"Will do."

"I'd love to go out with you again. Tomorrow, maybe? We could go back to my place, and you could meet my roommates. Or we could just hang out in my room or whatever." His implication was clear, and Lila knew she needed to nip this whole thing in the bud.

She sighed. "I don't think so, Eli. I've had fun going out with you, but I don't really see this going anywhere, and I don't want to lead you on."

He seemed disappointed but took it on the chin like a champ. He gave her a quick hug and commented that he'd see her around, and then he drove off. Lila blew out a sigh of relief and turned to head back inside.

She went to open the door just as it swung back, and she collided with whoever was exiting. "Oof, sorry!" she managed to get out before she tripped backward. Given the fact that everybody inside had almost a foot and at least 100 pounds on her, it felt like she'd just bounced off of a brick wall.

Large, strong hands grabbed her waist, steadying her. And then she looked up, right into King's dark, chocolatey eyes. "Sorry, La. Didn't realize you were on the other side of the door."

"No worries," she said, proud of herself for keeping her shit together, because it had been so long since he'd put his hands on her. This was also the most they'd said to each other since he'd ended things. Lila had forgotten how good his hands felt. How they managed to fit her somehow. And she'd definitely forgotten how much she liked the velvety depth of his voice and what caused said voice to turn all gritty and growly and sexy and...

No, Lila.

She needed to abort this mission ASAP, or her body would start trying to influence her mind, and she'd end up doing something irrational like humping his leg or kissing his face off. Or something.

"Um, I'm going to need my hips back at some point, King." She looked down to where he was still gripping her tightly, his thumb lightly tracing one of her hip bones.

"Right," he said, releasing his hands and taking a step back. "Sorry."

"No worries."

They stood there in silence for a minute, locked in place, unsure of how to proceed.

"You leaving?" Lila asked.

King nodded. So she unzipped his hoodie and started to take it off to give back to him. "Thanks for the loan..." she started to say.

"Hold on to it for now," King said. "It's colder than balls in there. I'll just grab it from Knight next time I see him or whatever."

She hesitated but then shrugged back into it and zipped it back up. "Okay. Um, thanks. That's nice of you."

"I'm trying to be nicer to my friends," King replied.

"So we're friends, huh?" Lila raised a skeptical brow.

"I'd like to be."

Her heart soared and sank in equal measure because King wanted to be friends. Which was great, but that also meant that he was past whatever else they'd been before. Lila didn't know if she'd ever fully get to the point where she felt okay about that, but she was sure as hell going to try.

"Okay, then. Goodnight, *friend.*" She tried out the word carefully with a tentative smile and didn't hate the way it felt coming out of her mouth, but she didn't love it either. Maybe eventually she would.

And he smiled too, just barely. Blink and you'd miss it. "Goodnight, La."

Chapter 24

"Keep this pace up, Spencer, and I'm going to pass out or puke before we complete another lap," Knight managed to stutter between sucking in huge spurts of air.

King wasn't even winded, but he slowed their pace to a brisk walk. "Punking out on me already, Patrick? We've only done six miles." He'd already run two by the time Knight joined him on the track. It was early in the morning, before the summer sun beat down too forcefully, though their shed shirts were an indication that temperatures were rising quickly.

They walked one more lap around the track and then veered off into the grass to stretch and grab their water bottles.

After stretching, King splayed out on the grass and closed his eyes, breathing for a minute. He'd forgotten how potent Lila's proximity was. It had been torture to sit so close to her and not be *with* her. Though he'd known going in that Lila was bringing her date home, it had been more difficult to see her with the guy than he had anticipated, even if he could tell by her body language that she wasn't really into it. But seeing her date with his arm around her, his hand in hers, did something awful to King's chest.

The past two months of counseling had been really helpful to him, and he was finally starting to feel like he was capable of being the kind of guy he'd always wanted to be but thought was impossible to become. He'd also set some boundaries with his parents (in the form of blocking their cell numbers and only communicating via email) that had helped him to get his mind right.

He channeled his former inclination toward self-destruction into healthier outlets, like running and other forms of exercise. He'd also started reading a lot more. And he'd made the decision to officially return to the soccer team for his last year. He was only two classes away from a double major, so he'd filled the remaining holes in his schedule with classes he'd always thought sounded interesting but hadn't really fit in with the course load he had to take. If they also happened to be classes Lila mentioned she was interested in taking way back when, it was purely coincidental.

Bullshit.

"So, how serious are Lila and glasses guy?" King stretched his arms behind his head and hoped his voice only sounded mildly interested in the answer.

Something soft hit him in the face, and it took a moment to register that it was the hoodie he'd loaned Lila the other night. It smelled faintly of her, a heady combination of their scents, and he tried not to be a creep and inhale too deeply. Knight would notice and never let him live that shit down.

"Oh that's totally done. She let him down gently on movie night," Knight chuckled. "Honestly, I don't think she was ever that into him. I think she was definitely trying, though, for whatever reason." Knight paused for so long that King lifted the hoodie from his face to see what was going on, only to catch his friend suggestively wiggling his brows in King's direction. King groaned and dropped the hoodie back down on his face.

"I wonder what reason that would be?" Knight prodded. "Perhaps the arrival of an old flame tipped the scales? Or maybe it was a total and complete lack of chemistry." He shuddered. "I might have walked in on them kissing one time, and I felt really bad for the girl. Dude had absolutely zero finesse."

King tried to stop the growl that erupted as soon as he'd heard she kissed the guy. But, based on Knight's laughter, he'd been unsuccessful in his attempt.

"Look, man, just because this particular person wasn't her jam doesn't mean that she won't meet somebody else. Hell, most of the guys are half in love with her but are too afraid of you to make a move." Knight plucked the hoodie off of King's head. "You need to up your game, King. She practically forced this into my arms when she heard I was meeting you for a run."

"Just taking it slow." King took the hoodie back and tucked it under his head. "We're trying the friendship thing."

Knight snorted in reply. "Yeah, I'm sure you both are going to be great at the 'friendship thing,' as you call it." He scratched at the dark stubble on his jaw. "Bro, I think that now's the time to put our plan into action. Otherwise, all bets are off."

"You're right," King agreed as he sat up. "It's time. Hell, it's past time. Let's do it."

Knight clenched his fist. "Yesssssssss. It's about damn time. Phase two of 'help King be less of a dick' is officially underway. I'm thrilled you're finally pulling your head out of your ass."

"Yeah, well, you might be the only one who feels that way."

"Psssh. I failed to mention that when Lila was passing off your hoodie, she kinda looked sad about it. There's still feelings there, my friend. You'll see."

"I'm taking it slow, man. Super slow," King reiterated. "Super fucking slow."

"Fine," Knight agreed. "But you need to come over tonight. Around 11:30ish. Lila's closing, so she'll be bringing food home. I'll give her a heads-up that you'll be there so she's not taken off guard. Since now you've decided you're friends and all."

"Okay, I guess it'd be good to ease back into things, given the fact that phase two is about to start. And obviously, I'm not gonna turn down free food."

"So you're in for food tonight and finally ready for phase two. How soon do you want to move on that?"

"I see what you did there...and I don't know, maybe next weekend? That way it'll be right before school starts back up again?"

"Sounds like a plan."

King studied his friend for a minute. "Have you talked to Wren?" His friend still hadn't shared much about what had happened that night beyond what they'd initially discussed, but King knew that Knight still had it bad for Lila's fiery friend.

"I've been writing her letters. Sometimes she answers; sometimes she doesn't. There have been a few FaceTimes. She seems to be doing okay, which is good. She needed to get away from some stuff."

"Do you think Lila knows what happened?"

Knight nodded. "She knows." He cleared his throat. "She's holding out hope for us, which means a lot."

King sensed that he needed to lighten his friend's mood a bit, so he pivoted. "Well, you are a great human, Knight. And I bet you're especially skilled with your throwing hand." He couldn't mimic Knight's superior eyebrow waggle, but he sure as shit tried.

Knight punched him on the shoulder and barked out a laugh. "You know it." And then, more quietly: "Thanks, man."

King nodded. "I've got your back. Just like you've got mine." As they left the track, they parted ways even as Knight ribbed King for running home after his run.

"I've got a lot of tension to burn off." King shrugged.

"Just remember, 11:30 tonight."

King gave his friend a mock salute. "I'll be there."

* * *

Given the enthusiasm with which Knight and Bear greeted Lila when she walked through the door, you would have thought she had Wren and Demarcus inside the bags she was holding instead of dinner. But when various portions of their favorite foods began to emerge, along with Lila's accompanying smile, King totally understood the reaction.

She pushed a to-go container in front of him. "Buffalo chicken salad and shoestring fries?" She posed it as a question, but her knowing smile said it all. She'd remembered his favorite meal.

"Thanks, friend," he managed to eke out.

Her smile dimmed just slightly before she replied, "Anytime, friend." She turned her attention back to the food as she fished out a sandwich and salad for herself. They all ate and joked, and Bear convinced Lila to tell King about what had happened when her boss found out that she was living with athletes.

"So, for a little context, Bryan's always been a total ass to me. Well, he's pretty much an ass to everyone except for a couple of the blondes he hired as hostesses who magically got promoted to server and given the best sections within a couple of months." She rolled her eyes.

"I remember," King said softly.

She stilled for a sec before rebounding with aplomb. "Anyway, he was being his typical drill sergeant self until he noticed Knight, Bear, and Will in my section. So obviously, he goes over and starts talking shop and kissing ass." Lila shoots an adoring gaze Knight's way. And even though King knew better, he had to briefly remind himself that it was definitely a familial adoration and not a romantic one. "And Knight just goes on and on about how I'm the best server they've ever had..."

"Who makes the best raspberry lemonades," Knight interjected.

"And always remembers to put my dressing on the side," Bear added.

Lila laughed. "Right. And so they're talking me up, and Bryan all of a sudden is just singing my praises and saying that he hired me personally, etcetera etcetera."

"At that point, I casually mentioned that she was moving in with us, and I thought the guy's head was going to explode," Knight said as Lila laughed.

"So after they left, I nonchalantly asked Bryan if I could bring home food from time to time on nights when I'm working the closing shift. And also promised that the guys just might tag The Pub on their social media."

She paused to take a bite of her sandwich and a drink. "He looked like he was about to wet his pants, he was so excited. Then he said I could take whatever I wanted, within reason." She raised a brow. "So now I get a ton of free food, *and* I'm getting assigned better sections." She ended with a raised shoulder.

"And making way better tips," Knight chimed in.

"Hashtag truth," Lila agreed. "Which is nice since my rent is exorbitant and my roommates are so hard to live with," she joked.

"So high maintenance," Bear teased. To which Lila lovingly gave him her middle finger. King loved seeing her like this, comfortable in her own skin and aware of how fun she was to be around. He'd missed her more than he realized.

Once their food was finished, King shot Knight a look, and he nodded. Knight stretched his arms above his head and yawned. "I think I'm going to call it a night, Li." Then he not so subtly elbowed Bear.

"Yeah, um, me too." Bear's fake yawn was super obvious. "G'night guys!"

Once they'd hustled up the stairs, the awkwardness settled in. Lila seemed unsure of what to do, so King spoke first. "Do you, uh, want to go sit on the couch and chill for a minute?"

"Sure."

Once they were seated next to each other but far enough apart to be platonic, Lila reached for the remote. "Want to watch something?"

King put his hand over hers lightly. "Actually, I wanted to say something to you first, if that's okay."

Lila leaned back, breaking the contact between their hands, and drew her legs up to her chest. "Yeah, of course. What's up?"

King angled his body so that he was facing her, his elbow hanging over the back of the couch, and she mirrored the movement. "I just wanted to apologize to you for...well...for pretty much everything that happened between us last year."

Lila's speechlessness and shocked expression pushed him to continue.

"I was in a pretty bad place mentally and emotionally, and even though that doesn't excuse my behavior, I'm sorry that you were caught up in that. That you became part of the fallout of my insecurities and poor self-worth." King sighed. "I'm so sorry, Lila. I'm sorry for hurting you, for saying dickish things to you, and for not treating you like the queen you are. It's taken a fair amount of self-analysis and counseling to figure all of this out, and I have a long way to go. But I'm really grateful that you're up for being friends in spite of everything I've done."

King blew out a breath and waited. He'd said what he felt he needed to say and tried to apologize without making excuses. How she chose to receive it was up to her, and frankly, she was entitled to feel however she felt. He'd royally fucked up, after all.

Lila studied his face intently for what seemed like forever before she finally broke the heavy silence. "I didn't realize how much I needed to hear you apologize to me until you actually said the words. Thank you, King."

She bit her bottom lip then inhaled another breath and exhaled, seeming to measure her words before speaking again. "Also...I want you to know that I forgive you. I know that you were and are dealing with circumstances that are challenging and were doing the best you knew how to do at the time." She smiled faintly. "But I can see the change in you. The self-awareness and the confidence. The maturity. It's a wonderful thing to see. I admire you for seeking help when you realized you couldn't tackle everything on your own. That takes real courage."

"Thanks, La. That means a lot coming from you."

"You're capable of great things, King Spencer. I'm glad you're starting to realize it."

"Back 'atcha, Lila Alexander."

They were silent for a minute, sizing each other up in a reassessment of sorts. "Your hair's gotten even longer on top," Lila mused. "I like it."

"I'd hope so, since I believe you were the one who suggested it in the first place," King said with a smirk.

"I did, didn't I?" Lila smirked right back. "No offense to your old 'do, but you have such a great head of hair, it was a shame you kept it so short all over. Though I like that you kept the shorter sides. You're lucky you have a friend with such great taste in hair. And a barber that knows how to blend."

"I am." King tried to smile, but the word "friend" just felt wrong coming from her lips.

Baby steps. Baby fucking steps.

They ended up turning on a movie, and King could tell Lila was getting tired. She sprawled out so that she was lying on the couch, her feet close to where King was sitting. He reached over to grab a pillow and placed it on his lap. "Feet," he said, tapping the pillow expectantly.

Lila hesitated, just for a second, then sat up and scooted the couple of extra inches so that she could prop her feet up on his lap. She lay back down and sighed when he rubbed the arch of her left foot.

"Damn, that feels good. Thanks, King. I owe you."

"I'll hold you to that," King chuckled, even as he tried to will his growing erection away. He loved touching her, loved the sounds she made. He tried not to picture all the ways he'd had her, all the ways he knew her. Thank fuck for throw pillows. Otherwise her feet would have been stabbed by now.

King blew out a frustrated breath then looked over and saw that Lila's eyes were closing. Within minutes, she was asleep. He slipped out from under her and gently picked her up, cradling her body against his. She stirred then let out a sigh and burrowed into his chest, and he tried to focus on getting her up the stairs and safely tucked into bed rather than dwell on how great it felt to have her so close. He laid her gently down on her bed and covered her with a blanket.

As he looked at her, he couldn't fight the urge to bend down and kiss her forehead softly, breathing her in for just a moment. Then he made his way back downstairs, turned off the TV and the lights, and made sure the door was locked behind him as he walked out into the balmy summer night.

Chapter 25

"I appreciate you agreeing to meet with me, darling," King's mom, Eleanor, said from across the table. After a particularly emotional email from her, King had agreed to meet up, in spite of his misgivings. He'd chosen The Pub, mainly because it was familiar and because they'd seat him in Lila's section if he asked. Today, he needed all of the moral support he could get.

"Yeah, well, it's been a while since we've seen each other without Solomon present." He couldn't help the bitterness that tinged his words.

"True. I didn't get the chance to congratulate you for your national championship..."

King held his breath, waiting for her to finish the sentence. He hoped that perhaps it would be an apology, but he was almost positive she was going to take him to task for something.

"Because you stormed off like a spoiled child."

And there it is.

He rubbed at Lila's crown necklace hidden beneath his shirt to calm himself.

"I'm not going to apologize for feeling blindsided by Solomon and some random MLS scout. But I am sorry I didn't come over and say hello. That was rude of me."

At that moment, Lila approached with a smile. "Hey King." She turned her head to take in King's mom, most likely noting the family resemblance in their hair and eyes, and her smile grew. "I didn't realize you had an older sister." It was cheesy as hell but just the kind of compliment his mom reveled in.

"Oh, my precious girl, you are *too* much. I'm actually his *mother*."

Lila's expression was appropriately awed and stunned, and King couldn't help but appreciate her efforts to charm his mother. "My goodness, Mrs. Spencer, you must let me know what's in the water you're drinking, because you look incredible. I could have sworn you were in your early 30s."

King's mom was 56. Needless to say, Lila had just become her new favorite person.

Eleanor trilled with laughter. "Now how do you know my Solomon?" King noted how Lila stiffened when she heard Eleanor refer to him by his first name and tried not to find her protectiveness completely sexy.

"I met King last year through a mutual friend." Her subtle emphasis on his preferred name only increased his admiration. "Here at the restaurant, actually. Our friend Jason used to work here with me, and he sent me over with refills when their glasses were already full."

"Such a trickster, that Jason," King added with a smile.

"Agreed." Lila's smile lit up her face in such a way that made King want to kiss the shit out of her, and it was a much better feeling than the one he was experiencing when he was left alone with his mother.

"Anyway, sorry to chat your ear off. I'm sure you two are ready for some drinks? Maybe an appetizer or two?"

Eleanor closed her menu. "Actually, I think we're ready to order. I'll have a lemon water and a garden salad with no dressing, please."

"I'm good with my usual, La. With a raspberry lemonade because I'm feeling dangerous today."

"Coming right up."

Once Lila had left them, Eleanor looked at King knowingly. "I like her."

"I'll make sure to let her know," King replied, and they both shared a smile. It was a pleasant moment, one that was short lived because of what his mother said next.

Her face fell. "Solomon, I wish you had more respect for your father," she remarked sadly.

"Mom, first off, please stop calling me Solomon. I go by King now, and if you can't respect that boundary, then we're not going to be able to see each other. Okay?"

Eleanor gave him a look that resembled her *We'll talk about this later* expression, but she nodded nonetheless.

Their conversation paused when Lila put down their drinks, along with a small bowl of freshly sliced lemons for King's mom. "In case you want more than one," she said with a wink as she whisked away to another table.

Eleanor's expression was one of pure elation. "She's getting a great tip." Then she focused back on King. "As I was saying...King...I do wish you'd respect your father. He's a great man who has provided a charmed life for the both of us."

King suppressed a frustrated groan. "Look, I don't want this to come out the wrong way, because I think you did the best you knew how, but I wish you would have protected me from him. I wish that instead of laying your hands on me, you would have left that lying, toxic bastard behind and started over." He cleared the emotion out of his throat. "I would have been happier sleeping on a dirt floor with a hungry stomach than feeling like a prisoner in that man's mansion."

Eleanor rocked back like she'd been struck, and her eyes filled with tears. "How *dare* you." She shot forward, apparently forgetting that A: They were in public, and B: There was a table in the way.

"Are you going to slap me, Mom? Gaslight me when I come to you crying that I'd seen my father having sex with my nanny?" King sighed and ran a hand over his face. "This was a terrible idea. I honestly thought we could attempt to have a civilized, adult conversation about all of this, but we're not there yet."

"I'll never be ready to hear you disparage your father in such a manner," Eleanor snarled as she shot out of her seat. "As far as I'm concerned, you're cut off."

King shook his head sadly. "I've been cut off for a long time, Mom. Going on two years now. You just never noticed."

Eleanor paled, just a little bit, and then stalked out of the restaurant.

King sat there in silence, trying to modulate his irregular breaths.

"Scoot over."

Lila's voice penetrated his daze, and he automatically shifted down the bench. She sat down, putting her head on his shoulder, and he could feel her soft braid grazing his arm.

"That looked intense, King."

"Yeah" was all he could muster.

"I don't know the circumstances, but I'm sorry regardless," she sighed. "I'm sorry she doesn't appreciate how wonderful her son is. Because you're pretty damn great."

King slid his arm around her waist and squeezed her in a side hug. "Thanks, La."

She lingered a minute more, which helped King calm down. Gave him a quick kiss on the check. Just a brush, but he felt it down in his core. Too soon, she was back up on her feet. "Be right back."

A few minutes later, she brought his meal out in a to-go box. "Lunch is on me today." She held up a finger to silence King's protest. "Nonnegotiable." Lila gestured her head toward the box. "It's boxed up so you can take off, or you're welcome to stay as long as you want. Let me know if I can get you anything else, okay?"

King couldn't look at her because his eyes were blurry, so he just murmured his thanks in the direction of the table. She put a hand on his shoulder and squeezed it gently, and then she was off to work again.

Chapter 26

"And this..." Wren's phone camera scrolled across the square, "is the Trevi fountain. Obvi." She flipped the view back so that Lila could see her face again as she wandered to find a place to sit down in the busy square. From her vantage point sitting on her bed, Lila was delighted to see that Wren looked serene and happy. Spain, Greece, and now Italy had been treating her friend well. Thank heavens for technology so they could FaceTime each other.

"It's beautiful, Wrenny. We'll have to go back together someday."

"Trust me, bestest, I've already planned our itinerary."

"I'd expect nothing less." Lila grinned. "I'm impressed you've been able to travel so much and do school at the same time. I need my summers at least partially off to recover."

"That's because you get 4.0s in college like that's normal or something," Wren snorted. "Some of us are fine with Bs. They get degrees, after all."

"Fair point."

"Besides, it's actually easier in a way, because we're seeing all of the art and architecture we're studying in real life. Ionic columns are a lot cooler once you've seen them at the Parthenon, you know?"

"You mean the ones at the admin building on campus don't do it for you?" Lila teased.

"Dammit, I miss you," Wren sighed.

"Same. But I'm proud of you. I think the distance is just what you needed." Wren looked pensive for a minute. "How's Knight doing?"

Lila rolled her eyes affectionately. "I could grab him and you could ask him yourself, you know."

Wren blushed. "I actually talked to him yesterday. Because that particular conversation was long overdue."

"And it went okay?"

Wren nodded. "I don't know how, but I have this calming feeling that everything is going to work out the way it's supposed to." She smiled at her friend. "The letter idea was a good one, Li. My first one back was an apology for everything after Jock Jam, which made it easier to start talking again."

"You were going through a lot, which I think Knight understands, but I think it's nice that you acknowledged what happened. He might look like he's super tough, but the man is a marshmallow inside," Lila mused. "In the best of ways."

Wren nodded. "That's one of the things I like about him. Before yesterday, we'd been FaceTiming a bit. Obviously, there's a lot to say, you know? A lot's changed since that night."

"I know. I'm trying to be here for both of you without inserting myself. But I think that since there are obviously some strong feelings there, you need to both put aside your insecurities and talk it out so that you can figure things out.

"Even though this is all big and scary, and frankly life-changing, I have a good feeling about your future. Even when one or both of you is acting ridiculous."

"Speaking of ridiculous... How are things with your new bestie, King? You realize I still want to cause him some bodily harm that may or may not involve handing his balls to him in a paper bag, right?"

"Again with the shockingly violent and shockingly specific maiming scenarios. Are you listening to murder podcasts again?"

"Guilty." Wren raised her hand. "But stop avoiding the question."

Lila raised a shoulder. "Things are fine. He's been coming around more and hanging out with the guys. I already told you that he gave me a damn fine apology." She shifted to uncross her legs. "So we're doing the friends thing. It's a relief, actually, to know where he stands."

"Mmhmm."

"Seriously. He's made it abundantly clear that he just wants to be friends. So I'm not overanalyzing everything like I did before." Lila started to ramble. "Actually, it's better, you know? I don't have to worry about what's going on if he doesn't text me back or wonder if we're done or wonder if he's with someone else. It's a delightful place, the friend zone."

"Aw, babe. You're still feeling feelings, aren't you?"

"Trying to stop," Lila mumbled.

"I hear that," Wren replied solemnly.

"We're quite the pair. Even with thousands of miles between us."

"Best friends for life. Soulmates forever."

"And ever."

After hanging up with Wren, Lila meandered downstairs. Bear was having breakfast with Demarcus. They'd just decided to upgrade their relationship from self-proclaimed "fuck buddies" to boyfriends, and they were sickeningly adorable. Hell, they'd even styled their cornrows in the same exact pattern in preparation for the season.

"Morning, boys. Heading to conditioning soon?" Football had started back up for her roomies, so they were gone a lot more.

"Yup," Bear answered, sliding a coffee her way. "Cashew milk and sugar, right?"

"Okay, you are officially my favorite this morning." She took a contented sip and sighed.

"Working today, Lila?" Demarcus asked.

"Closing." Both Demarcus and Bear's eyes lit up at the prospect of being fed. "And yes, I'll bring you two food."

"What about for your big bro?" Knight sauntered in, shirtless, hair still mussed from sleep.

"There will always be food for you, my friend."

"Appreciate that." He headed over to the fridge as Bear and Demarcus headed out.

"Don't you have practice with those two?"

He shook his head. "Defense is doing three-a-days. Offense is just doing two-a-days. So I'm good for another couple of hours."

"That sounds positively terrible, especially in this heat."

"Eh, it's all worth it for the six-pack," Knight joked as he patted his flat stomach.

"I mean, all of those abdominal muscles are a definite perk for sure."

Knight laughed and angled his head toward the carton of eggs that he'd just grabbed. "Want an egg?"

"Sure, thanks," Lila said as she settled into one of the barstools arranged around the kitchen island.

"Toast?"

"Yes, please. With lots of butter."

They sat in companionable silence while Knight worked, not speaking until they were halfway into their breakfast.

"So our new roommate is moving in tomorrow," Knight said casually. Like it wasn't kind of a bombshell.

Lila swallowed the bite she was chewing. "So that's actually happening? I kind of expected there to be a line of applicants and an extensive interviewing process. I was also kind of selfishly hoping I'd have a bathroom all to myself for the rest of the year. I'm so spoiled now," she teased with a whine.

"Sorry, Li. Our landlord, aka one of Bradley U's biggest donors, won't allow such a desirable room to remain empty. Especially not when an athlete wants the slot. So unless you want to pay double rent…" He winked at her feigned shudder. "But, trust me, he's been thoroughly vetted by Bear and me. He'll be on his best behavior as far as you're concerned. You'll always be safe here, Lila."

"Thanks. I'd be lying if I said I wasn't a bit nervous. But honestly, living with you guys has been so much fun and so much easier than what I had to deal with last year. And I can still walk around in my underwear during the summer because you're both not sexually attracted to me. So it's a win–win." She gestured down to the longline bralette and matching boxer brief–style bottoms she was currently wearing.

Knight laughed. "I'm sure our new roomie wouldn't mind if you kept that up."

"I mean, it's the same as wearing a bathing suit, so honestly, I don't know why some people are so weird about it. My own parents included. Like, you should have seen their faces when I told them I was living here. You'd think that we were having orgies every night or something." She laughed and rolled her eyes.

"Orgies just sound exhausting," Knight replied with a smirk.

"More exhausting than practicing 37 times a day?"

"Oh definitely. For reasons we will not get into right now, because then we'd have to get into feelings and how I'm only emotionally equipped to handle one woman at a time."

"How refreshingly non-cliché of you to desire monogamy in spite of being one of the most desired and sought after males on campus."

"What can I say? I'm just full of surprises."

"Indeed. I'm assuming our new roommate plays some form of sports ball?"

"I feel like it's okay for you to admit that you enjoy watching sports now, Lila. At least when it comes to football and soccer," Knight chuckled. "Hell, you even learned the rules and everything. And yes, new roommate plays... sports ball. Yeah, we'll go with that for now."

"Well, at least there will be something I can talk to him about, then."

"I think you'll get along just fine." Lila couldn't quite identify the cause of the gleam in Knight's eye and decided to redirect the conversation.

"So, abrupt subject change. I just got done talking to Wren..." At the mere mention of her, Knight Patrick blushed. Actually blushed. "And I'm just happy to hear that the two of you are talking, and I feel hopeful for what's to come. Obviously you're both crazy about each other, and I have every confidence that once you all process some things, you'll be able to work everything out."

"I think we're getting there," Knight said, shifting uncomfortably.

"And you're okay now that you know?"

"I'm...still processing. But I'm more than okay. I think I might be at a better place than I've been in a long time."

"And you're feet-over-ass in love with her."

His smile in response was tentative but also really tender. Lila almost felt the need to fan herself because of all of the love vibes wafting her way.

"Good. I love you both, so I'm here if you need to talk or process or whatever, but only if you ask me to. I'm fine to sit on the sidelines and watch this beautifully budding love story unfold before my very eyes." She punched his shoulder lightly. "Besides, I think you're both at a place now where you can hash things out on your own. And that's all I'll say about that," Lila finished with a wink, and Knight visibly relaxed.

She cleared their plates and put them in the dishwasher then returned to her friend and kissed the top of his head. "I'm going to hit the bookstore before it gets super busy. Have fun trying to not puke your guts out at practice."

He swatted at her playfully, and she headed upstairs to get dressed.

Chapter 27

Of course the book Lila needed was on the top shelf and she'd worn her sneakers. She had managed to score most of her textbooks online secondhand, but this particular tome was specific to her gothic literature in America class, so Lila had no choice but to brave the bookstore in search of it. She examined the bookcase closely. Maybe if she carefully stood on the lowest shelf...

"Need a hand?" a deep voice boomed over her shoulder as she was assessing her options. Startled, she jumped about a foot, much to her would-be savior's apparent delight. She didn't need to turn around to know who it was.

"Done laughing yet, King? Because I really do need help reaching the book."

Only then did she risk a glance over her shoulder and noted that King looked particularly edible in a plain white tee that stretched over his chest and thin cotton shorts that showcased his muscular calves and thighs.

Do not *think about his thighs.*

"My pleasure." He moved in and reached up to retrieve the book. Lila definitely did not notice how nice his ass looked or how tan his skin looked when his shirt lifted up and exposed a couple inches of his stomach. Skin that she knew felt surprisingly soft to the touch. Not that Lila was thinking about touching his skin or anything.

King handed her the book with an amused look on his face, like he knew exactly what she'd been thinking about.

Friends. Friends. Only friends.

"Thanks, friend," she said to reinforce her inner monologue. Then she noticed he'd tucked another copy of the book under his arm. "Wait, why do you have one too?"

"I'm taking the class. Word on the street is that we get to read *The Shining*."

"I'm *aware*." She smiled. "So I guess we're in the same class, then? Since Dr. Danger only teaches one American gothic class a semester?"

"Guess so." King snapped his fingers as his dark-brown eyes glowed. He looked like he'd just been struck with the best idea ever. "We'll have to be study buddies." Lila swore he was closer to her than he'd been a few seconds ago. Also, was it getting hot in there?

"Study buddies sounds good," Lila replied.

Just then, a group of girls turned down their aisle, and the one who appeared to be the de facto leader zeroed right in on King.

"OMG, girls. It's *King Spencer.* The star of our soccer team."

"Who can definitely hear what you're saying," King replied with a tight smile. "How's it going, ladies? You all soccer fans?"

"We're definitely fans of what you have to offer."

Lila was equal parts annoyed and in awe of this girl's boldness. She definitely took the "Go for the things you want in life" pep talk they all received during freshman orientation to heart.

The group flocked around King, pointedly ignoring Lila. She was getting prepared to shoot him a wave and let him take care of his groupies, but then she noticed the way his body had stiffened and how inappropriately forward the women were being. He was a person, not a piece of meat. So she thought on the fly.

She wedged herself in between the girls and King, her back to his front. Thankfully, the group instinctively backed up.

"While I appreciate you all taking in the utter deliciousness of my *boyfriend*, I'd appreciate it if you would keep your hands off him."

She studied each of their shocked faces intently. "Which is just kind of a good rule of thumb in most situations when you encounter somebody you don't know. Because, body boundaries and consent and all of that."

Lila flashed them what she hoped was an intimidating smile, as King's free arm circled her waist and pulled her back so she was pressed against him.

She could feel King everywhere when he moved her hair aside and grazed his nose down the crook of her neck, and she tried to suppress her body's reaction. "I'm sure he'd be willing to sign autographs if you'd like. If not, I think we'll be on our way."

He spun her around so she was facing him and put his hand on her lower back, dangerously close to the swell of her ass. "Maybe I'm not in the mood to sign anything because I want to get you home as soon as possible." His grin was positively wicked, and when he licked his full lips, her ovaries wept.

While they were in the middle of some serious, prolonged eye fucking, Lila registered the ringleader of the group stammering out an apology and saw the group of embarrassed girls quickly retreating down the aisle from the way they'd come.

She reluctantly took a step back, and King dropped his hands. "Sorry about throwing that whole scenario at you. But I figured it was better than getting mauled by a group of superfans."

"I mean, I think we did a great job at improv just then, and I am very grateful for the save."

"And to think I was initially planning to just slink away and leave you to your own devices."

He shuddered. "Super glad you chose option B."

"Happy to help." They wound their way over to the registers. "I'm closing tonight, so you're more than welcome to come over later and partake in all the free food gloriousness."

King pursed his lips. "As tempting as that sounds, I'm actually busy tonight. But I appreciate the invitation."

"Got a hot date or something?" Lila word vomited, because she was actively trying not to think about all the ways she'd been "busy" with King in the past. She definitely didn't want to think about him being "busy" with anyone else. But friends talked about this kind of stuff, right? So she needed to toughen up if she wanted to make this whole platonic thing work.

"Or something," King replied, the left corner of his mouth curved into a sort of half smile. Then he slung an arm around her and pulled her into his body. "The groupies just looked over here," he whispered into her ear.

"Ah. So our exercise in improv continues."

"At least until we exit the bookstore, apparently." King chuckled. "There's some pretty hardcore hate-staring happening. All directed at you, of course."

"Internalized misogyny strikes again," Lila remarked solemnly. "Next thing you know, everybody will blame me if you don't score a goal every game."

"Forget people like that. I've had people try to control me and tell me how to live my life from the time I was born. I've got zero fucks left for that kind of bullshit."

King dropped his arm so Lila could pay for her book, and then she hung out when he paid for his. They walked outside side by side, eyes alert for the approach of any more rabid fans.

"Looks like the coast is clear," Lila remarked. "See ya around, King. Thanks for the two-minute quickie fake relationship."

King's forehead furrowed, just slightly, and then he nodded, giving her a little mock salute and an almost smile before walking off in the opposite direction.

Chapter 28

Billie Eilish's latest was playing as Lila gave the bathroom counter one last swipe with a Clorox wipe. Admittedly, the bathroom was pretty clean already, but she wanted to make sure that everything was in perfect order for when her new, mysterious roommate showed up. She just prayed he'd be amenable to putting the seat down.

She'd put all of her toiletries and hair-styling implements in one of the two drawers and ensured that all of her shower stuff was in a caddy underneath the sink closest to her bedroom. There was a double vanity, a toilet and a pretty decent-sized walk-in shower, all decorated with light-gray subway tile and white granite. She'd spent a little money on new, fluffy, dove gray hand towels and some of her favorite hand soap for each sink. Not like most guys would even notice, but she did it anyway.

Lila also nervously double checked that she'd taken her vibrator out of the shower. One of the double-edged swords of "dating" King was that she realized that she had a pretty high sex drive. Which would be great if she were having sex on the reg, which she was definitely not. Besides the failed attempt to date Eli, Lila hadn't gone out with or hooked up with anyone else.

It wasn't like she didn't get the occasional number slipped to her at work or that she didn't notice the interest in some of Knight and Bear's friends' eyes. But she couldn't fake it if she felt zero sparks. Especially now because she knew how potent chemistry between two people could be. So she was content to wait it out until she found someone she felt something for. Thus, all the sex toys, which were now stored in a shoe box underneath her bed.

Satisfied that the bathroom was in good shape, Lila headed back into her room, turned off the music, and made sure the deadbolt lock on her side of her bathroom door worked.

Check.

Such a nice feature, really. The handle locked from the inside of the bathroom, and the deadbolt locked the door from the other side.

Lila scanned her room. She'd gotten new bedding for her bigger bed when she moved in and picked a linen rose-colored bedspread with crisp white sheets. She'd hung up a full-length mirror on her closet door, and three poster-sized framed line drawings of abstract female nudes that she'd commissioned Dani to draw for her before she graduated with her degree in fine art on the wall. Even though Lila had only lived there a few months, she felt more at home in this room than she did when she visited her childhood bedroom.

She moved over to her desk and took stock of all of her textbooks. School was starting in a week, and she felt ready to start her last year. And even though some would say that graduating in three years was a little over the top, she wanted to get a jump start on graduate school, whether it was law school or something else. Hell, some people took a gap year before even starting college; she was just going to take one at the end instead.

The rumbling of male voices and the sound of heavy footsteps coming up the stairs was muffled, but she could only assume it was her new roommate. She suddenly felt nervous, unsure of how to play the situation. She'd been getting better at dealing with her social awkwardness and shyness. The more she practiced being outgoing, the more outgoing she became. But she felt tongue-tied and awkward and almost gave in to the inclination to hide herself away in her room.

Chiding herself, she sucked in a breath and walked out of her room and down the hall to say hello.

She heard Knight's uproarious laughter through the partially open door. He seemed to be talking to the new roomie, so she knocked before pushing the door open a little farther until the mystery guy's face was visible.

Her eyes widened as she took in the form of one King Spencer. He caught her gawking and half smiled. "Hey, La."

"Surprise!" Knight exclaimed, about giving Lila heart failure.

"Decrease the volume, bud. You just about scared me to death."

"Sorry." For the record, Knight did not look one bit sorry. "But, you have to admit, this is a fun little plot twist. We're all going to have so much fun now that you two are friends again."

She looked at Knight then King. "So you're seriously the new roommate?"

King nodded.

Lila tried to ignore the way her heart painfully twisted in her chest, because she still wanted him, dammit. And not in a friendly way. She was barely holding it together just being his friend. How would she be able to last the next nine months? How would she be able to handle it when he brought girls home? She pushed the last thought away.

"Earth to Lila," Knight said, verbally nudging her out of her thoughts. "This is so great, right?"

"So great," she parroted with enthusiasm she didn't feel. She gave herself an internal shake and added, "I was so worried about bathroom sharing with a random and feeling mildly guilty about threatening bodily harm if the toilet seat gets left up. And now I am fully absolved of that guilt." She smirked cheekily.

"I would never, ever do something so terrible," King deadpanned. He seemed to be analyzing her every word and facial expression, and the scrutiny was almost unbearable. Seemed like she needed to do a better job of hiding her feelings.

"Well, that's a relief." Lila looked around the room. "Need help with anything? I just cleaned the bathroom, and there's plenty of room for your bathroom stuff."

"Nah, I don't have a lot to unpack."

"Except your extensive sneaker collection," Knight interjected. "Have any size 13s in there by chance?"

"Sorry, they're all my standard 14s."

Knight put King in a mock choke hold. "That's it, I don't think this whole thing is going to work out after all."

King stuck out a leg and flipped Knight over so he landed on the bed. "I guess I better pack up all this shit, then." They both laughed.

"Well, I'll leave you two to it, then." Lila headed toward the door that led to the bathroom and started rambling. "King, we'll have to work out a showering schedule or whatever, though I usually do it at night, so maybe that won't even be a conflict. Except for when you're using it for...extracurricular activities when you bring girls over. So maybe we need a system for that...for ear plug purposes. In fact..." She took the thin floral scrunchie off of her wrist and threw it to him; he deftly caught it with one hand. "You can just put this on my bedroom door handle if you're going to be using the bathroom for sexy times, and I'll plan accordingly."

Knight was standing just behind King and was desperately trying to hold in his laughter. *Nice,* he mouthed to Lila, and she could feel her whole face bursting into an inferno.

King looked pained, and she tried not to think about how awkward she'd just been. His brow furrowed, and he worried his bottom lip with his teeth. "What about when you, ah, need the shower for, what did you call it, extracurricular activities?"

Shit, this is awkward.

"I'll do the same. I have more than one scrunchie." She shot the guys an awkward little finger wave and then darted through the bathroom and into her room. After both doors were closed, she flopped down on her bed and put her hands over her face.

"Fuck," she whispered. Yup, this definitely warranted an F-bomb. She sat up, got out her phone, and started typing.

LILA: *911. King is my new roommate. Repeat, King fucking Spencer is my new fucking roommate. Who I will be sharing a fucking shower with. Who has agreed to put a scrunchie on my doorknob when he's using said shower for "extracurricular activities." FML.*

WREN: *The plot thickens...hopefully in a fun way?*

LILA: *...*

WREN: *I'm sorry, babe. It'll be okay. Maybe this will just help move things in the direction they're supposed to move in.*

LILA: *Unfortunately, that direction seems to involve my shower.*

WREN: *Hang in there, bestest. I'm always here for you, eight-hour time difference notwithstanding.*

LILA: *heart*

WREN: *heart*

She lay back down on her bed and grabbed a pillow and put it over her head. She may or may not have shouted an expletive or two into the pillow. Her head was starting to ache.

"Knock, knock," Knight said as he shuffled into her room.

"Lila's not here," she said.

Knight grabbed the pillow and removed it from her face. "Say that again? Your voice was pretty muffled."

"Never mind," she groaned as she sat up.

Knight sat down on the edge of her bed and playfully hit her with her pillow. "Talk to me, Li."

"I can't, Knight."

"C'mon." He nudged her with his elbow. "I thought things were good between you and King now. I thought this would be a fun surprise. You don't have to share your space with some random dude."

Lila arranged her face into something she hoped resembled a smile. "You're right. We're like the best of buds right now. It'll be a party. And I've got a whole drawer of ear plugs ready to go, so...we're golden."

Knight studied her intently for a minute. "So you're telling me that you don't have any more sexy feelings towards our new roommate, and you're totally fine if he has sex with someone else within earshot?

"Yes?" Dammit, she'd made it sound like a question. This conversation was going downhill fast.

"Aw, babe. If you still have feelings for him, why don't you tell him?"

She scoffed softly, her voice rising a note or two. "I *so* don't. Besides, even if I did, hypothetically speaking, he's made it abundantly clear that he just wants to be friends. Also, he's the one who imploded everything before—twice—and I don't know that I could ever trust that it wouldn't happen again."

Lila faked another smile. "And so it's all fine. We've got a system already.

It's great. He can bang whomever he wants to bang."

"Was the term 'bang' ever really a thing?"

"It is now."

"Okay, Li. Whatever you say." He kissed her on the forehead and then left her alone.

And she tried really, really hard not to cry tears of frustration. But failed quite miserably.

Chapter 29

It was a great morning for a football game. Due to Bradley U's successful season last year, they'd secured a slot on ESPN's College GameDay, which meant that the Bradley U Bulldogs had an earlier kickoff time than usual. King had come to tailgate with some of his teammates before they made their way to their seats right on the 50-yard line. He knew that Lila was planning on sitting by them and bringing her little sister, Layla, who was visiting for the weekend.

They'd officially been roommates for six days, not that he was counting or anything, and he didn't think he'd ever forget the way she looked at him when she realized who she'd be sharing a bathroom with for the foreseeable future. It was shock and dread and sadness quickly masked by a friendly smile. And he saw, maybe for the first time, how much damage he'd caused the year before. She'd forgiven him, but there were, understandably, still scars underneath. When she suggested they set up a sexy time shower schedule? He almost lost his mind thinking about it. Because the only person he wanted in that damn shower with him was her.

Especially after their little act in the bookstore.

Shit, he'd almost forgotten how heady it was to touch her body, to breathe her in. The way she'd been able to perceive how uncomfortable he was and come to his rescue was hot as fuck. He'd had to veer off to calm his erection down like a 14-year-old boy.

He knew that Knight had gone in to talk to her, but he didn't say anything to King except to say that both King and Lila needed to talk it out.

"Omigod, these seats are amaze!" an excited voice squeaked.

King turned his head toward the end of the row and saw Lila looking completely fuckable in a navy skater skirt and a cropped white tee. The girl next to her, who he assumed was Layla, couldn't look more different from her sister if she tried. She had blonde hair, blue eyes, and had definitely more of a tomboy style in cutoff jean shorts and an oversize striped tee.

Lila smiled at her sister as they made their way over to where King, Will, and Benny were sitting. "Hey guys. This is my sister, Layla. Layla, this is Benny, Will, and King." They exchanged waves and even a "What's up" from Benny.

Layla turned to her sister and loudly whispered, "Wait. King as in, like, *the* King?"

Lila quickly shushed her and then made a point to actually whisper in her sister's ear so he couldn't overhear the rest. But the fact of the matter was, she'd talked to her little sister about him. Interesting.

"Yup," King rumbled with a knowing smile. "I'm *the* King, whatever that means." He held out his hand for a fist bump, and Layla shot her sister an apologetic look as she returned the gesture, but Lila seemed surprisingly unruffled. She'd had the same exact affect around him the past few days they'd been living together, and he desperately wanted to know what was going on in that brain of hers.

"Layla's just a huge soccer fan," Lila said smoothly. "Right, sis?"

Layla nodded, a little too vigorously if you asked him. "Yup… I love all of the…kicking that happens."

Lila stifled a laugh as they both settled into their seats. King had arranged it so that she was sitting next to him.

They all made small talk until it was time for kickoff, and then they all got caught up in the game. Lila pointed out Knight, Bear, Demarcus, and their other friends on the team, and Layla seemed to have a better grasp of the game than Lila had when she first started coming.

Lila more than made up for that now. "*Come on, Knight!*" she yelled when he held onto the ball and ran instead of passing it and swerved away from a potential tackle. When he crossed into the end zone, they all jumped up to cheer. King watched as she took a video of Knight's victory dance and then furiously started typing as she sat back down.

He did the same, right as she looked up and noticed that he was watching her and gave him her eyebrow face. "I'm sending it to Wren," she explained, and then her focus shifted back to her phone.

"So they're still talking?" King couldn't help but be curious. Normally he and Knight could talk about everything, but this was one instance where, beyond what they'd initially talked about, Knight was acting like Fort Knox with his version of events.

Lila hummed. "I plead the fifth." Then she shifted her gaze to his. "Honestly, I've mostly been staying out of it, so I don't really know. All I know is that she doesn't get mad at me when I do this kind of thing."

"As long as she doesn't hurt him again." King's tone came out harsher than he'd intended. "Because he was a mess."

Lila wrinkled her nose. "Who do you think got rid of all of those takeout containers?"

King glanced at her in surprise. He hadn't realized she'd been the one to clean his room. He should have, though. It made perfect sense, because that was just the kind of thing that Lila would do.

"Also, and I'm saying this because we're friends now, you don't know shit about what happened. They've each got some demons, and they both have to figure it out."

King felt appropriately chastened. "You're right, sorry. That came out harsher than I meant it to."

"Thanks. And I get it. It's Knight, and he's the best. For what it's worth, I think the universe will find a way of working things out. If that makes sense."

"Not really." King mimicked her eyebrow face. "But I'll take your word for it."

"Smart man."

"Not always." He couldn't help the feelings of remorse that crept in when he thought about how poorly he'd treated her. How he'd had this wonderful woman who was intelligent, beautiful, kind, and sexy as hell, and he thought it was a good idea to push her away. Twice. He didn't know what the future held for them, but he knew with a sinking certainty that he'd regret what he'd done for the rest of his life.

"You got pensive all of the sudden." Lila nudged him with her elbow. "Doing okay?"

"Just regretting how awful I was to you last year," he confessed. Her eyes widened in surprise. "It just hits me all at once sometimes. The regret."

"Not everything about last year was awful," Lila murmured as she turned her head to look at him. "In fact, some of it was wonderful. A lot of it was wonderful, actually."

"Hard agree," King said, nostalgia hitting him right in the gut.

Lila shifted her focus back to the football field. "When I decided to accept your apology, I made the decision to hold on to the good and let go of the bad. Otherwise our friendship would have never had a chance."

"I'm glad you gave us a chance, La."

"Same. I guess it's a good thing that you're pretty great at apologizing." She lowered her voice so only he could hear her. "Plus, you made me come twice my first time. I'm pretty sure you get major brownie points forever just for that."

"Did you just..." King was speechless. Also turned on.

"Bring up the fact that we've spent sexy naked time together? Yup. I mean, it's a thing that happened, so it's silly to pretend it didn't."

"It is definitely a thing that happened. Many times," King managed to grind out even as he tried to surreptitiously adjust himself.

Lila just smirked and turned her attention back to her sister. "Want a soft pretzel, sis? Maybe a churro? I'm hungry."

Chapter 30

King glanced over the syllabus for the gothic lit class that he'd basically had to use all of his connections to get into with heightened interest. Lila had talked about the class last year, and he thought it actually sounded interesting. Since it was only taught once a semester, a spot in this class guaranteed that he'd be in it with Lila, which was his main motivator, if he was being totally honest. Dr. Danger (yes, that was her real name) insisted on doing everything old school, so the syllabus was printed on paper (sorry trees), its multiple pages stapled together. Word on the street was, Dr. Danger also preferred her students to handwrite notes because laptops were "distracting."

He was prepared with all of the things, just in case.

The class was tiny, only 15 students, so their seats were arranged around a conference room–style table, with Dr. Danger lording over them like a CEO. Personally, King respected the flex.

"This seat taken?" Lila smiled down at the chair that was currently being inhabited by his laptop bag.

"Actually, I was saving this for a friend...but I guess it's fine if you sit here." He removed his bag with a smirk.

"I guess your friend's gonna miss out. I hear it's assigned seating for the rest of the semester."

Oh, King was already well aware of this policy, which was why he chose the narrower section of the table where there were only two seats right next to each other. Hell, he'd gotten to class 20 minutes early just to accomplish that feat.

Lila tucked a strand of hair behind her ear, and they were close enough that King could smell the subtle scent of her perfume.

Before he could dwell too long on how much that simple gesture affected him, Dr. Danger entered the room and began class. King was glad that he'd brought a notebook and a pen because no one else got out their computers. They were, indeed, locked into their current seating arrangement for the remainder of the semester, which was supremely satisfying.

Class participation was a big portion of their grade, so King forced himself to focus so he'd have something to say. Lila was positively luminous in this environment. Her intelligence was obvious, but she only spoke up when she felt she had something valuable to contribute. He'd never really seen her in her element before, and it made her all the more enticing to him. Her quiet confidence and eloquent answers were pretty damn sexy.

Class flew by, and soon they were exiting the room and heading over to grab a coffee at the Brad. Instead of heading for the big common area where they usually sat, King led them down one of the vestibules to a much smaller but similarly high-ceilinged room that was furnished with a few couches and a smattering of tables and chairs.

"Embarrassing confession... I've been here two whole years and had no idea this room was even here," Lila remarked as they sat down next to each other on one of the couches.

"It's kind of a secret that's not really a secret," King replied. "I usually come here when I need to catch a ten-minute power nap between classes. There are rarely any people in here. Also, this couch is shockingly comfortable."

"Agreed." Lila took a sip of her coffee. "Thanks for showing this to me. I might have to use it for power naps too sometimes. I usually just find a bench and use my bag as a pillow."

"It's quite the bag. I bet you could fit an actual pillow in there if you wanted."

"A travel pillow," Lila confirmed with a raised brow. "But it took up too much space. So textbooks it is."

They sat in companionable silence as they drank their coffees. King took a pull of his before turning to Lila. "So I never really thanked you for the other day when my mom came into the restaurant." She tried to wave him off with her hand, but he reached out to still it and lower it back down. Their fingers were laced together before he realized what was happening. He wasn't even sure if it had been initiated by him or if it had been Lila.

"Seriously, La. You were brilliant with her, read her like a book. She looks down her nose at everybody, but she actually likes you. I'm sorry she left and didn't pay for her food. Thanks for being so chill about everything afterwards." He'd ended up staying in the booth to eat, taking comfort in Lila's busy, efficient movements.

"Well, you didn't have to leave me such an asinine tip." Lila squeezed his hand. And it was an asinine tip. He'd left her $50. "Lunch was on me, remember?" She kept their fingers linked but managed to nudge him with her shoulder.

"You did something nice for me, so I wanted to do something nice for you. That's what friends do, isn't it?"

She nodded. "I know it's not my business, but if you ever need someone to talk to…I'm here. You know, if you need support or whatever."

This time King was the one who squeezed her hand. Then the words just emerged from deep inside him, unbidden, flowing out until she knew about the neglect he'd experienced, the abuse, how his mother always took his father's side every time… Everything. How his fear of becoming like his father had affected him deeply. How he'd been working through everything in counseling.

He hadn't even noticed when she had gently taken away his drink and set it down, how she'd dropped their hands and had put an arm around his back. His head was resting on her shoulder, her fingers combing through his hair. When his words were finally spent, he let out a relieved breath. She sighed deeply.

"Thank you for trusting me with your story, King. You've had to deal with so much from the time you were just a little boy." Her fingers continued tracking through his waves. "Holy shit, you are miraculous," Lila whispered. "You've forged your own path, formed your own family. And you're fiercely loyal to and protective of those you care about." Then his heart stopped when she softly repeated her words from months ago, the words that he still carried with him every day:

"You are not your father. You're a king."

He raised his head off of her shoulder, their faces impossibly close to each other. Her amber eyes were bright, almost golden, with emotion. If he leaned in just a couple of inches, he could kiss her. And maybe that desire was written all over his face, because her pupils expanded and she looked like she wanted to be utterly consumed. He reached up to tuck a strand of her hair behind her ear.

That movement seemed to snap Lila out of whatever daze she'd been in, and she backed away slowly, putting much-needed space between them. She smiled, but the look in her eyes was harder for King to interpret. "We should probably get going. My next class starts soon."

King nodded, and they gathered their things.

As Lila was turning to go, King called out to her. She turned back, a question on her face. "Just...thank you" was all King could manage to say.

She nodded in understanding and then waved goodbye. Damn if he didn't hate watching her go.

Chapter 31

After an especially brutal practice, King tiredly entered his house and immediately heard a lively debate that was happening between Knight, Lila, and Bear. They were so deep in conversation, they didn't even notice King had entered the room.

"...I'm just saying that perhaps a party whose name sounds like it could be a fungal infection should be retired, or at the very least put on hiatus in lieu of another themed party." Lila lifted a shoulder.

Bear mumbled a "gross" as Knight barked out a laugh.

Knight shook a finger. "Yes, my friend, I think you're onto something with the rebrand idea. Jock Jam is a terrible name."

Bear shook his head. "It's like an institution at this point. Do we really want to be the ones who mess with tradition?"

"I mean, you could still have it in the spring, with a better name, if it makes you feel any better," Lila offered. "I just think that it could be fun to mix it up a bit. Something like, 'Nothing but the 90s' and have it be all about that vibe. The clothes, the music, etc. Bear, I know for a fact that you have more than one flannel shirt in your closet. Channel your grunge rock self and work it."

Knight perked up. "I like the 90s idea. I'm pretty sure if I used enough gel, I could recreate spiky boy band hair. Do they have temporary dye that would mimic bleached tips? Or I could literally just go for the gold and actually bleach it."

Lila vigorously shook her head. "There's no way in hell you're messing with your perfect hair color, Knight Patrick, temporarily or permanently. I will not allow it."

"Fine," Knight conceded. "No bleach, but the boy band hair is happening. And think about the musical possibilities!" Knight cleared his throat and sobered a bit before continuing. "I also feel like there's some negative Jock Jam energy that needs to be purged." He cast a sideways glance at Lila, and something that looked a lot like pain was communicated between the two of them.

"If we plan it, the people will come, regardless of the theme," King said, finally making his presence known. "Though I have to say I'm also on board with the 90s theme. I'm pretty sure Will has a secret collection of bucket hats that are just dying to be exposed."

Knight turned to Bear triumphantly. "Come on, Bear. You know you wanna see Demarcus rock a bucket hat."

Bear looked stern for a minute and then finally broke into a smile. "Okay, fine. It's a good idea. Why the hell not?"

King's work done, he headed up the stairs to go take a shower. Coach Klopp was being super intense with the team since they'd tied their first two games of the season, so King was especially beat. He dropped his bag on the floor in his room and quickly stripped out of his sweaty practice clothes and set Lila's necklace gently on the top of his dresser.

Clad in only his black boxer briefs (because he always made sure the door adjoining Lila's room was locked before he got naked), he stepped into the bathroom. He jumped as he turned the light on and saw Lila, fully clothed, exiting the shower stall, a flustered look reddening her features.

Her eyes darted over to the door leading to her room, and she began inching toward it without a word.

"Any reason why you're hiding in our shower in the dark and then trying to sneak out like a ninja?" King asked, amused.

Lila gulped but stood up straight, tucking one of her hands behind her back. "I just remembered that I left something in the shower and realized that you were about to use it. So I figured I'd hurry and grab it and whatnot."

She started rambling about how sometimes he showered in the locker room after practice and she wasn't sure if he'd done that today and that she wouldn't need to be sneaky again because she'd just assume that he'd be showering at home after practice from now on, most of which King tuned out. Because he was very interested in what she was hiding.

"And what, exactly, did you leave in the shower, Lila?" King teased.

"None of your business," she threw out sassily.

"Oh really? Why are you being so secretive? It's not like you left a vibrator in there or something." Though that would have been fucking hot.

When Lila's face reddened ever more, King realized that he'd inadvertently guessed what she was hiding. He didn't even try to conceal how much that turned him on. And, judging by the way her eyes darted south, he knew she'd noticed too.

"Show me." King barely recognized his own voice as he growled out the command.

Lila stood still for a minute and then steeled her shoulders. She held up a small purple silicone clitoral vibrator in the palm of her hand. Her expression had morphed from embarrassed to determined, and it just made King harder.

"You use this often, La?"

"Maybe," she said, her eyes once again drifting down to take in his arousal. "It's not really any of your business. Though I do suppose you're partially to blame. You're the one who helped me realize I have a super-high sex drive."

"Dammit Lila," he groaned. "You're killing me right now." His dick was begging for release, and it was taking all of his willpower to not bend Lila over the bathroom counter and fuck her senseless.

"Now you know how I feel," she murmured so softly he wasn't sure he even heard her right. He was also pretty sure those words weren't intended for his ears, but he answered them anyway.

"You feeling frustrated, La? Like you're about ready to explode if you don't get off right now?"

Lila tried to appear impassive, but his words were affecting her. He could tell by the way her nipples beaded underneath her shirt, the way her eyes took him in hungrily.

"Maybe," she said quietly.

"Then let's help each other out, yeah?"

"What do you..."

"I want to see you use that toy on your pretty little clit while I stroke my dick. I want you to sit on the bathroom counter with your legs spread wide open while I look at your perfect pussy and watch your face as you let yourself go. I want you to see me watching you and see how that affects *me*. I want you to watch me come all over because the sight of you uninhibited like that drives me crazy."

He held his breath, bracing himself for her refusal. Instead, she walked over to the bathroom vanity and slowly dropped her bottoms so she was bared to him from the waist down. He advanced on her slowly, his hands gripping her hips as he lifted her up onto the counter. Then he backed up, watching as she spread her legs wide. The sight of her wet and ready put him into a daze. He wanted between those thighs again so badly.

"Your turn," she said, and he slowly removed his boxer briefs. Her eyes widened at the sight of his erection. "I'd almost forgotten how monstrously huge you are," Lila breathed as she turned on the vibrator and positioned it just above her clit.

King took his cock in his hand and started leisurely stroking himself, his eyes never leaving Lila. The way she writhed and the sounds she made reminded him of how good they were together, and his dick wept for the chance to be inside her again.

Someday.

The room was filled with Lila's soft moans and King's guttural groans as they both neared their climax. "Can't hold on much longer, La. Need you to come with me." King's voice was pure gravel and sex, and it was enough to get Lila off. He came right then too, the intensity of it almost causing his knees to give out.

Once they'd both come back down from their respective highs, they stared at each other, the silence thickening with every passing second. Then Lila jumped down and retrieved her underwear and shorts and gave King a little nod before slipping into her bedroom. He heard the finality of the lock firmly clicking into place behind her and wondered if he'd just fucked up everything. Again.

Chapter 32

Driving gave Lila time to think. And she had a lot of thinking to do. Along with their propensity to vacuum perfectly symmetrical carpet lines as pristine as the mowed grass at Yankee Stadium and their proclivity to gather weekly for extended family dinners, the Alexanders were legendary for their love of driving. Which might seem to be a strange identifier, but there was something woven into the Alexander family DNA that practically dictated that road trips and long drives were necessary for their survival. Lila had fond memories of her Grandpa Alexander driving in his car, a custom-sized cup holder for his 64-ounce soda clipped to the inside of his door.

Her parents were the same, driving around the country in their decidedly fuel-inefficient Suburban, and Lila had fond memories of the open road, of seeing the landscape morph and change.

After what had happened with King in their bathroom, after what had *continued* to happen in the days since, Lila knew she needed a little space. After their first encounter, she'd been left reeling. Seeing King like that again, after all this time, was overwhelming. After the first time in the bathroom, she vowed it was just a one-time thing, something brought about by a sudden burst of lust that would hopefully wane quickly.

But then, the next day, she heard a faint knocking on her interior door and opened it to find King standing there, again stripped down to his underwear, a feral gleam in his eye, his arousal visible. Like he knew she needed relief as much as he did. Silently, she'd retrieved another vibrator from her stash and followed him into the bathroom. This time, however, she'd stripped down so she was just wearing her bra, much to King's delight. Last night? She'd almost taken the bra off too.

They didn't talk about it. Whatever happened between them in the bathroom stayed in the bathroom. And then they'd go to class and he'd come into the restaurant with the guys, and she'd go to his games, and they were the textbook definition of friends.

But it was all messing with her head. She tried to rationalize it by telling herself that everything was fine because they weren't actually touching each other; that maybe this was a thing that friends could do together. The problem was, she *wanted* him to touch her. She wanted to be the one touching *him*. She wanted to feel him inside of her...and that was a huge problem. Because she'd been down that road, and it hadn't ended well.

So she'd thrown an overnight bag into her old Toyota 4Runner that she'd aptly inherited from her Grandpa Alexander and made the hour drive north to her childhood home.

It was late, so the freeway was mostly empty. Normally, Lila would listen to a playlist or a podcast, but that night, all she wanted was silence as she processed things out on the open road. Her mom had left a key under the mat, and Lila let herself in quietly. Though it was well past midnight, Lila's mom was up waiting for her in the kitchen, clad in one of her floral-patterned house dresses that she favored as pajamas.

And, even though it was barely fall, Diana Alexander had a cup of hot chocolate with extra marshmallows ready and waiting for her daughter.

"Thanks, Mama." Lila took a sip, and of course it was the perfect temperature.

"Anything for my angel girl," her mom replied with a tender smile, taking a sip of her own hot chocolate. They made some small talk about classes and how Wren was doing before Lila gathered up the courage to talk to her mom about what she actually wanted to talk to her about.

"So, Mom, first off, I'm sorry that I haven't been coming home as much. Work and school are busy, but that's not an excuse."

"While we'd love to see you more, I completely understand why you'd want to stay down at school, especially now that you don't have womb sounds for a roommate anymore," her mom responded with a tiny grin.

"Are you still bothered by the fact that I live with a group of guys?"

Her mother seemed to measure her words carefully before answering. "Lila, I'll admit that it's been difficult in some ways to see you grow up and to see the way that your life is diverging from the things that your father and I had always envisioned for you." She smiled a little sadly. "But I realized how narrow my vision was for you. Just because I didn't graduate college, married young, and had a bunch of babies doesn't mean that you should feel like you have to live that same life."

Diana took another drink. "I love my life; I love being your mom. I was lucky to find a man like your dad who has always loved and valued me and grown with me. We've fit the roles that were prescribed for us, and they've worked out for us just fine. But I understand that the opinions I've formed about marriage and gender roles based on how I was raised don't always fit into what's happening now."

She chuckled, "This is all my long-winded way of saying that although I may not always understand completely where you're coming from, I will always love you, and I will always try to be open and listen, without judgment. And if you feel like living with these roommates is the best thing for you, then I trust that to be the case. Because I trust *you*, Lila. You are strong, and intelligent, and brave, and are capable of the world."

Lila's heart warmed as she received her mother's loving words. It was one of the first times her mom had made her feel truly seen, and she was so glad she'd followed her gut and come home, if only for a day.

Her mom paused and then looked slightly pained. "And I'm really sorry we weren't better about having the sex talk with you. Expecting abstinence until marriage is really naive, so I hope that if you are sexually active, you're being safe. We're trying to do a better job with your siblings."

"I'm not going to pretend that this doesn't feel awkward, but I appreciate you bringing it up." Lila paused. "I'm being safe." She reached over and squeezed her mom's hand. "And thanks for always supporting me and loving me. You and Dad gave me a wonderful childhood full of so much love. I'm beginning to realize how rare that is."

Her mom looked at her knowingly. "What's his name, Lila?"

"King," she mumbled.

"That handsome, slightly broody athlete Layla and I saw when we came into the restaurant last year?"

Lila nodded.

"He's one of your roommates, isn't he?" Her mom tried to keep her voice modulated, and Lila smiled at her efforts.

"Yes, but things were over long before we were ever roommates. He and Knight kind of surprised me with it, and it really took me off guard." She exhaled. "Things didn't...end well with us, but he genuinely apologized and we're trying to start over as friends. He's made a lot of positive changes in his life. And he's overcome a lot."

"But...?" her mom prompted.

"I think I may still have non-platonic feelings for him. So I don't know if the whole friend thing is going to work out super well for us."

"For what it's worth, Layla said that he's crazy about you."

"Wait, what?" Her sister hadn't mentioned this juicy little detail to her, and they'd spent the whole weekend together.

"She said he didn't take his eyes off of you at the football game. Or ever, really, the entire time she was visiting. Plus, he went out of his way to make sure that your sister had a good time and felt comfortable. Which leads me to believe that he might feel the same way that you do."

"Doubtful," Lila snorted.

"Then he's an idiot, honey," Diana said matter-of-factly. "You've got a big heart and a great head on your shoulders. I doubt they'll steer you wrong."

"Thanks, Mom."

They sipped the rest of their hot chocolates in comfortable quiet and then headed up to bed.

* * *

The next day included her waking up to two eager sets of eyes, in the form of her two youngest brothers, Lance and Landon, ages nine and eleven respectively. Back when Lila still lived at home, this lack of privacy would have bothered her, but now, she didn't mind it so much.

She pulled back her covers so the three of them could all snuggle for a minute before they headed upstairs to join her parents, Layla, and her 14-year-old brother, Leo, for breakfast. In classic Erik Alexander fashion, her dad had made a delicious breakfast consisting of all of Lila's favorites: French toast, hash browns, and super crispy bacon.

The boys had various sports ball games, so Lila spent the bulk of the day with her family watching a couple of fall baseball games (Leo and Lance) and a soccer game (Landon) before she headed back down to Bradley.

While they were watching Leo's game, Layla sidled up to her sister and put an arm around her waist. "I've missed you."

"Same." Lila kissed Layla's cheek affectionately. "You'll have to come down for another visit sometime soon."

"So I can watch you and King make sexy eyes at each other the whole time? Count me in." She craned her neck to make sure their parents and brothers weren't paying attention and lowered her voice. "The sexual tension between the two of you is off the charts, sis. Off. The. Charts. Like that old-school video of Beyonce and Jay-Z when they're all up in that phone booth. Or, like, whenever Camila Cabello and Shawn Mendes did their thing pre-breakup."

"And why exactly were you watching music videos made before you were even born?" Lila evaded.

"Because Ashley's mom is a huge fan and was playing the album the other day. So I did a Google deep dive. And voila! Phone booth shenanigans."

"Look at that internet coming through." Lila smiled. They turned their attention back to the game, but Lila knew that Layla wouldn't let the topic drop for long. "We're just friends, Layla. It's better that way, trust me."

Layla just snorted a laugh and said, "We'll see."

When it came time for her to drive home, she hugged everybody and made a firm promise to come to the next extended family dinner. She put on a 90s hip hop playlist she'd created to try to psyche herself up for the upcoming rebrand of the party formerly known as the married name of jock itch and toe jam.

With Wren's electronic help, she'd already picked out her outfit for the party. A thrifted vintage yellow baby doll dress that hit mid-thigh paired with platform sneakers that would've made the Spice Girls jealous. She figured if she got excited about the music and fashion elements of the party, she'd feel less anxiety. Because, if she was being perfectly honest, the last one hadn't ended well. Neither had last year's Halloween party. Lila was pretty sure that she had some Jock Row-related party issues, but couldn't avoid attending, seeing as how her place of residence was kind of the epicenter of the whole damn thing.

Her phone picked that moment to ring. Knight. She carefully put her earbuds in and answered the call.

"Please tell me you're on your way home," he whispered. "Someone has been really cranky since you left."

Of course her mind jumped directly to King, and her heart immediately started performing an elaborate gymnastics routine in her chest. But she played it cool, glad Knight wasn't there in person to read her facial expressions. "Bear? Pssh. Tell him I'll be home soon."

"I'm not talking about Bear and you know it," Knight hissed. "Seriously, Lila, he wasn't showy about it, but he kind of freaked out when you left. Almost like he thought you weren't coming back or something. Hold on." She could hear footsteps and stairs creaking, followed by a door closing. Knight's voice returned to a normal volume. "Seriously, Li, it's not like there's a sign-out sheet for our house, but we worry about you."

Lila winced. "I mean, I let *you* know I was going, you know, for safety purposes. I just figured you'd pass the message along."

"Fair point," he conceded. "But I know another person who would most likely disagree with that statement. What the hell is up between you two? Actually...nope. I don't want to know. I'm staying out of this shitshow."

"Be nice," Lila laughed-winced. "Nothing's up. We're friends, and I went to visit my family for a minute and now I'm coming back. End of story."

"Hardly. But again..."

"You don't want to know."

"Exactly."

"Duly noted. See you soon."

"Later, Li."

Lila ended the call and clenched the steering wheel until her knuckles turned white. She was just so tired. Tired of fighting the combustive chemistry between her and King. Her heart was already fucked, so why not just go down with the sinking ship full of orgasm-induced endorphins?

The rest of the drive passed by too quickly, and she was greeted by a chorus of "Heys" when she let herself into the house. A bunch of guys had congregated and were having some sort of a gaming competition with the latest PS5 sports game. She waved, went to the fridge to grab one of her lemonades, and then climbed the stairs leading to her bedroom.

Once she'd unpacked the few things she'd taken with her and had a few sips of her drink, she opened the door to the bathroom. King's door was open, and she moved across the cool tile until her feet hit wood flooring once again. King's lamp was on, casting light on his strong, tall body propped up with a couple of pillows. His large frame seemed to overtake every inch of the king bed he'd managed to wedge into the room. His laptop was open on his lap, and he appeared to be watching something on the screen.

She knocked softly on the doorframe, and finally, his eyes, jet black in the low light, landed on her.

"What're you watching?"

"A movie." His jaw was tight, and he looked upset. But that couldn't be because of her, could it? Because that would make everything even more convoluted than it already was. Maybe he was just mad to miss out on the high that their collective orgasming seemed to create. Yeah, that was probably it.

"Glad to see the verbosity is out in full force tonight." Lila leaned against the doorjamb. "Not in the mood to hang with the dudes tonight?"

"Nope." Lila was low-key impressed because King popped that "p" like it was his job.

"Wanna tell me why you're being so grumpy right now?" Lila ribbed gently because what the hell was up with him? She sincerely hoped that his nightmare parents hadn't pulled something messed up, but she wouldn't put it past them.

King drew in a large breath, held it, then exhaled slowly, intentionally. Lila entered his room and made her way over to him. His eyes tracked her movements like an apex predator. She stopped when she got to the side of the bed closest to where he was sprawled.

"Why'd you leave?"

Had Lila not already talked to Knight, the question would have surprised her, so she was grateful to her friend for the heads-up.

"Just needed to see my family. It's been a while since I made the trip. Which is kind of terrible of me since it's not that far of a drive."

"It didn't have anything to do with the fact that we've been fooling around?"

"I don't know that I'd classify mutual masturbation as 'fooling around,' but I suppose I can concede to that phraseology for the purposes of this conversation."

"That's not a no."

"It's not a yes, either," she retorted. "Why are you asking in the first place? Did you miss me?"

"Yeah. I fucking did."

Lila froze, unsure of how to respond. All she was certain of was the pull she felt whenever King Spencer entered a room. The pull she was feeling now, even as she schooled her expression to the best of her abilities.

King studied her for a minute then scooted over so he was on one side of the bed. He patted the spot next to him. "Wanna watch this with me?"

"Depends on what movie it is," Lila replied, even as she stretched out next to King on his bed.

"*The Shining*. You know, so we can compare and contrast it with the book and all that for class."

"Spoiler alert: the Overlook is basically just a supernatural representation of the patriarchy." Lila paused. "But I'll watch it with you if you don't say I'm emotionally dead inside for laughing at some of the cheesy parts."

"There are no cheesy parts in this movie. It's terrifying. At least, I thought so when I was ten."

"I sort of feel like that may have been too young to watch this movie?" Lila wrinkled her nose. "Then again, my parents didn't let me watch anything other than G and PG movies until I was 13, so I can't really judge."

"I'd take overprotectiveness over negligence any day."

She reached out and squeezed his hand in silent acknowledgement of his fucked-up childhood.

King unpaused the movie, and before long, Lila found herself tucked inside the crook of his arm, her head resting on his broad chest. Enveloped by his warmth, relaxed by the rising and falling of his chest, she closed her eyes and drifted off.

Later, in the middle of the night, she woke up, momentarily confused where she was. The movie was long over, and King was fast asleep, spooning her from behind. She figured she should probably leave to go sleep in her own bed, but when she tried to gently slip out of King's grasp, his grip tightened, just a little bit.

"Please stay," he murmured into her neck, his voice vulnerable in its sleep-drenched state.

So stay, she did.

Chapter 33

Lila had to admit that the "Nothing but the 90s" party had turned out to be pretty great. The music was spot on, and the fits ranged from Tommy Hilfiger everything to various shades of Nirvana-esque flannel. Also, there were lots of butterfly clips happening, and Lila wasn't the least bit mad about it.

She did, however, miss Wren something fierce. Though she'd temporarily lost her wingwoman to the museums and the architecture of the Old World, she took comfort in the fact that every time they talked, Wren's smile seemed to be brighter, the weight on her shoulders a little lighter.

Lila also missed Vicky and Dani, who'd both moved back to their hometown after graduation. Julia and Nate were still going strong and now living together, so even though Julia was still at school, she wasn't at the party tonight. Lila couldn't help but feel like many of her girlfriends were moving on without her, which made her even more grateful for her boys. Things were simpler in a lot of ways since she'd moved in with them. Except for the large asterisk that loomed next to King's name.

"You're not dancing," Knight chided as he slid next to her against the railing of their front porch. He was clad in what was his best approximation of the "boy band in the late 90s" look. With spiky gelled hair and everything. Seriously, it was crispy to the touch and more than slightly terrifying.

"Nah." She shrugged. "I guess the mood hasn't hit me just yet." She leaned against the railing and turned her head to look at him. "Why aren't you out there?"

"I felt like adopting more of a supervisory role this time around."

"I'm here for that energy." Her lips curled up in a nostalgic grin. "Can you believe it's been a year since we tore up the floor with our wicked dance moves?"

He chuckled heartily. "We were the best ones out there, for sure." Knight's expression turned from joyous to pensive as he continued, "Not to get too cheesy on your ass, but I'm so glad that our paths crossed back then. You know you've got a brother for life, right? No matter what?"

Lila's throat suddenly felt all lumpy as she gently hip checked her friend. "Same. No matter what, no matter where, no matter when."

Knight stuck his pinky out, and Lila linked hers with his. Then they turned back to survey the party. Déjà vu pricked at her consciousness as she glanced down to the side of the house and saw King leaning against the side of it.

Knight cast a knowing look her way. "Go get him, Li."

Lila's brows furrowed. "I don't know that he wants to be. Gotten, I mean."

"Are you sure about that?"

She shrugged. "Honestly? I don't know. All I know is that I'm scared." It came out barely above a whisper. "I don't think my heart can handle the aftermath of another rejection." Though in her heart, she knew that wasn't quite right. Not anymore. Not with how much King had changed. Still...

"You love him though. Don't you?"

Lila paused, debated. Then she decided to go with honesty. Because it was Knight, and he was one of her best friends. She nodded, swallowing the lump that had suddenly formed in her throat. "Yeah, I do. So much it aches."

"Then what are you waiting for?" Knight raised his brows but didn't wait around for an answer. He just smiled, chucked her softly on the chin, and made his way down into the dancing crowd.

Almost as if her body was on autopilot, she made her way down the couple of porch steps and headed left to where King was perched. He pushed off the wall and advanced so they were almost standing toe-to-toe. Again, he hadn't dressed up for the theme, though he looked edible in the black tee and dark jeans look he was currently rocking.

The left side of his mouth slanted up, exposing a dimple that was simultaneously adorable and sexy as hell. "Tell me something. You still think you can handle my dance moves?"

"You saying you want to dance with me, King?" Lila's stomach was a kaleidoscope of butterflies.

He nodded. "I'm saying I want to dance with you, La." King's index finger traced a line from her temple down the slope of her jaw, and Lila was totally gone. Whatever this was, it was happening. And she was going to let it, consequences be damned.

She stepped back without a word and turned away from him, throwing a devilish look over her shoulder. "Let's see what you've got."

"Trust me, you can't handle it."

"We'll see."

Lila was keenly aware of the heat of his body as he followed her to the dance floor. The beginning notes to "No Diggity" started playing, and King whirled her around to face him. Keeping a hand on her waist but space between their bodies, he started to dance, and she moved with him. Unlike last year, when hers and Knight's dancing was hilariously silly and over-the-top, this dancing was pure and utter sex.

King pulled her closer and the space between them vanished. His strong hands angled her so that she was practically riding his muscular thigh. The rough material of his jeans caused all sorts of delicious sensations in her lady parts. She could feel him, too, thick and hard and heavy against her stomach.

They danced until she thought she'd explode, and then King's lips were next to her ear. His gravelly tone was gloriously lust-laden as he grunted, "Inside. Upstairs. Now."

The moment she nodded her agreement, he grabbed her hand and practically dragged her through the throngs then inside and upstairs until they'd gotten to his bedroom.

As soon the lock clicked on the door, they were on each other, their mouths and tongues fighting for control as King grabbed Lila by her ass and lifted as she hitched her legs up around his waist. She locked them around him and furiously grinded her body against his dick. He walked them over to the bed, dropping her on the mattress then covering her body with his. King moved his body against hers with frenetic energy, his bottomless eyes clouded with need every time they snagged hers. He moved his mouth down to her pulse point. He traced it with his tongue and then bit down softly.

"Goddammit, La. I want to be inside you so bad it hurts."

"Be inside me, then."

She arched up into him, loving the way that the friction made him hiss, and reached for the button of his jeans. As soon as she'd flicked it open, he pinned her hands above her head, just for a second, before he let go and divested himself of his jeans and sheathed himself with a condom from his nightstand drawer. Then his skilled hands reached underneath her dress and wrested her underwear down and off, his hard dick filling her before she had a chance to breathe. And the feeling in her chest at that precise moment was one of profound relief.

"Fuck, La. You feel…"

King leaned down to take her mouth, holding himself still inside her as she adjusted to him. Then he started to move, long, hard strokes that threatened to shatter Lila at any moment. It wasn't precious or soft. It was desperate, untamed. Utterly feral. And Lila wondered how they'd lasted so long without *this*, without this feeling of riotous contentment. Of completion.

She felt the delicious sensation of sparks licking up her spine as King brought her up and over the edge, the sparks spreading over her body and dancing behind her eyes. Then, impossibly, he increased his intensity and thrust into her even harder as he chased his own relief. When it came, he was beautiful, letting everything go as he gazed at her intently before closing his eyes as pleasure overwhelmed his features.

He collapsed on top of her, and she welcomed the heaviness that covered her body like a blanket. He propped himself up on his forearms. "Fuck, La, that was…"

"Everything," she finished quietly.

He nodded. "Yeah."

The implications of what they'd just done swirled around them, but neither of them spoke. They just stared at each other. Lila mapped out the shadowed planes of King's face so that she'd always remember the way he looked in this moment. The softness in his eyes. The curl of hair that had fallen over his forehead.

She wanted to tell him that she loved him, that she'd loved him before they separated and probably had never stopped, but she stayed silent, willing the words to stay inside. For the moment, at least.

Reluctantly, King separated from her to clean up, and Lila smiled at the sight of him still wearing his shirt.

"We didn't even take the time to get naked," she said as she sat up with a laugh, looking down at her dress.

King smiled at her as he emerged from the bathroom. He reached and grabbed his shirt at the back of the neck and pulled it up and off. "Better?"

Lila took in the perfection of his perfectly toned form and felt her desire start to rise again. "Much," she murmured as he advanced on her, and she had the feeling that round two was going to be even more enjoyable than round one.

Her hands were at the hem of her dress, ready to pull it over her head, when she noticed the glint of the necklace hanging around King's neck. And then her stomach bottomed out.

Was that... It couldn't be...

She scrambled off King's bed to get a closer look.

King's expression morphed from playful to panicked as he realized what she had focused her attention on. As she got closer, her suspicions were confirmed. It was her crown necklace. The one that her grandmother had given her right before she died. The one he'd said he lost.

Lila's brain whirled as she tried to process how she felt. A minute ago, she'd felt like everything was finally falling into place, and now? Now, she wanted to know what the hell kind of a game he was playing with her.

She tried to arrange her words into a coherent sentence, but all she could do was extend a finger and touch the crown charm.

King stiffened under that touch, his chest starting to inflate and deflate quickly. "Lila, I can explain..."

His words snapped Lila out of her trance. "Explain why you lied about losing my necklace? Why you've hidden it from me all this time?"

She felt so foolish. She'd actually thought that King wanted to be with her, for real this time. But the presence of this old talisman brought up all of the feelings and insecurities she'd had when he'd told her he lost it. When he'd watched her crumble in front of him at the pain of losing something so precious. Which wasn't even about the damn necklace. It was about him. Because though she'd given it to him with no intention of ever asking for it back, she'd also underestimated how much their "breakup" would decimate her. And how the thought of him having something she treasured when he'd discarded her so easily made her sick to her stomach.

"I'm sorry, La. I should have told you I still had it." He gulped. "I should have just given it back when you asked for it."

"Why didn't you?" Lila had to know why. His honesty in this moment felt necessary, vital. Because if they didn't have trust between the two of them, what the hell was the point?

His face was tormented as he scanned her face. "I... I don't know," he finally uttered in a pained, whispered tone.

"You don't know?" Lila tried to keep the frustration out of her voice as she repeated his words. They stood there for what seemed like an eternity, staring at each other, and she willed him to answer. She *needed* him to answer.

When he didn't? She swallowed a disappointed sob and maneuvered around him, crossing the threshold of their shared space and then entering her room. She clicked the deadbolt, locked her other door, and then slowly slid down the wall, crumpling into a ball on the floor.

Chapter 34

King hadn't slept at all. He was still reeling from the whiplash of what had happened the night before. How, for those wonderfully brief moments he'd thought that he might actually have a shot at being with Lila for real. How much of a relief it'd been when he was finally inside her. It had been so long but still felt just as intense and consuming as it had before. More, even, because they knew each other better. Because he loved her.

It felt like coming home.

And then, he epically and most likely irreparably fucked things up. Again. The damned necklace. Why hadn't he just told her he still had it? And why couldn't he find the words to explain himself last night? She'd given him more than enough time, and he'd frozen. The look on her face stabbed him in the gut, and in the moment, his old hang-ups had risen to the surface. Thoughts that he didn't deserve someone like her, how there'd be no way she could ever be truly happy with a fuckup like him.

Around 3:00 that morning, he'd written her a note, which he'd left to the side of her sink, her necklace gently draped on top of it:

I'm so sorry, La. For everything. I'm sorry I let my fear and insecurities affect my actions. I'm sorry for not being completely honest with you.

This belongs to you, and I shouldn't have kept it. But I'm ready to tell you why I did, if you ever want to know. If not, I can respect and understand that. I'll leave it up to you.

Whatever happens, I hope you know that you are incredible. Your kindness saved me when I really needed it, so even if you come to regret our time together, I don't.

I can't.

K

After leaving the note, he'd gotten dressed and run over to the track, where he pushed himself to the breaking point until the sun came up, his legs and lungs burning as he ran mile after mile. He showered in the locker room, changing into the spare set of clothes he'd stashed there for emergencies. As he sat down on the bench in front of his locker, he couldn't help but remember the night Lila had come to him. The night he'd fallen ass over feet for her. The night she'd given him the best gift he'd ever received before or since.

You are not your father. You're a king.

King propped his elbows on his knees, his head bowed low, and cried. He cried until there were no more tears to wrench from his body. He couldn't remember the last time he'd full-out sobbed. It was probably the night when he'd told his mom that their bags were packed and that they should leave.

Fuck. Would anybody ever want him? Stay with him?

After, he just...wandered around the empty campus for a bit. It was a Sunday, so other than the few weekend studiers who used the library, it was pretty much a ghost town. He didn't want to go back to the house yet because he wanted to give Lila some space. At the very least, he could give her that much, especially since they'd be stuck in class together tomorrow. After walking a while, he began to feel lightheaded, so he decided to head back to where his car was parked near the house so that he could go get something to eat.

King made the slow walk towards home and then snuck into his car like he was a spy on a secret mission, all while ignoring texts from Knight and Bear. And then Demarcus. And then Will. And then even Jason from across the damn country, for fuck's sake. He finally just turned off his phone to stop all of the vibrating.

He stopped to get some fast food, which he knew he'd regret later, and then drove up to the overlook. It had been a long time since he'd driven up there, but it was the only place he could think of to go. He pulled into his typical spot, turned off his car, and stared at the valley below in silence. Even here there were memories of Lila.

At the time he'd brought her here, he didn't understand why, but now he did. There'd always been something about her, from the first time he saw her, that had spoken to him on a cellular level. Perhaps it was just her kind spirit identifying a hurt that she could help heal. Or maybe it's because all his life, he'd been searching for someone to love, for someone strong enough to love him back.

Lowering his head to the steering wheel, he breathed deeply, trying to find some semblance of peace. So wrapped up in his own head, he didn't notice the form standing just outside his passenger window until a soft knock wrenched his body upward.

He blinked a couple of times because it couldn't be who he thought it was. Not in a million years.

But when she knocked again and motioned to his locked door handle, his lucidity fully returned. *Lila.* He hit the unlock button, and she slid inside, locking the doors again once the door was closed. She got out her phone and quickly typed out a text.

"You've been gone for hours, King. Knight was about to send out a search party," Lila mused, her attention directed at the windshield.

"Sorry," he whispered.

"I made him promise to hold off until after I looked for you here." Her smile was both heartbreakingly sad and heartbreakingly beautiful as she turned to face him. "And here you are."

"Here I am." He managed a wan smile as he took in the face of the woman he loved more than anything else in his life. "I'm sorry."

"I know," she replied kindly, her brows slightly furrowed. "I read your note, and I'm ready to hear what you have to say."

King exhaled in relief. "That's... Thank you. Thank you for hearing me out." His breath stuttered a bit, and Lila reached out to lace her fingers in his.

"Take your time," she said softly. "I'm not going anywhere."

King's heart sped as he tried to organize his thoughts. "So, you know about how fucked-up my family is. All my life, the people I've loved have left me, whether it was physically or emotionally. I thought that was just how my life was going to be with everyone. That I'd always feel alone." There was a hitch in his voice, and Lila's gentle pressure on his hand encouraged him to continue. "Then I saw you."

He hesitated before continuing, "I've never told you this, but the day that Jason introduced us wasn't the first time I noticed you. It was the year before. I had gone in to pick Jason up because his car was in the shop, and you were working the salad bar. Your hair was hanging down your back in one of your signature braids. And when you smiled at a customer, it felt like a kick right to my gut."

King heard Lila's breathing stall, but she stayed silent, so he continued. "After that, I stayed away for a while. At the time I had no idea why. Now I realize it's because of the way you made me *feel* things. Not specific emotions, but emotions in general. I'd been so closed off that I couldn't even identify my own feelings."

The sun started to set, and the valley lit up with an array of oranges and yellows and purples and blues. King turned his head toward Lila's. "I was scared to feel at all, but especially to feel for you. Because, you? You're Lila fucking Alexander. There was no way I could possibly deserve to be with someone as wonderful as you. But damn if I didn't want you anyway.

"When you gave me that necklace, you said I was different from my father, that I was capable of more. And for the first time, I actually felt it. I actually believed it for myself."

He raised his free hand and gently stroked her cheekbone with his fingers. "Lila, that was the night I knew I loved you. That I always would. And after, I was an asshole and pushed you away—again—because I was scared I'd fuck it all up. That you'd eventually leave me because of it." He shook his head, frustrated by his complete and utter idiocy. "But I couldn't give you the necklace back, even after you asked me for it, because it was all I had left of you, of your faith in me."

A tear slipped down Lila's face as her glassy golden eyes looked into his, like she was trying to determine whether he was telling her the truth.

"I was miserable without you, but the memory of what you'd said to me helped inspire me to change. To heal. Which I hope you've seen. But I should have come clean about it. I'm still working through some insecurities, but it's not an excuse. I should have told you once we were back on better terms. I should have given it back. I'm so sorry."

When Lila unlinked their hands, King's heart sank. He waited for her rejection, of her exit from his life, and convinced himself that, no matter what, he would eventually be okay. That he'd done his best to answer for his mistakes, but that those mistakes might still come at a cost. He took comfort in that, even as he dreaded her rejection.

She reached into her pocket and pulled out her necklace. The tiny crown reflected the last bits of sunlight in the sky as she held it up for him to see. She leaned forward and wrapped the chain around his neck, fastening the clasp. She ran a hand down over where it now laid on his chest, circling the charm with her thumb.

"This is yours." Lila moved her hand up to the side of King's neck, her eyes molten gold as she pulled him closer. "So am I, if you want me."

His heart pumped faster and he exhaled a relieved breath, words temporarily leaving him as that tiny sliver of fear tried to reemerge. The fear that he wasn't good enough. That Lila would eventually leave. But he quashed it, his thumb reaching up to smooth the furrow that had appeared between Lila's brows as she waited for him to respond.

Nothing would keep him from her now. Not ever again, if he had anything to say about it.

"I want you," King murmured as he closed the gap between them and kissed her.

* * *

Later, King woke up next to Lila. After they'd made good use of the back seat of his car, they reluctantly separated so they could drive home. Knight and Bear gave them knowing smiles when they entered the house, saying nothing as Lila gave them a quick wave before King threw her over his shoulder and hauled her upstairs. Sometime after round three, she had rolled over to cuddle against King's side, her arm draped over his abdomen as she slept. The sheets were tangled low, exposing the delicate notches of her spine.

His hand softly traveled the length of it, tracing up and down, as she roused from sleep. She looked up at him sleepily, her smile the one she reserved only for him. Her fingers started tracing the indentations of his abs, and he flexed automatically as desire pooled low and his body responded, tenting the sheets in the process.

"I love you, King," Lila whispered.

King hauled her up so she was lying on top of him. He'd never get tired of hearing those words coming from her lips, not ever. "I love you too, La."

"Wanna show me?" Lila moved her body against his, and he could feel how ready she was for him.

And obviously, he did, in fact, want to show her, especially when she was moving her body like that.

"Dammit, La, let me grab a condom," King eked out, though the thought of having her bare was almost too much to process.

She stilled and propped herself up on her hands so she could look down at him. "Is there a reason we need one?"

He shook his head. "We get tested as part of our annual sports physical. I'm good. Hell, I have the lab results around here somewhere if you want to double check." King paused and then confessed, "I haven't been with anyone else since I was with you the first time."

Her breath caught, and her face lit up with the sort of expression that was more than just a smile. It was tenderness and joy and relief and trust. It was everything. "I haven't been with anyone else, either. Also, I have an IUD, so we're covered."

"Fuck yes we are," King growled as his control began to slip.

Lila sat up and reached down to line him up with her entrance. Then she lowered herself down slowly, inch by delicious inch, until there was no more space between them. She rode him hard, unabashedly taking what she needed until she came apart, and then King inverted their bodies so she was beneath him. He teased her with long, slow strokes before pulling out of her completely.

"What are you doing?" Lila's voice was adorably breathless and thoroughly pissed. "Don't stop."

"Shower. Now," King demanded as he picked her up, wrapping her legs around his waist as he led them into the bathroom to their walk-in shower. He turned it on and tested the water temperature before setting her down partially underneath the spray. His eyes caught a flash of purple, and he got impossibly harder at the sight of Lila's vibrator.

He picked it up and waved it in front of her face. "Forget something?" he teased.

Lila's brow arched as her eyes darkened with lust. "Nope." And then she reached out and stroked him, gripping him tightly just the way he liked it.

King kissed her, hard, before spinning her around. "Hands against the tile, legs spread," he whispered in her ear. He turned on the vibrator and positioned it between her legs but didn't make contact with her body just yet. King chuckled at her frustrated moans as he grinded against her perfect ass. "Trust me, baby. I'm going to take care of you."

"You better," she sighed over her shoulder, rising up on her tiptoes.

He entered her just as he pressed the vibrator against her clit. She exhaled a pleasured, pained moan at the sensation, her arms buckling where they were pressed against the tile.

"Close, La?"

She nodded and reached down to hold the vibrator.

He wrapped his newly freed hand around her stomach and braced the other against the wall as he kissed her neck then thrust into her over and over until she tightened around him and came again, his name on her lips. He followed, his vision flooded with white, his body shuddering from the intensity of it. King rested his head in the crook of her neck as they both slowed their breaths.

Then she turned to face him, a sated look on her beautiful face as she threaded her arms around his torso. "That was better than anything my imagination ever came up with."

"You're saying you've thought about us fucking in the shower?" He looped his arms around her, his thumbs tracing the indentations at the base of her spine.

"I'm saying that it wasn't a coincidence that my vibe was ready and waiting in said shower," she replied wickedly.

"I like the way your mind works." King smirked.

"You seem to bring it out of me."

"You're welcome."

Lila's giggles vibrated against King as her arms tightened around him and she laid her head on his chest. "Sometimes I get overwhelmed by how much I love you, King," she murmured.

"I know the feeling." King stepped back to reach for his body wash and then spent a fair amount of time washing Lila's body then her hair. She made contented sounds as she let him love her with his hands, and then she returned the favor, her hands traveling over the lines and planes of his body then softly raking her nails through his scalp.

Then, when the water started to run cold, they went back to his bed and dozed until the first rays of the sunrise sliced through the blinds, signaling the start of a new day.

Chapter 35

"Are you sure you're ready for this?" Lila asked as soon as King put the car in park. "My family is kind of extra."

"Please. If I can handle you, I can definitely handle your family," King said with a teasing twist to his smile. It had been almost a month since they'd figured their shit out, and King couldn't remember a time when he'd felt this happy. There was something supremely satisfying about being with Lila officially and publicly. Every time he spotted her front row center at his games, wearing a Bradley U jersey with his name and number on the back, his chest swelled with pride and love for the woman who had come into his life and torn down his walls like a wrecking ball.

She swatted at his chest and went to open the door, but he gently grasped her wrist to stop her. "Wait one sec. I have something I want to give you first."

Her expression turned downright sinful. "We can't do anything worth doing in my parents' driveway. At least during the day." Her brows danced mischievously.

"Mind out of the gutter, Alexander. I'd be lying if I said that I didn't love it, though." He opened the center console between their seats, pulled out a small box, and set it in her hands. "Since you gave me yours, I wanted you to have one of your own," he murmured as she lifted the lid.

"King..." Her voice wobbled as she pulled out the necklace. It was an exact replica of the one he was currently wearing, except the crown was studded with tiny pavé diamonds. "It's beautiful. I love it. I love *you*."

"Not as much as I love you." He leaned in to kiss her chastely.

"Doubtful." She kissed him back, not so chastely. Then her eyes darted to the front of her parents' house. "We have an audience," she laughed as King turned to see four pairs of eyes peeking at them from behind the curtains. "Help me put this on before we go inside?"

King fastened the necklace and kissed her once more before they both exited the car and headed up the short walkway to the front door, their fingers intertwined. It swung open as soon as their feet hit the front porch.

"Lila!" a chorus of voices shouted out, and she was mauled by her younger siblings, so much so that they knocked her back a step.

"Whoa there, peeps. You about took me out right there," Lila laughed as she tried to wrap her arms around all four of them. Then she took a step back and put an arm around King's waist. "Boys, this is my boyfriend, King. King, this is Leo, Lance, and Landon. And you remember Layla."

Their laser-like attention shifted from Lila to King. "Hi everybody. I'm the boyfriend."

"And we're so happy to finally meet you, King." Lila's mom poked her head out of the door and greeted him with a motherly grin. "Come on, kiddos. Let's let Lila and King get inside, shall we? It's starting to get chilly out."

Once they'd all funneled back into the foyer of the house, King took brief notice of an office to the right and a formal living room to the left. Then the space opened up to a family room/kitchen area, and everybody made a beeline for the large sectional that was set opposite a big flatscreen TV.

"Erik's just finishing up making some lunch, so I hope you two are hungry?" Lila's mom asked.

"I can't speak for Lila, but I'm always hungry, Mrs. Alexander. Especially for something made by someone who knows what they're doing," King joked.

"Please call me Diana. And please don't hold it against Lila. She could burn a pot of water if left unattended for too long," Diana laughed.

"Mooooom," Lila groaned. "I'd actually managed to keep my kitchen deficiencies under wraps until now; you've ruined everything!" she deadpanned.

Diana just laughed and headed toward her husband in the kitchen.

Lila looped an arm through King's, and they followed her. "Dad, this is my boyfriend, King."

"Nice to meet you, King." Erik Alexander extended a hand for King to shake. "And please, call me Erik."

"Nice to meet you as well, Erik. Thank you both for inviting me to your home."

"You're welcome here anytime. We're glad you both could make the drive up. It was a bye-week for soccer, right?" Diana remarked.

King nodded. "Yeah, we have a couple more games until we break for winter, and then we start back up again in February."

"Diana and I have been talking about bringing down the kids and seeing you play. We'll make it happen before the end of the season," Erik said as he put the finishing touches on a pasta salad. "Landon plays soccer, and Lance is thinking of making the switch from baseball to soccer, so I think they'd love seeing a more competitive game than what they see in their youth leagues. We've heard you're quite the athlete, King."

"I can hold my own," King answered with a small shrug. But inside, he was warmed with pride as he took in the genuine compliment that seemed refreshingly devoid of any ulterior motives.

Lila snorted. "Please. He's got scouts checking him out at every game. He's the star of the team. Multiple Major League Soccer teams have him on their radar."

"No doubt a product of exceptional talent coupled with an impressive work ethic," Diana commented. "That's something to be very proud of, King."

"Thanks." He ducked his head, suddenly overwhelmed by all of the positive energy being thrown his way. It felt nice, but it would definitely take some getting used to. Luckily, lunch was ready, and they all helped themselves buffet style to sandwiches and salads and the best damn chocolate chip cookies he'd ever eaten. That was one recipe Lila assured him she could duplicate.

"They're the ones I made for your roommates that one time," she whispered.

"The 'sorry not sorry we're having loud sex' cookies?"

"Is there any other kind?" she laughed as she went to grab another.

The Alexanders were loud, expressive, and obviously loved the shit out of each other; it was no wonder that Lila had such a capacity for patience and compassion. Her siblings all seemed to adore her, and she interacted with each brother individually and shared a giggled whispered conversation with Layla as the latter's eyes drifted over to King.

They all treated him like he was one of the family. Joking with him, asking him questions, but seeming to know which topics to steer clear of. He had no doubt that Lila had prepped them ahead of time in that subtle way of hers, not revealing any of his personal business but also setting boundaries. Like when they invited him to Thanksgiving dinner, somehow knowing he didn't have anywhere to go, but not making a big deal about it.

Watching the wonderful way that Lila's parents engaged with each other, their devotion and love apparent, gave King a startling sense of déjà vu. Like he was seeing himself with Lila years into the future. It reaffirmed his belief that she was going to be his forever someday.

And the way her eyes shifted to him, wholly open and filled with more love than had ever been thrown his direction before, he knew deep down that she felt the same way.

Chapter 36

Lila's knee bounced subconsciously, bumping the "Welcome Home" poster she'd made with every upswing, as King pulled into the parking lot of the airport. "It's too bad you're not excited to see Wren," he commented teasingly as he parked, noting that Knight had pulled into the spot right next to them.

"I'm just so excited she's home early!" Lila exclaimed. "And there's so much you don't know. So *you're* in for a treat, my love," she continued cryptically. Lila had been notoriously tight-lipped about Wren's early return from Europe. Apparently it was something that had been in the works for a while, because Wren had needed to get clearance with the university to ensure that she'd still get credit for all of her classes.

Lila jumped out of the car and threw herself at Knight, who caught her expertly, his surprisingly pale, nervous face brightening. She whispered something in his ear and kissed his cheek, seeming to calm Knight even more, and King was able to watch it with the security of knowing that his girl was a kickass friend and that he had no reason to be jealous. Which was kind of a huge milestone for him.

She linked arms with King and Knight and practically skipped to the area of the airport by the baggage claim. They were stationed at the foot of a bay of escalators, which was where Wren would be coming from. If she hadn't had prepped him, King would have been surprised that it was just the three of them greeting Wren at the airport. But Lila had explained that it was a request that came straight from her best friend. Wren's family was waiting to greet her back at her childhood home.

Soon, King spotted Wren's bright auburn hair as she descended the escalator. Her face lit up when she saw Lila's poster and then warmed even more when she turned her focus on Knight. Lila shot a look at Knight, and he nodded, nudging her forward. Lila dropped the poster and ran over to her friend, hugging her tightly as soon as Wren had stepped clear of the escalator.

They held on to each other for a while, speaking in muted tones that didn't carry over to where King and Knight were standing. When Lila stepped back, Wren's trench coat fell open, revealing... Holy shit, was that a baby bump? King's eyes shot from Wren's belly to Lila, and she gave him a nod through her happy tears. Then he looked sideways at Knight and caught the tears in his eyes. Lila touched her friend's stomach softly and kissed her cheek. Then she took her friend's carry-on and led Wren over to Knight.

Speechless, Knight took a single step then fell to his knees and cradled the sides of Wren's stomach with his hands. When he leaned forward and kissed her bump tenderly, resting his forehead against it, King's eyes started to water. Wren's shaky hand combed through Knight's hair for a moment. Then Knight stood, a hand still protectively resting at the side of Wren's abdomen. "How are my girls?" he whispered.

"Missing you," Wren said, eyes filled with tender tears, and then she leaned in to kiss him.

King turned to Lila, who was now a beautiful mess of tears. "Well, this is...a lot to process," he said softly.

"I know," she murmured back, eyes slightly downcast. "I'm sorry I didn't tell you. Wren swore me to secrecy before we got back together. It wasn't my story to tell."

King put a reassuring arm around his girlfriend. "No worries, La. I get it. You've always gotta show up for your girl. Anyway, this is probably the sweetest damn thing I've ever seen in my life, so I'm not mad about it." He shook his head in wonder. "Knight is going to be a dad. Who would have thought all of this was even possible a few months ago?" He wasn't just referring to Knight and Wren, who were still in the process of their happy reunion slash makeout. No, King was thinking about him and Lila, how close he'd been to fucking everything up.

Lila went up to embrace her two best friends, her short stature almost comedic as she wrapped an arm around both of their waists.

Then King approached. "I hear congratulations are in order," he said with a smile and was taken aback when Wren leaned in to hug him.

"Thanks for getting your shit together and taking care of my girl, King," she said in a low tone before she stepped back, a hand on her belly. "And sorry for the subterfuge. This is something I played close to the vest."

"Understandable." Then King turned to Knight, and the two of them grinned and embraced. "Congratu-fucking-lations, Daddy."

"Thanks, King. I wouldn't be here if you hadn't helped me get over myself and all of my self-pity. I owe you, man."

"Nah, that's just what brothers do for each other."

"And godfathers," Knight said with a huge grin.

King's eyes widened as Wren nodded her agreement.

"We'd be honored if you'd be our daughter's godfather." Wren motioned her head in Lila's direction. "Especially since you're currently banging her godmother."

"And now I know where Lila got that word from," King joked. "Or did you get it from her?" They all laughed. Then King sobered, straightened. "It would be an honor, guys. Truly."

"It's settled, then," Knight said, slapping King on the back. After another round of hugs and the retrieval of the rest of Wren's luggage, they all walked out to the parking garage together, making plans to meet at the house later after Wren got settled in. Because obviously Knight and Wren needed a little alone time, and she still had family to see.

Once Knight and Wren had driven off, the shock of what had just happened finally hit King like a lightning bolt. "I cannot believe all of that just happened." He shook his head in happy disbelief.

"Oh, it happened, all right," Lila replied. As they made the drive home, Lila filled him in on a few more details about Wren and Knight's situation. Some of it, King had known, but the rest was surprising. He couldn't imagine what it would have been like for Wren to discover she was pregnant a couple of months into her semester abroad or what it would have been like for Knight when he found out. The fact that Wren wanted to keep quiet about it was something that King could respect. Especially when things were up in the air with Knight.

Lila explained that while Wren was gone, Wren and Knight started working through their feelings for each other and deciding what to do about the baby, which had been an emotional process. Wren found out that she needed to come home before the start of her third trimester, so she had to coordinate with the university to make it happen.

After hearing Lila fill in all of the blanks, King understood his friend's reactions more clearly. Though it seemed like it had been a long road for Wren and Knight to get to this place, they were committed to giving their relationship a real shot and raising their baby together.

"Which means we'll need a new roommate in a couple of months," Lila said a little sadly as he pulled his car into a parking spot near their house. "And when Knight gets drafted, she'll go where he goes. She's moved up her graduation to the spring, just like me. So this is our junior and senior years all wrapped up into one."

She sighed. "It's the end of an era really, but I'm excited for them both. It's an unconventional beginning, but I have a feeling that they're endgame."

"Like us," King replied. Because she was it for him.

"Oh yeah? You think we're endgame, huh?" She curled a strand of her hair around her finger.

"I don't think. I know."

They looked at each other for a long moment and then raced inside, ending up in their bathroom, shed clothes strewn everywhere as the shower was turned on and began to steam as they loved each other frantically under the warm spray.

After, King watched as a still-naked Lila brushed through the length of her freshly dried hair, his desire to care for her almost overwhelming.

"Can I?" King asked as he approached from behind, making eye contact with her reflection in the mirror. He felt suddenly shy but pushed it aside. Because he wanted to be vulnerable and open with Lila, always.

Lila's expression wrinkled in confusion for just the briefest of seconds, and then understanding lit up her face. Instead of turning around, she reached for his hand and then placed the brush in it, holding his gaze the entire time. The moment King began to slide the brush bristles through her long strands, she sighed contentedly.

"I love your hair," King gritted out as he felt his body respond to her sounds, to the thrumming, constant desire he felt for her.

"It loves you right back." Lila's expression morphed from satisfied to smug as she felt his arousal nudging at her from behind. "I'll even teach you how to braid it sometime if you want." She leaned back into him, slowly grinding her ass against his hard length. "But right now…"

King set the brush down and grabbed Lila by the hips. "Right now, we have more important things to do," he growled softly into the shell of her ear.

She shivered and nodded her agreement then gasped and gripped the counter of the bathroom vanity as he slid inside her, all hair brushing–related activities temporarily forgotten.

Chapter 37

King smiled at the fan section that Lila, Knight, Wren, and Lila's family had created. It was the last game of their fall season, and the Alexanders were repping in head-to-toe Bradley U soccer gear. Even Wren had made a point to dress in school colors, which meant more to King than he could actually verbalize. In the weeks she'd been home, he'd gotten to know her on a whole new level and had been able to see how good she was for Knight. He sometimes felt the need to pinch himself because he'd never imagined living a life filled with so much love. A life filled with...*family*.

Notably absent was King's mother, who still wasn't speaking to him. And though Solomon wasn't visible from the field, King had the feeling that he was lurking somewhere in the wings, ready to pounce. But for the first time ever, that prospect didn't faze him at all. He had found his own family, and their ties were thicker than any blood connection could ever be. Because they'd chosen each other.

King dribbled the ball around a defender and sliced it over to Will, who was waiting at the wing. Will headed it towards the goal, and the ball slipped past the keeper, cementing their lead by another goal. They fist bumped as they ran back to prepare for the opposing team to kick off.

The rest of the game flew by, and King managed to score a goal in the second half, much to the delight of Lila's brothers, who started a chant and the wave in their section of seats. He gave them a couple of claps above his head in salute as he ran past, and Lance and Landon acted like it was the best thing they'd ever seen.

As soon as the referee's whistle signaled the end of the game, he made a beeline over to his woman. She jumped over the cement barrier, and he caught her in his arms as she attack-hugged him and then wrapped her legs around his waist. Then he kissed the shit out of her, to the supreme delight of their small audience. "Love you, La."

"Love you, my King."

Just as he was prepared to take her mouth again, the sound of a clearing throat interrupted them. Coach Klopp stood there, looking as grumpy as ever, even though everybody knew he was secretly a teddy bear inside.

"Sorry to interrupt, but I need you in the locker room right now, Spencer."

King nodded and set Lila down before lifting her back up and over the cement partition. "See you soon?"

Lila nodded and pecked him on the mouth quickly. "We'll wait here."

King followed his coach into the locker room, where most of his other teammates had gathered. But, instead of stopping, they walked straight through to Klopp's office, where his coach motioned for him to sit down.

"Good work out there, son," Coach Klopp remarked gruffly. "I just wanted you to know that I've been contacted by scouts from Europe, notably from La Liga and the Premier League. They've got their eyes on you."

"That's... Wow" was all King managed to say.

"I'm not surprised. You're probably the best forward I've ever worked with. I know that MLS has been following you too. But I think you should sincerely consider playing abroad. You're definitely talented enough to be competitive, even if you are getting a later start than some of the European players."

"I appreciate the advice, Coach," King said, his mind reeling. Playing soccer professionally at all would be a dream. But in Europe? It would be phenomenal.

What about Lila?

He knew he couldn't expect her to follow him wherever he went; she had plans too. But the thought of them being separated for any amount of time made his chest tighten. Luckily, they still had months to figure things out. Hell, he still had half of a season to play. But this information definitely changed things.

Thanking his coach, King grabbed a quick shower and then headed out to greet Lila and her family. Knight and Wren had gone ahead to grab a table at the local pizza place, where they'd all decided to eat afterwards.

King exited the tunnel and headed towards Lila and her family, where he was met with a chorus of cheers and even some hugs from the two youngest. Their exuberance was something he was still getting used to, but he didn't hate it.

The heightened energy continued throughout dinner, as Lila's brothers did their best to each eat an entire large pizza. Leo succeeded, but he looked a little green afterwards. Wren and Lila were talking about baby names, and Knight was always making some kind of contact with Wren, whether it was an arm over the back of her chair or a hand on her knee. King was surprised how well his best friend had settled into the role of boyfriend and father-to-be. If anything, he seemed even calmer. Happier. More whole.

Wren had, for all intents and purposes, moved in, so Lila and Wren were finally able to be roommates, even if it was in a slightly different way than they'd always envisioned. More often than not, King and Knight would arrive home from practice and find them curled up on the couch watching their favorite shows and snacking on their special mix of buttered popcorn and peanut butter M&Ms.

When dinner was over and they'd said their goodbyes to Lila's family, King drove up to the overlook. As if sensing he needed her close, Lila climbed over from her seat and straddled King's lap.

"What did Coach say?" Lila asked while running her fingers through his waves.

"He thinks I have a shot at playing in Europe."

Her fingers halted suddenly, elation readily visible on her face. "King! That's incredible!" Her hands moved down to shake his shoulders as she peered down at his face and her expression sobered. "Or maybe it's not so great?"

King sighed deeply as he traced a hand up her side. "It's great. A dream, actually. I never thought that playing over there would be a possibility. Hell, I thought playing professionally here would be a stretch."

"So what's going on in that big, beautiful brain of yours, then?"

King squeezed her side and leaned forward to kiss her softly. "You." Her brow wrinkled and his chest squeezed. "I don't want to leave you, and I don't expect you to drop your life and come with me. I don't want to take you away from your family and from Wren and Knight. Fuck, I feel like we just found each other again. I don't want to lose this. You're more important to me than a game."

Lila pressed her forehead against his, her scent flooding over him like a wave. "I love my family, and I love Wren and Knight. But..." She cupped his face with her hands. "I love you the most. You're the most important person in my life."

"But law school..."

"Might be something that I still want to pursue. But honestly? I am graduating college in three years instead of four. I'm kind of burned out. I can afford to take some time to figure out what I really want to do and not what I've put pressure on myself to do just because it fits some prescribed path I envisioned years ago."

She lowered her face to his as she started to make little movements back and forth over his lap. "There are really amazing law schools in Europe, you know. I wouldn't be mad about channeling Amal Clooney and going the international law route. After a bit of a break, of course."

When her tongue grazed his bottom lip, he couldn't help but bite it.

"I fucking love you." He gripped her hair loosely at the base of her skull and pulled so that her neck was exposed to him.

"Same," she hummed as he kissed and sucked and bit the length of her throat. "We're in this together. We'll figure things out together. Endgame, remember?"

"Endgame," King hissed as she freed him from his pants and started stroking him. After some surprisingly dexterous maneuvering, Lila extracted herself from her jeans and then lowered herself onto King's throbbing cock.

They didn't talk again for a good, long while.

Chapter 38

King pulled on the jacket of his newly acquired charcoal gray suit and assessed his appearance in the mirror. He'd unbuttoned the top couple of buttons of his white dress shirt because he was only going to wear a tie if something threatened him with bodily harm. Even then, it was a tossup. He aimed his voice at the partially open bathroom door.

"How's it going in there, La? You almost ready?"

She stepped into his room, and the sight of her damn near took his breath away. She was dressed in a spaghetti-strapped floral sundress and strappy heels, her hair styled in waves that fell down to the small of her back. Her navy graduation robe was draped around her shoulders, unfastened. Lila gave him a little twirl. "Well, what do you think?"

"I think I may have to bend you over the counter before we leave," King growled, only half joking.

Lila's light laugh was one of his favorite sounds in the world. "Promise?" she teased. "Or we can just skip it altogether. I mean, I'm done with classes. The diploma's already in the mail. I've already graduated. Walking is just a formality. And *you* aren't walking. So." She popped a hip at him.

"That's because I've been here for five years and it would be anticlimactic. You're walking. End of discussion," King said, channeling his old, grumpier self before breaking out into a smirk. "Also, your mom would kill me if we ditched. I have a vested interest in staying on her good side."

"Please, she loves you more than me," Lila replied with a smirk. "Not that I blame her. So do I."

King made no effort to hide his grin. He couldn't help but marvel at the fact that they were standing here, happy and together, after everything that had happened between them.

The past few months had flown by in a whir of events, all life-changing in their own magical little ways.

Right on the heels of Knight leading the Bradley U football team to win the National Championship, he and Wren welcomed their daughter, Ivy Lila Wright-Patrick to the world. Lila had been by Wren's and Knight's side the entirety of the 24 hours of Wren's labor, while King had paced the floor of the waiting room and had done food and drink runs. The new family of three found a non-student apartment a few miles away, and Lila and King visited often, even babysitting once in a while for their friends. They had to get in their friend time while they could, because Knight had been drafted in the first round by the New York Giants, and he and Wren were planning to move to the city in a couple of weeks.

King knew for a fact that one of the things that Knight was packing was an engagement ring. A family heirloom, in fact, that Knight had made sure to get Lila's stamp of approval on before getting it cleaned and sized to be ready for Wren. King knew that while Lila was thrilled for her friends, she was going to miss them a lot. And hell, so was he.

After Knight moved out with Wren, Demarcus had moved in, and so Lila, much to King's delight, continued walking around the house in her underwear, which usually led to sexy shower time. Or sexy counter time if Bear and Demarcus were both out of the house. After one last Halloween bash, where Lila blessedly wore her costume from the year before (and he rewarded her accordingly), they ceded the parties to Will and his roommates across the street, and all had watched bemusedly as Jock Jam made its reappearance in the spring, the younger athletes and students more than happy to pick up the torch they'd left behind. Because some things never changed.

As for King... He had hit the ground running once soccer season recommenced. He'd started getting calls from scouts at the beginning of the spring season. Lila helped film him at games, and they were able to access official game tape so that he could submit footage. After a scout from London made the trek over to see King score two goals and have an assist in the championship game, King had signed with Chelsea, a Premier League team. He and Lila were planning to move to South London near the soccer stadium around the same time as Wren and Knight were moving to Manhattan so that King could get over there and start training with his new team.

He was also going to be making a shit ton of money, which meant that Lila could attend law school wherever. She was thinking she might apply to University College London, which was one of the best programs in the country. For a while, she had insisted that she was going to pay for it herself, but King had shut down that line of thinking with a half a dozen orgasms until Lila finally relented. After all, his money was her money. They were a team.

Lila retrieved a lipstick from her purse and walked over to the wall mirror to put it on.

"Wait a sec." King whirled her around and kissed her deeply, his tongue dancing with hers in the way that always got him instantly hard.

She sighed against his mouth, and he allowed himself one more second of consuming her before he reluctantly stepped back. And then adjusted himself in his slacks.

"It's a good thing you did that pre-lipstick. Otherwise we would have definitely been late and covered in red." Her eyes connected with his in the mirror. "I love the shit out of you, King Patrick Spencer."

Oh yeah, and he'd legally changed his name a couple of months ago. He'd chosen Patrick as a new middle name in honor of Knight's last name. And yeah, maybe it was cheesy as fuck, but when he'd told his friend what he was thinking of doing, they both cried, so... That was a thing that happened, and he was completely fine with it. It was just another way he was forging ties with his own chosen family.

He sat next to Knight at the ceremony, while Ivy napped inside some sort of baby wrap carrier contraption that King was impressed that Knight knew how to tie around his body, with Lila's and Wren's families flanking them. Though the two besties had both graduated early and shared a major, their last names on opposite ends of the alphabet ensured that both groups were locked in for the entire ceremony.

"Can you believe this is our life?" Knight whispered, his face a picture of wonder with a side of befuddlement. "I'm a dad, for hell's sake. We're both getting paid insane amounts of money to play a *game*. What is this magnificent thing we've stumbled into?"

King got choked up, in spite of himself. "It's pretty fucking—" he glanced down at the sleeping child "—er...freaking amazing." He cleared his throat. "And I know I tell you all the time, but thanks for convincing me to move in with you guys and to fight for Lila. If you hadn't helped me with the whole roommate thing, I don't know if I would have been able to get her back."

"You would have found your way back to each other," Knight answered confidently. "But I accept your praise. And you were there for me when I was doubting myself in regards to Wren, so, in a way, we kind of saved each other."

"Brothers." King held out a fist.

"Brothers," Knight repeated as he bumped King's fist with his own.

Miraculously, Ivy stayed asleep through the effusive cheers for both Lila and her mommy. King watched with pride as Lila walked across the stage. Summa cum laude, with a perfect 4.0 GPA. Yup, he was in love with a genius.

When the ceremony was over, the large group made their way to where Lila and Wren were standing, their arms wrapped tightly around each other. He had a feeling there would be quite a few trans-Atlantic flights in the friends' future. And thankfully, they'd be able to afford it.

There were choruses of congratulations and hugs all around, an evening full of celebrating back at Lila and King's house. And then, much later, there was the simple quiet of the two of them in bed together, limbs entwined, lips pressed together.

And King thought of the engagement ring he'd bought as soon as he signed his contract, already picturing the moment he'd get down on his knee and officially ask her to be his, forever.

Epilogue

The chanting for King that echoed through the stadium was something Lila was still getting used to. It was loud and thoroughly electric, thousands of fans screaming out the name of her fiancé like they knew him personally. He'd just scored a goal, and his gaze traveled to where he knew she was sitting and he blew her a kiss.

They'd been in London a little over six months, and King was already proving to be formidable on the field. Lila had applied to and been accepted to law school at University College London and was prepared to start the next fall. She enjoyed the downtime as she and King settled into their new routine and had found part-time work at a little bookshop near their flat. Though she missed her family, she and King had already booked a flight to visit once the season was over. And she loved all of the random messages and FaceTime exchanges she'd been able to have with them.

In some ways, she missed Wren and Knight and her little goddaughter even more, and thankfully, she'd already been able to take a trip to visit them all in New York, cheering on Knight as he played in one of his first professional games. Ivy looked absolutely adorable wearing the tiny noise-canceling headphones Wren had found for her and a onesie with her dad's number on it. They also made an effort to text and Marco Polo almost daily and FaceTime once a week. Their text message conversations were still legendary.

Cosmically, or perhaps predictably, because their respective partners were best friends, Lila and Wren had ended up both getting engaged on the exact same day. Lila had known that Knight was planning to propose, because obviously she'd had to sign off on the ring on behalf of her best friend, but she was completely shocked when she'd come home from running a quick errand to find King waiting for her with a bunch of bouquets of her favorite flowers filling their small living room.

He'd gotten down on his knee almost immediately. Like he couldn't wait another minute before asking her to marry him. His dark eyes had been filled with tenderness when he'd taken her shaking hand and said, "You're already my home, my family. But I want to be connected to you in every way possible. I know we're young, but I also know that you are the best part of my life. My endgame. Please say you'll be my wife."

She didn't hesitate even a little bit. Though the ring he'd bought was just shy of ostentatious, she loved the fact that he'd designed it himself and that it was so meaningful to the two of them. It was a row of three pear-shaped diamonds, the center stone the largest, the two stones set next to it slightly smaller in size, with tiny pave diamonds glittering around the thin band. A crown. A crown for the girl who fell in love with a broken king who eventually came into his own power and created his own kingdom. And showed her more love than she'd ever thought was possible.

How could she not be excited about marrying a man who loved her with everything he had? Who'd overcome the circumstances he was born into and decided that he was capable of so much more?

King hadn't had any contact with his parents since that disastrous day with his mother at the restaurant. For a while, Solomon had tried to lurk around at the remaining college games King played, but the team successfully ran interference and finally had him banned from attending at all after he'd left threatening messages on King's voicemail. Even though Lila's heart ached for the boy inside King who'd been neglected and abandoned by his parents, she knew that the family they had formed was filled with more than enough love.

And maybe, someday in the future, they'd have a child or two of their own, who Lila knew King would love fiercely and completely. Just like he loved her. Someday. Maybe. If they both wanted. Right now, the love that they shared with each other was more than enough.

After the game, she waited for him by the players' exit and greeted him by jumping straight into his arms and kissing him deeply. "Great game,

Spencer."

He squeezed her butt. "Great ass, Alexander."

"Take me home?"

"We're already there, baby," he said as he pressed their foreheads together and breathed her in deeply. "Home is wherever we're together."

About the Author

Lola Gregory is a contemporary romance writer living in the Mountain West with her husband, two human children, and one cat child.

Endgame is her first novel.

You can connect with me on:

🌐 https://lolagregory.com

🔗 https://www.instagram.com/lolagregorywrites